THE
CHOSEN
MAN

Published in the UK in 2021 by TOTO Publications

Copyright 2021 Tony McLaren

Paperback ISBN 978-1-7398177-0-1
eBook ISBN 978-1-7398177-1-8

Cover design and typeset by SpiffingCovers

THE
CHOSEN
MAN

TONY McLAREN

CHAPTER ONE

The Californian sun was burning down on the oiled chest of the chosen man. Chosen to have cancer and die in about four week's time. That's if he believed in God; otherwise it was just a cruel lottery. Whatever, he was dying. Frank Gruber had already survived two months since the doctor at Cedars-Sinai Medical Center gave him the bad news. He'd decided not to touch chemo – he loved his hair too much – and he'd heard all about the side effects. He'd philosophised deep about the life of the wretched mayfly, destined to live only for a day. With the end near, his thinking became alarmingly clear. He measured his life, his achievements and failures, his loves, his regrets. He fantasised how he could spend his final days – getting revenge on his old rivals, confessing to things he wish he'd never done, being really kind to strangers for the first time in his life.

Frank was taking it easy in the midday sunshine, lying by the tiny roof-top pool of the Beverly Wilshire, where Julia Roberts came visiting in "Pretty Woman", chomping on a burger, washed down with a good Moet, his blonde locks and tanned jaw belying his sixty years.

Behind him, the signs of a sick man, an oxygen cylinder on wheels.

Beside him, two giggling young girls in bikinis, who he was plying with bubbly. Still life in the old dog, just. He had them laughing, then lapsed into a coughing fit.

The ancient pool attendant, in white shirt and black bow tie, shuffled over.

"For you Mister Gruber," and handed him the poolside phone.

"Thanks Arnie," said Frank, coughing again. "Frank Gruber." He listened then got to his feet. Puffed out his chest. And winked at the girls.

"Sorry ladies – gotta go." And, without explanation, grabbed his oxygen cylinder and limped off.

*

The bar at the Beverly Wilshire, even around lunchtime was always heaving, mostly with rich bastards who could afford a glass of fine wine around thirty dollars. There were botoxed ladies looking to lunch, gelled salesmen looking to buy, Ukrainian dolls looking to sell.

Frank recognised no-one. But he smelt the money.

The mannered barman, "Ivan" on his lapel, leant across. "You Frank?"

Frank nodded, wheezing.

"You Russian?" he asked, wondering why this jerk's in his pet hotel.

"Red jeep. Rodeo Drive. Parked outside Louis Vuitton," said Ivan snappily in a strong Muscovite accent, then turned away, smiling cheesily at his next customer.

"I ain't buying fucking handbags," muttered Frank, and made for the exit.

*

He was nearly knocked over by the jostling tourists taking selfies on Rodeo Drive, Beverly Hills' shopping paradise where every doorway had its own armed guard. A seductive palm-dotted haven of luxury boutiques where you forgot world poverty, watching starlets and Saudi princes silently cruise by in their gleaming electric Maseratis and Ferraris. The privilege was tangible. Cut it with a diamond.

Frank saw the red Jeep parked outside the handbag store. Someone in the driving seat.

He tapped on the window and a thick-necked burly hunk with a grizzled crew cut unlocked the back door.

Frank slid in behind.

"Been a long time Frank," said the driver.

"I thought we'd finished," sighed Frank.

"One more job then it's over."

"Listen, I'm dying..." pleaded Frank.

"I hear you have a month, more or less.."

"Can't you leave me alone? After all I've done..."

"Boys at Langley appreciate your work... big fans."

"Bullshit. I was just a number."

"We're trying to get a citation – from the White House – for your services..."

"Really?"

"Really."

Frank coughed a moment.

"No."

"What?"

"I can't do it. Won't."

"Come on Frank. All that TV shit. Without us. We made you."

"It's too late. I'm over. End credits..."

Silence.

"You got a daughter. And she's got a daughter. Tara. Very cute..."

"You wouldn't..."

"We love you Frank."

"Jeez – you bastards..." He paused long. "OK. OK..."

"When were you last in London?"

"London?" The old country. Shit. Somewhere he thought he'd never see again. A lump in his throat. "Years back. Visiting family."

"We've one last mission. Big one."

"In London?"

"Yup. But, being sick, we want you to find someone to go with you. Help on the job. Someone 'disposable'. You get me?"

"I get you. What's the mission?"

"Can't tell you yet. Very sensitive. Once you're there you'll get instructions."

He passed an envelope to Frank. "Twenty grand in there for

fares and hotel. For two. Hilton on Park Lane."

"This is for real. And you want me to find someone. 'Disposable'?"

"It's for the U.S.A., Frank. Go find that person. Get to London. And we'll be in touch."

"That's it?" asked Frank.

Mike, the driver, nodded and started the Jeep.

Frank stumbled out of the back seat and stood blinking on the sidewalk amongst the browsing hordes as the vehicle roared off. This was not what he'd planned for his final days.

*

Hollywood Boulevard to the uninitiated sounded like the glossy glitzy heart of show biz, where billboard movie stars wined, dined, and romanced. The reality was the opposite. It was the arsehole of Los Angeles. Riddled with homeless, hookers, and druggies. Not somewhere to linger at night unless you wanted to get mugged or worse. Which is why when Frank emerged from the cab with his breathing cylinder, he wanted to get in and out mighty quick.

Almost immediately he saw what he'd come for.

A beggar sat on the sidewalk. Male. About thirty. Long matted unwashed hair. Needed a shave. Tattered purple t-shirt and shorts. A cardboard sign that said "Army Vet". A few dimes on a dirty towel in front of him.

Frank stopped by him, wheezing. "What's your name son?"

"Dwayne." No eye contact.

"Where'd you serve?"

"Afghanistan."

"What's the capital of Afghanistan son?" tested Frank.

"Fuck you sucker!" spat Dwayne.

"You don't know?"

"Kabul. I was there at the airport!" shouted Dwayne, seriously pissed at being questioned like this. "Saigon 2..!"

"Shit show." Frank paused. "Ever eaten at Dan Tana's? On Santa Monica."

"Slept outside it." snarled Dwayne.

"I'll buy you steak there. Tonight at eight." And threw ten

$100 bills onto the dirty towel. "Take a shower and get some new clothes."

"I'm not for sale..!" cried Dwayne, snatching the cash.

"Be there..." said Frank as he shuffled off along the sleazy sidewalk.

*

A few minutes further along, he stopped at another beggar. A girl. Probably a druggie. Real short hair, looked like cut by herself, and a ruby red nose. Sniffing.

Her handwritten scrawl on cardboard read "Singel Mom."

Frank hovered above her. "How many kids?"

The girl focused slowly. No-one had ever spoken like this, only shouted at her.

"Two. Boy and girl." She peered hard at Frank.

"Where are they now?"

"My Mom. Wanna see them?"

Frank sighed. "You ever worked?"

"Sure. Strip joint. I can dance for you?" as she tried to get up.

"No no... I got a better idea..."

And Frank invited her to Dan Tana's for a steak, leaving her $1000 for a wash and fresh clothes.

*

A block further he found a third street beggar. Black with a blinding smile.

Wearing a red bow tie and a tattered jacket. Sat with a ukulele, strumming to himself. His cardboard sign simply gave his name.

"Why you begging Sonny?" asked Frank.

"Ain't got no home, ain't got no shoes, ain't got no money, ain't got no class..." he sang.

"Nina Simone," laughed Frank.

"I'm beggin' mister coz I lost my home, my dog, my job. That's why. In a fire. So now got sweet fuck all."

Frank dropped $1000 in Sonny's lap. "You got a free meal tonight if you want it."

"Jesus loves you man…" whispered Sonny, his eyes welling up.

*

Dan Tana's Italian eaterie was a West Hollywood institution, holding down its spot on Santa Monica Boulevard since 1964 and hosting more famous people per square inch than anywhere else in town, from Sinatra to Nicholson, Burton to Clooney, one of La La Land's favourite watering-holes. Although only a few miles from the seedy strip where Frank had met his street beggars, this place had class.

As Frank sat opposite his three guests he pondered his involvement with the CIA. They'd come to him early. Back in his twenties, wide-eyed, just off the plane from Heathrow, when he was starting up his own TV production company in Hollywood. They offered him funds and an office, on condition he did them favours from time to time. So when he started travelling to Moscow and Istanbul and Berlin, making his crap game shows for the local audiences, he'd get the call in his hotel.

Always late at night. Always a secret mission, no questions asked. He'd meet a stranger in a park and collect a parcel; he'd pretend to be a foreign agent and lure someone to a remote meeting place; he'd lie to the authorities and give someone an alibi. Sometimes he woke sweating wondering how many people he'd led to their death; how many would still be alive today if he'd told his unseen masters to go fuck themselves. But they had their vice-like grip on him, through his funding, and those veiled threats on his daughter and family back in the U.K. And now here, in the twilight of his life, dying of cancer, they were fucking with him again. His final days.

One last black op. And probably taking down one of these grinning saddo's sat in front of him, singing for their supper, as well.

The three lowlifes had all made an effort, observed Frank.

Dwayne had shaved, had a hair cut, wore a fresh shirt and jeans.

The single Mom, called Maxy, wore a new frock with long sleeves, probably to cover up the syringe marks on her tattooed arms, her ruby nose shiny and clean.

Sonny sat proudly in a new jacket and tie, very spruce, ukulele at his side.

Frank took a whiff of oxygen from the mask attached to his cylinder and leant back. "So here we all are," he said. "Four total strangers. Enjoy your meal?"

"First steak in years," said Dwayne, emptying his glass in one.

"Cool, thanks mister," croaked Maxy.

"You're a true gentleman, sir" smoothed Sonny.

"My pleasure," beamed Frank, wondering which would draw the short straw and become his "disposable."

"Whaddya want mister – you some kind of perv – get a kick meeting shit like us!?" muttered Maxy, desperate for her next fix. "Where we going after – back to your fuckin' bedroom!?"

"OK, OK.," said Frank, taking another breath from his mask. "So here's the thing. As you can see, I'm not that well. But, I'm planning a trip, and I need a buddy, a travelling companion, to come with me. No strings. Nothing weird. Just someone to watch my back. They'll get paid. Be away a few weeks. Then that's it. You come back here or go where you like. Simple."

"Why us mister? Got no friends?" asked Dwayne, onto a new glass of wine.

"Not many. I just thought, I'd experiment. Try help guys like you. I've got the money. Can't take it with me. Perhaps might kick-start a new life."

"Where's this trip Frank?" asked Sonny, trying hard not to be too curious.

"London."

The three suddenly woke up, like they'd won the lottery. Dwayne spilt red wine down his trousers; Maxy's gaping mouth revealed her rotting teeth; while Sonny pinged his uke strings.

"So," continued Frank, "trouble is I have to choose which of you to take with me."

All three raised their hands.

"Let me play a truth game. You've had your meal so you can walk out on me any time." He paused. " I think you've all been lying…"

All three feigned shock and hurt.

"Dwayne. You said you were in the army. Afghanistan. I don't think you've ever worn a uniform, except jail. I suspect you've lived off crime for years to pay for your drink problem."

Dwayne stood seething, then dropped to the floor and did ten one-arm push-ups. He then sat calmly again. "You ain't seen a fitter man – that's Marines!"

"My mistake son..."

He turned to the girl. " And Maxy. You got drug issues. That's OK. But I suspect you've no kids, you're not a single Mom..."

Maxy glared at Frank then spat across the table. "Fuck you asshole!" and stormed out, taking the half-empty bottle of wine.

"And then there were two," smiled Frank. "Sonny - what really happened to you – was there a fire..?"

Sonny sighed. "You got me. I did lie. No fire. I worked in a bank. Then one day stole some cash, and more and more till I got caught. Jail. Lost everything. A sucker who ends up on the street homeless."

"So. Tough choice. Dwayne – can see you're mighty fit, which is good. Sonny – vivid imagination, also good." Frank put a brown envelope on the table. "In there is fifty thousand dollars. If you can prove to my attorney you've turned your life around in one month, you'll get one more payment. One of you gets this... The other... comes with me to London."

Dwayne and Sonny looked nervously at each other.

Frank stood up. "I'm going to the john. When I get back I'll give my decision." He limped off to the restroom.

Dwayne looked at the envelope with fifty thousand.

"We could take that while he's gone and split it 50/50..." he whispered.

"I could hit you over the head and keep the lot!" threatened Sonny with his ukulele. "Or, one of us might get a better life... the other, who knows..?

Dwayne strummed the table impatiently. "You think this guy's straight?"

"I think he's dying," said Sonny. "Needs a carer."

"Shit."

Frank returned and stood at the table.

"Dwayne." He paused long, too long, like naming the winner on one of those tacky TV talent shows. "Here's your big chance.

Go find a new life." And gave him the envelope with fifty thousand dollars. Then turned to the other. "Sonny – grab your uke – you're coming to London!"

Hours earlier Frank had never met these two strangers, homeless and begging for food. Now he'd thrown Dwayne a lifeline and was taking Sonny on a journey where anything could happen, good or bad. Probably bad.

*

The red Jeep was parked on Mulholland Drive overlooking the thousand twinkling lights of Los Angeles at dusk. Each home, condo, hacienda, hiding a drama of its own.

"Hey. It's done," said Mike on his cell. "Gruber's back in play. I told him take someone 'disposable' to London, keep him company. But him on borrowed time, he's the 'disposable'." He sucked on his Havana. "We got our very own suicide bomber, and he doesn't fuckin' know it."

CHAPTER TWO

The inflatable red dinghy was fast approaching the Spanish beach, taking the tourists by surprise. It slammed ashore and fifty migrants leapt onto the sand, running for the dunes.

One suddenly stopped, took off her Ray-Bans, and looked back at Africa.

Zafira. A tall, elegant, Sudanese beauty. Her body pumping adrenalin, fists clenched white numb, eyes glowing with a driven energy, a hidden goal getting closer.

Beside her, two skinny boy soldiers, Chindi and Sami, weary faces wizened beyond their years, collapsed and kissed the sand.

Charlie froze the holiday video on his iPhone and asked the cabbie to turn into Piccadilly. He wondered where they were now, what they were doing, those migrants.

The memory was clear as yesterday… rubbing oil into Tara's glistening breasts on the Playa de los Alemanes – just across from Morocco where the Germans landed their killing machines in World War Two - when the Africans crashed his beach party.

His photo of them landing made the front page that same day.

*

Charlie Lomax – an assured shaggy blonde in jacket and jeans who could be a city broker or South Ken estate agent - had been working as a reporter at "The Evening Standard" for three years. It was in his blood, getting out there, sticking his nose in, lifting up stones, revealing the unknown and unspeakable to the world. But, sometimes there were dreary slow news days when he had to fill with fluff, the lightweight dross that readers loved way more than his serious stuff.

Today was one of those days... A self-publicity story on some singing detective. Jack Albert Duffy, aka Duffy...

Charlie paid his cab then pushed his way through the shoppers into Fortnum and Mason, the luxury store around since 1707, best known for its picnic hampers and inventing the scotch egg, heading for the winery in the basement.

He wasn't difficult to spot. Sitting in the corner of the bar. Early thirties.

Purple shirt and jeans. Dark bro flow hairdo, stubble, broken nose. Like some Head and Shoulders model waiting to be discovered. Almost a little too cool. A twinkle in his blue eyes. Perhaps he was taking the piss. Out of himself. He stood tall and held out a bronzed hand with a dangling red string wristband. The air of a charming rogue.

"Sherlock the rock star?" beamed Charlie.

"Better than 'the singing dick'..." shaking the journo's hand. "Duffy."

Charlie was won over already.

"Charlie Lomax. Evening Standard."

"My pleasure."

They sat and Duffy ordered bubbly for two from Toto the black barman.

"Mind if I tape this?" asked Charlie.

Duffy nodded and the journo started his mini-recorder.

"So what's the big story ?"

Should I give him the short version or the long, thought Duffy..?

How he was raised in a Harrow slum with an outside bog and a single Mum who had an affair with a rich married geezer from the City who paid for his boarding school which he ran away from to sail the world as a cruise entertainer where he disastrously met and married snooty barrister Zandra to live in Belgravian luxury before she bunked off with her trainer and our kid turned sleuth to get his revenge.

Nah. Short version.

"I got a crazy sales gimmick."

"Try me," said Charlie.

He showed Charlie the app sitting on the screen of his smart phone.

"Basically, I'm a private eye... tap this, swipe, tell me your problem... and with you in minutes..."

He tapped his app and his image filled the phone screen, white suit and teeth astride a Harley, introducing himself... "Hi there, I'm Duffy, your very own private eye. You want someone found, followed, look no further. Just swipe and we can talk."

"I'm impressed," said Charlie. "Where's your office?"

"You're in it."

"What?"

"No office, no home..."

"You what?"

"My office is this bar ... till I'm thrown out. And home is where I lay my head. Nightclub, girlfriend, wherever..."

"Very gypsy", said Charlie both impressed and a little stunned. "Tell me about the singing."

"Love the old pop songs – see a mike on stage – try keep me down..."

"A singing detective, with no home, no office." said Charlie sipping his bubbly. "You're a one-off mate..."

"Sad to say, but the coronavirus did me a favour – it's wrecked lives ... divorces, people losing jobs, more crime... they need a helping hand..."

Suddenly Sheryl Crow interrupted with "All I Wanna Do is Have some Fun".

Duffy answered his phone, mouthing to Charlie –"first job off the app?"

He tapped his screen and an anxious female around forty, short black fringed hair, green eyes, runny mascara, appeared.

"Mr Duffy?"

"At your service madam." he answered soothingly.

"Julie Slade. My husband's missing. I know something's wrong. Been gone for two days. Can you help?"

"This happen before Mrs Slade – gone to a party - not come home..?"

"Never. I keep calling him but he doesn't answer. I'm really worried."

"Let's meet. How about today at four. The London Eye?" said Duffy.

She paused, bit her lip.

"I'll be there, thank you ever so much," and faded to black.

Duffy turned to Charlie. "Magic's working already Charlie…"

"Way to go Duffy."

And both clinked glasses.

*

The Houses of Parliament, Big Ben, Westminster Abbey, looked like tiny Toytown models sitting beside the gray curdling Thames, as the London Eye – Europe's tallest ferris wheel - moved gently on its half-hour snail-like rotation through the sleeting rain. The capsule was crowded with excited Chinese visitors, all exceedingly well-dressed in the very best English tweeds and Barbours, carrying the latest i-Phones, and making far too much din.

Duffy sat in a far corner, handed Mrs Slade an Americano in a cardboard cup, then offered her a KitKat. She sipped hesitantly at the coffee but declined the chocolate bar.

"Tell me about your husband Mrs Slade," said Duffy.

"John. We been married twelve years. Two children. When we met he was an accountant. Then he got an offer, to join the Treasury."

"Well done him."

"It was a huge break. A mate of his from school had put his name up and very soon he was in there, pin-striped, working just across there in Westminster with the government's top money people. I was very proud," she sighed.

"What's his job now. Before he disappeared ?"

"He was personal advisor to the Economic Secretary, Cyril Sharp. All seemed to be going swimmingly – John was working very hard – late nights – then suddenly three days ago he simply vanished!"

"Vanished?" repeated Duffy, waving away a shouty tourist, squeezing between them to take more photos.

"Didn't come home Monday night. Didn't answer his phone.

And his office haven't seen him. I didn't know what to do then I saw your app... Please help me find him Mr Duffy."

Duffy took a hipflask from his pocket and handed it to Mrs Slade.

She took a nervous swig, her hand shaking.

"Of course I will my dear," said Duffy, patting her on the arm. "We'll find your John, never fear."

*

The next morning Duffy was cruising on his Harley down Whitehall when he was cut up and nearly knocked over by a convoy of dark tinted Humvees racing towards Downing Street. Too flashy for the new P.M. Must be a VIP visitor in town.

Getting into the Treasury offices was more difficult than buying a ticket for Twickers when the All Blacks were playing. He'd already been waiting an hour to meet the Economic Secretary, Cyril Sharp, when he spotted "The Evening Standard" in a stand beside the receptionist. Splashed all over the front page was a photo of the richest woman on the planet – ex-wife of a Qatari prince – the exotic Saladine. It must have been her and her entourage that nearly bowled him off his bike. No doubt buying up more London hotels, or closing the Dorchester Grill so she could eat lunch alone.

Saladine had been a dancer from Sheffield who found Allah and became the first wife of Sheikh Hamad El-Tadi. On their separation she invested her £100 million settlement in the country's oil-fields and became an overnight zillionaire. Now she travelled the world as a maverick, dabbling in business deals from Beijing to Hanoi, Las Vegas to Moscow. Very much an elusive enigma.

"Mr Duffy." cried the receptionist. "Cyril will see you now."

Duffy nodded and turned to page three of the newspaper.

There he was, all guns blazing. A huge photo of himself at Fortnum's Bar – "The Sofa Surfin' Singing Detective!" Charlie had done a bloody good job. Must send him a bottle.

"Lovely photo Mr Duffy," smiled the receptionist, leading him into Cyril Sharp's office.

A sweaty bald little man, early sixties, with a pot belly, open stained shirt, and yellow teeth rose from behind a massive desk and held out his podgy paw. The Queen stared down from one wall, Marx from the other. Weird times we were living through.

"See you made the 'Standard' today Mr Duffy – take a seat."

Duffy judged Cyril was a professional jobsworth – probably worked in this dump all his life – treating the Treasury cash like it was his own – never travelled, never got drunk, never took risks. Then again, first impressions could be wrong.

Duffy sat. "You can guess why I'm here Mr Sharp."

"John Slade. Never made it home Monday." sniffed Cyril.

"Exactly. His wife's asked me to investigate. See if we can find out what's happened."

"It's very upsetting for Julie but here at the office we've no clue," sighed Cyril. "Very conscientious, good time-keeper, loved his job…"

"Didn't have a secret girlfriend..?"

"Lord no – devoted to his wife. Perfect family man."

"Is there anything – anything Mr Sharp – out of the ordinary that might seem strange about his behaviour Monday… something worrying him, money problems perhaps?" Duffy persisted.

Cyril shook his head.

"Genuinely sorry Mr Duffy. Run out of ideas. Just hope it might be one of these freaky memory lapses and he'll turn up on the doorstep…"

"Could I see his office?"

Sharp stood. Hesitantly. "Follow me." And lead him into the adjacent office.

It was smaller than Sharp's; Constable's Salisbury Cathedral on one wall, Jack Vettriano's Singing Butler on another. On his desk a computer… a photo of Julie at a royal garden party… three sharpened pencils each an inch apart… back copies of "The Economist"… and a travel book on German river cruises.

"He and Julie were cruising up the Rhine next week," sighed Sharp.

That was enough to kill anyone, thought Duffy.

"What's on his computer Mr Sharp?"

Sharp stalled. "No can do. You'll understand, as personal

advisor to my office, a lot of confidential information in there…"

"No probs mate – understand."

Sharp headed to the door. "Sorry can't give you any clues – bloody strange business…"

Duffy nodded and shook Sharp's hand. "Appreciate your time – thanks."

Handed him his business card. "My card, if anything crops up." And let himself out.

He stopped at the receptionist.

"John Slade on Monday when he left. Did he seem OK?", he asked.

"Perfectly. Big smile as usual – went home happy as a baby," she replied.

Duffy nodded. He didn't like this. Slade was obviously very bright – a numbers guy – probably a bit dull, bit risk averse, but not someone who'd get pissed and do something silly, not someone who got into the wrong company, or top himself… this was beginning to look more sinister…

He headed out to his Harley as the phone rang. It was Charlie, the journo.

Seemed the band at a friend's wedding gig had pulled out and they were desperate to find a performer. Someone who could sing those old pop classics…

"When?" asked Duffy, grabbing his helmet and straddling his bike.

On the pavement opposite, a crowd of tourists had gathered round a bloke with a table and three cards playing 'Find The Lady'. Little guy with a shaven head, black beard, cut across his left eye, wearing a dirty grey hoodie. He was dealing the cards with lightning speed like a Vegas croupier. The crowd cheered as a player won some cash.

"Tonight!? Where?" asked Duffy. "The Chelsea Barn. OK. Hope they like my stuff. See you there Charlie… Thanks." And roared off down the street with a smile.

Across the road the crowd had suddenly dispersed; the cards and table gone; the 'Find The Lady" dealer done a runner.

*

Duffy had dropped in to visit Julie Slade at their fifties brick bungalow in a shady cul-de-sac in suburban East Sheen. Just the sort of place he'd expect a suit to live. Safe, respectable, probably a member of the local rotary club.

He handed the monthly bank accounts back to Mrs Slade.

"Nothing out of the ordinary here – no strange transfers or deposits. Just the usual bills, eating out…"

"It's a mystery," agreed Julie Slade.

"What about family?"

"The kids are grown-up – see them mostly at weekends. They can't believe he's missing…" she said with a damp distant look in her eyes.

"There could be a simple reason Julie – a stroke on his way home - could be lying unconscious in a private hospital somewhere… Let me check the medical lists," said Duffy. "These things come out of the blue when you least expect them. "

"If he'd been mugged, the police would have been in touch, wouldn't they..?"

"Soon as. I looked round his office today – nothing out of the ordinary. Did he have a computer here at home?" asked Duffy.

Julie led him through to a small study. Desk and a large iMac. Those same three sharpened pencils each an inch apart. A crumpled copy of "Private Eye."

"This is…was… his private den," sighed Julie, turning on his computer.

On the screen a large confidential file, flagged red.

Duffy took out a USB flash drive.

"Can I take a copy Mrs Slade?"

She nodded.

Duffy downloaded the iMac contents onto his USB stick.

"Let me see what I can find. There's got to be some clue where he's gone."

He made for the door. "I'll be in touch…"

Julie Slade watched him depart and nervously closed the door.

*

The Chelsea Barn was a converted nightclub in Tite Street, just off the Kings Road.

Tonight it was hosting a post-wedding party for Jenny and Richard, two finance wonks from the City. With speeches and the "Dirty Dancing" number over, Duffy had the room thumping as he sang the finale to Fats Domino's "My Blue Heaven." He was wearing a white tux and dangling bow-tie as he gyrated on stage. Just inches from him a gaggle of twenty-something posh totties were heaving on the floor. He was spoilt for choice – the lanky brunette with the pixie fringe in the low-cut red satin number, the busty blonde with her crazy beehive in her sparkling party dress, or the stunning black diva in her purple drape. Call Duffy a poseur or a chancer, he could sure get the girls' attention.

As he hit the last note, Charlie joined him on stage and thanked him for filling in at the last moment. Several drop dead party girls jostled him with their cards for future engagements, business or personal.

"Come and meet Tara," said Charlie, much inspired by his new friend's talents.

Duffy pushed through the crowd to a cool young redhead in the corner.

Tara.

She who'd been oiled and massaged by Charlie on that Spanish beach many weeks earlier when the migrants came crashing ashore.

"Babe. Meet the amazing Mister Duffy. Duffy – Tara," enthused Charlie.

"Your babe..." added Duffy. "My pleasure."

Tara still glowed from a sun tan, probably fake, and wore a yellow dress that looked like it was sprayed on. Her eyes locked with Duffy's.

They shook hands. A long moment.

"And mine. You certainly can sing – awesome," cooed Tara. "And good to meet a real dick these days – never know when you might need one..."

"You got a problem?" asked Duffy.

"My parents. Just got thrown out of their home by the Equalisers..."

"The Equalisers? Shit. Where do they live?" asked Duffy, realising this was politically dangerous stuff.

"Dorset," replied Tara. "Helluva shock, but Dad's ex-army – he can look after himself."

"We think he was SAS but never admits it," added Charlie.

"Tara – let me know if I can help..." said Duffy, handing her his card.

She fondled it thoughtfully. "Who knows Mister Duffy, who knows..."

"Charlie – where's the little boys' room?"

Charlie gave directions and with a nod Duffy headed to the loo.

As the door closed behind him there was a sudden vicious blow to his neck and his knees buckled.

As he collapsed he saw a little scar-faced bearded guy in a dirty grey hoodie standing over him. Seen him somewhere.

A steel-toed boot slammed his ribs and he blacked out.

All went quiet then Sheryl Crow blasted through his bloodshot aching mist.

"All I Wanna Do is Have Some Fun."

His ringtone.

He was aching all over. Everything stank of piss. Still lying on the toilet floor. Ribs on fire.

He stabbed his phone.

Julie Slade on screen. In a state. No makeup. Crying.

"Duffy! I been burgled. They've taken the computer and left this." She held something in her hand, like a large marble. Duffy tried hard to focus. "It's John's! He... he had a glass eye..!"

Duffy heaved himself painfully up onto his elbow, bent over his phone, and spewed all over Julie's face.

CHAPTER THREE

Politics in Britain these days seemed like a chapter out of "Alice in Wonderland", only far more lethal.

It had started and ended with the infamous Brexit referendum, where a slim majority had voted to leave the European Union, under a Tory government. This split the country into "Brexiteers" and "Remainers"; the former mostly the old, out of London and without higher education; the latter mostly the young, in London, Wales and Scotland, and university academics.

The invigorated Labour party became more and more extreme as it found its core base were the first-voting students who could become their lifelong supporters.

And with every move Left to a Marxist Statist project, the wide-eyed youngsters, Remainers all, looking for cheap homes and free education, queued to join the new cause.

But, following the 2019 election, the Tories won a landslide victory and looked like they'd stay in power for years, having banished the Left to the wilderness.

Until the coronavirus struck, sweeping across the planet, infecting millions, killing thousands in its wake.

The Tory Government struggled to cope, making mistake on mistake, U-turn upon U-turn, with the highest deaths in Europe, followed by mass unemployment, alienating students and pensioners with their incompetent blunders, then the farcical pingdemic and travel chaos, which brought them a staggering election defeat in 2024, when Labour renamed itself the New Dawn party, and everything changed.

Boris and gang had hoped the 2021 Oxford vaccine bounce

would win them approval but by then it was too late – Brexit had angered the farmers, the fishermen, and brought violence back to the streets of Northern Ireland – then the Health Minister's love antics were caught on camera, and the Tories were brutally thrown out, just as Churchill was dumped having won World War Two.

The new revolutionaries kept their promises, spending billions on public sector salaries, dwarfing those in the private industries, repaying student debts, and building new homes. But soon their finances began to unravel; the rich and talented fled abroad, and the country slowly steamed to bankruptcy. As quickly as they spent, cabinet ministers desperately travelled worldwide to try borrow more, but not even the IMF would lend to the seemingly out-of-control new government.

But it was not just finance, it was also how the Marxist doctrines were changing the whole fabric of society. The sinister New Dawn youth wing – the "Equalisers" – were hunting down and harassing Tory supporters, the "cancel culture" mob on Twitter getting them fired from key positions, threatening their homes, and driving many to suicide. Britain in these edgy times had almost become a 21st century police state where the young were pulling down statues, gagging free speech, rewriting history, even binning Enid Blyton. A veritable powder keg.

Then there was defence, or lack of it. The big unions had successfully taken over all the key public necessities – gas, oil, hospitals, railways, schools, the police, and now were effectively disbanding and emasculating the armed forces.

The result was a sterile fearful society where the State, the Party, and the Equalisers protected and policed life from cradle to grave, making Orwell's terrifying totalitarian "1984" look like a bland Disney cartoon.

*

It was during these fragile and unpredictable times that the new Prime Minister, Godfrey Young, face of the extreme Left, and feisty Tory opposition back-bencher Suki Carter, protector of traditional values, fell into their otherworldly forbidden relationship. Godfrey had been living with his Jamaican activist girlfriend for ten years in Brixton; Suki married to accountant Henry, with two kids, six hens, and a rescue lurcher near Petworth in Sussex.

The unthinkable happened on a wet afternoon in the House of Commons when the parties were debating Labour's proposed Land Tax. The gender fluid Speaker – Jack or Jackie – depending on the way they dressed that day – was trying to maintain order in a very noisy angry House.

Jackie's quivering painted lips and quavering voice shrieked to its highest falsetto.

"Order, order my darlings!" they cried. "The Prime Minister..."

Godfrey rose to his feet, blood colouring his bearded face.

"This Land Tax will bring relief to nurses in the NHS, teachers in the classrooms, and the starving poor all over the country. It's a blessing for all..." he shouted over the grumbling voices opposite.

Suki caught the Speaker's heavily mascaraed lashes.

"Hon. Member for Arundel and South Downs, Suki Carter..."

Suki stood and went for the jugular.

"Madame Speaker... This Land Tax'll bankrupt anyone with a lawnmower..!"

"Rubbish" cried a heckler.

"I agree," persevered Suki. "It is rubbish! Everyone wants a home with a garden - now they'll have to move house!"

"Balls!" shrieked another heckler.

"Mr... Madame Speaker", continued Suki, " we know he thinks 'property is theft', but if this government forces through the bill, they'll be facing their biggest defeat by those same nurses, teachers, and so-called poor!"

And sat down with a wallop.

The Speaker recalled the Prime Minister.

"I think the Honourable Member will find she's very much mistaken!" replied the Dear Leader with a patronising smirk.

As Suki shouted back: "This is class warfare - we're not living in a Communist State... yet!"

And Godfrey ruefully raised an eyebrow.

*

Later that evening the Prime Minister and his hardline Chancellor, Sean O'Leary, were tucked into an intimate corner of the Strangers' Bar with the Arabian zillionaire Saladine.

They were in earnest conversation, interrupted only when Suki entered and gestured across to Godfrey. He looked extremely irritated – it was an unwritten rule that in the bar you had privacy for meetings and to interfere was crossing the line. He reluctantly pulled himself away from the others and joined Suki at the bar.

"I'm having a private conversation," seethed Godfrey.

"And I'm having my life turned upside down!" retorted Suki.

"What – not gas boilers again?"

"If that Land Tax goes through, I'm ruined!"

"Don't be stupid love", sighed the Prime Minister. "It's no big deal - you can afford it…"

"Don't 'love' me ! You Commies have no bloody idea about real people!"

Her shouting caused others at the bar to stop talking and turn their way.

Suki took a deep breath and lowered her voice.

"Like many others, we're property rich, cash poor. Big house but nothing in the bank. Can't pay your twenty grand a year and end up in bloody jail!" She bit her lip and tried to hold back her fury. "All because of your fucking Marxist claptrap!!"

Godfrey sighed, grabbed a wine bottle with two glasses, and quietly escorted her from the bar, waving to Sean and Saladine, who looked somewhat bemused.

"What are you doing?" asked Suki.

"I think we both need some air and a drink…" soothed Godfrey as he ushered her into a lift, nodding to the armed policemen with their Sig Sauer assault rifles.

They hugged opposite walls, avoiding eye contact, as the elevator whined upwards and clanged to a halt.

"Ever seen the view from Victoria Tower?" as Godfrey led her from the lift, through a locked door, up some stairs and out into the starry night.

They were standing on the roof of the third tower above the House of Commons, with Big Ben at the opposite end of the building. The London lights were sparkling around them, the river

Thames glinting black velvet below.

Godfrey handed Suki a glass of white wine which she downed in one.

She took a deep breath as Godfrey poured another.

"You really get me going Godfrey," she sighed, half an apology, half irritation. Then noticed the view. "My God. Never been up here... it's stunning."

"Twelve floors of archives, and this secret little hideaway," chuckled the PM. "I find it helps get everything... in perspective..."

Suki took another deep swig and turned to him. "Didn't mean to get personal Godfrey. Sorry... Just that, I'm truly worried – that tax ... it'd cause real pain and..."

"Shush... forget that bloody tax..." He hushed her, his finger on her lips. Then pulled her to him and slowly, gently, kissed her.

Suki froze. Stunned. Confused. Stepped back and stared puzzled at Godfrey.

She hated this man. And yet. And yet there was a quiet sensitivity deep down.

A warm musky aroma. Her breathing started to race, to falter... felt sucked in by a stronger current... willingly out of control...

"I didn't mean..." Then suddenly grabbed the PM and embraced him hard and long.

They eased down onto the ground and began ripping off their clothes. Suki flung her bra over her head and the two let nature take its course.

What seemed hours later, they exited rather formally from the lift and walked out towards the Palace of Westminster gates.

Suki started to laugh.

"Was it that bad?" smiled Godfrey nervously.

She shook her head.

There high up above them on the palace walls was her bra draped over a snarling gargoyle, spotlit in all its glory.

"Have you ever been to Cannes?" asked the Labour Prime Minister to the Tory backbencher.

*

That trip to the Riviera, those nights at the Carlton in Cannes, now seemed a lifetime away. Suki was back with Henry and the kids in Petworth and Godfrey was still fighting capitalism and the greedy rich.

The Land Tax had been temporarily stalled at the P.M.'s request so an enquiry could determine if it would alienate their ageing voters, those baby boomers who bought homes at low prices years ago which had since escalated in value beyond their wildest dreams. The ones like Suki who were sitting on a million pound homes with zilch savings. Perhaps this guy had a human side to him after all.

But both Suki and Godfrey had realised what a dangerous game they were playing. Both were in relationships and could wreck their partners' lives. There were kids involved. More importantly, it was the politics. A hard Left Prime Minister with a ballsy Tory backbencher. And the febrile climate around the Commons following all those sex scandals. There'd been rape, suicide, and resignations. To be discovered having an inter-party affair these days would be the end of their careers and their private lives.

Which is why both decided to end it quickly and cleanly.

No incriminating emails, no ranting phone calls, simply a terse two minutes pretending to browse in the Commons' library. And it was over.

Back in her rabbit-hutch office, the relief was palpable. Suki called Henry and promised him his favourite venison sausage pie that eve. The guilt was still there but at least she'd turned a corner and was back in control again. She could breathe freely, and quietly started to plan her business week ahead without thinking endlessly of him.

Her mail had been neglected so she started to open the pile from irate constituents in West Sussex. Many were anxious about the proposed Land Tax as most of her voters had large gardens.

After an hour she was getting bored and longed for a stiffener but thought she should avoid the Strangers' Bar in case she bumped into Godfrey. Two more letters then she'd head home early.

The last was a big brown envelope with a cardboard backing.

She ripped it open and sat back aghast.

It was a photo of her and Godfrey on that balcony in Cannes weeks ago.

There was no note. Nothing. Just this terrifying evidence of her affair.

"Fucking hell!" she stuttered.

Thought a moment then grabbed the phone and dialled.

At the other end a secretary replied: "Prime Minister's office."

Suki held her breath then put down the phone and started to sob uncontrollably.

*

Duffy sat up in the hospital bed with his ribs bandaged and a bruised neck.

He was feeling better after his attack in the Chelsea Barn loo and quietly pleased he'd had free lodgings for a week or so, without having to chase a place to sleep. But he was still trying to fathom why he'd been beaten up – it wasn't a robbery as his phone and cards were still intact; it wasn't the usual jealous boyfriend or husband as he'd been a good boy since returning from Shanghai; it could only be something to do with a case. And the obvious answer was the missing guy from the Treasury – John Slade, who now it seemed, was the victim of a kidnapping. Which reminded him, he still had that computer file on a memory stick he'd hidden in his motorbike helmet.

Must get it checked soonest by his hacking geek, Marky.

"Someone to see you Mr Duffy," said the attractive black nurse, ushering in Julie Slade to his bedside.

"Thanks Zaffy – you're a star."

Julie, looking very distraught, pulled up a chair.

"Like a cuppa love?" asked Duffy.

Julie nodded.

"I'll magic you up something," said Zafira, elegantly vanishing out the door.

"That girl's a gem – just arrived from Sudan and already found her feet. Now. Any more news Julie?"

"Only what you know - they burgled the house - took John's computer - left his glass eye…" swallowed Julie, biting her lip.

"Which means he's alive. And kidnapped. No message anywhere? No phone calls?"

Julie shook her head. "Should we go to the police – they might be better equipped..?"

"Julie, if it was murder I'd say go to the cops. But kidnapping. Very sensitive as you might be aware. Mostly they like to think you're sitting trembling at home without getting uniform involved. Question is, why was he taken? What did he know, what did he see, who wants him out of the way..?"

"I've no idea. His job just deals with money. Government finance. Nothing dodgy. No money laundering. All above board."

Zaffy brought in tea and biscuits and put them on the beside table.

"You're a star Zaffy!"

"You said that last time. Next time it's a date," smiled Zaffy as she exited.

That's a promise I'd like to keep, thought Duffy.

"Must say it's good to talk - thanks for what you're doing..." said Julie.

"Should be out tomorrow then we'll see what's on that computer file...."

"You in much pain?"

"Na – right as rain. Only here for the meals..."

"Why were you beaten up?" asked Julie.

"That Julie, is what I intend to find out..." as he slurped his tea.

*

Jazza Al Britani had converted to Islam five years ago. He'd been brought up in Lowestoft in Suffolk, a quiet seaside resort, where he worked as a packer for Birds Eye frozen foods. By his late teens he was supplementing his salary with burglaries, targeting the many old dears who'd gone there to retire. Often he'd simply pose as a meter reader and steal what he could as he used their bog. But his luck soon ran out and it was in H.M. Prison Norwich – once home to Reggie Kray and Ronnie Biggs – that he found religion, said goodbye to Dave Chubb, and, taking on a new name, became a Muslim. This coincided very nicely with the creation of ISIS in Syria and Iraq. Before you could say "Allahu Akbar" our Jazza was down in the sand with his new-found brothers, marrying a Yazidi slave girl, and shooting up British Special Forces.

Over two years he led a lucky life, narrowly missing endless drone strikes, until Mosul and Raqqa fell to the Western and Russian troops. He then got involved in the Libyan slave auctions, nearly lost an eye, escaping home via Turkey and a rib from France, ending up living rough in the East End. Within weeks he found work in cafes and kitchens across the city until at last he heard from "13", his ISIS handler.

The understanding was that he'd lie low in London as a sleeper, until he was activated. He'd then be given some mission – to kill, to rob, to kidnap, to bomb.

Always no questions, and he'd get paid.

This last week he'd been busy. Doing his "Find the Lady" act in the street.

This came naturally as he always ripped off the other bastards in prison. Target was some ponce on a motorbike. Rough him up was the deal. See if he had anything of interest. Like a computer memory stick. He'd done the job. Found nothing. Now waited payment. They said it was for the cause.

He was standing at his little table, wearing his hoodie, playing "Find the Lady" on College Green, behind Westminster Abbey, across from the Houses of Parliament, as instructed.

A few yards away a BBC TV reporter was interviewing a Tory M.P., Suki Carter, about the Land Tax. She was not happy.

A small crowd had gathered around Jazza, mostly Chinese tourists.

His phone rang.

"Across from you is a new statue of Karl Marx," said the disembodied voice. "Meet me there in two minutes and you'll get paid."

Jazza went to speak but the phone was dead.

He collected up his cards, collapsed his table, and hurried across the green to Karl Marx.

A moment later from the shadows someone in a baseball cap moved silently to him, handed over an envelope, and vanished into the dark.

The mystery contact headed for the House of Commons, walked over the crossing, and took off his cap as he entered Parliament.

*

Julie was standing by Duffy's bed, about to leave.

"I'll be in touch sometime tomorrow," said Duffy, drawing himself up painfully, and extended his hand.

His phone rang.

Bloody Sheryl Crow again.

Duffy answered. "Can I help?" he groaned.

Suki Carter appeared on screen. In the background was Westminster Abbey – she was speaking from College Green. "Mr Duffy? I saw your article. I must talk…"

As she spoke, Jazza was walking in the background carrying his card table.

Duffy spotted him for that fleeting second.

"That man in the hoodie! Behind. Where are you!?" he cried.

"College Green. Westminster…" replied Suki, taken back.

"Where's that hoodie guy gone?" shouted Duffy.

Suki swiveled around but Jazza had vanished.

"I… I don't know. Why? What's this got to do with me?" she asked, bewildered.

"OK. OK. Sorry ma'am. How can I help?"

"I'm a politician. I have a personal problem. I need to meet."

"Friday at two. Fortnum's downstairs bar."

"I'll be there." And hung up.

"Never rains but it pours," sighed Duffy, putting his phone aside.

Julie was still standing there.

"Julie. Just seen the guy that beat me up. Was playing cards outside the Treasury. Must have followed me to the club. What the fuck's going on!?"

*

In a dingy dimly-lit room a naked man hung upside down from the ceiling, ankles tied by rope to a pulley, his head being repeatedly plunged into a bathful of water.

His masked jailer kept asking politely: "Who you told Mr Slade..?" Then dunked his head under water for half a minute.

Yanked on the rope, heaving the body free from the water, as the one-eyed head spluttered, gasping for air. "No-one I swear, no-one..."

Again the masked man whispered: "Tell me and you go home to Julie..."

Slade mumbled, spitting out water.

Another dunking. "I can't hear you Mr Slade..!"

And another until the body stopped threshing, violently twitching a moment, then hung motionless like a butcher's carcass.

CHAPTER FOUR

That night the Equalisers came and threw Harry and wife Viv out of their Dorset family home, ushering in a coachload of London homeless, was an experience neither would ever forget.

He'd called his old Army mucker Moggie and together they decided over a pint or three of real ale in "The Crown" at Alvediston how to get even with these Young Turks and reclaim their house.

These two had serious history.

They'd fought together as SAS in Afghanistan, Iraq, Libya, and South Sudan. The last two theatres had been as mercenaries alongside South Africans and French. The toughest and most ruthless years of Harry's life. He'd erased most of it from his memory. Regretted the killing, even though he believed he was always helping the good guys get into power and democracy. But that was firmly behind him.

Steel door shut. Key thrown away. Or so he hoped.

Harry was late fifties, very old school. Behind that cool steely blue gaze there was a confident certainty and control, that stolid Sandhurst military training wired into his brain, polished to perfection with that public school drawl, his rusty hair flecked with grey, cut en brosse like the French Foreign Legionnaires. He was gym fit with his ramrod physique, could almost strike a match on his jawline, and had a subtly ironic sense of humour.

"We could get a few of the lads, kick the doors in, crack a few skulls, and turf 'em out!", suggested Moggie, Harry's old sergeant. He was hewn from solid oak, could floor three blokes in one, an ace on the rugby field, and a champion sniper.

"No way – my Tudor doors you're talking about," sniffed Harry. "Something more subtle Mogs, though know you don't do subtle…"

"What exactly happened..?"

Harry sighed. "They turned up late one night… two yellow buses and them in Smiley Face tee-shirts… teens with guns…"

"Equalisers. With guns..?"

Harry nodded.

"Long story short. They gave us five minutes to vacate the house then this homeless lot got off the buses and went inside. Took over our home. Gone."

"Jeez."

"Viv said we'd call the cops and one of the kids – a girl – said 'we are the cops..'!"

"Tell me more about these geezers in your house…"

"Off the streets… old guys, young girls… been sleeping rough, whatever. They're trying to clean up London and thought we rich buggers were rattling round a big house so why not give it to the needy…"

"Threw you out there and then..?"

Frank nodded.

"But why you Frank… down here in deepest Dorset?"

"I think… I think I was targeted."

"By who?"

"Fuck knows… Listen, if I was a do-gooder, I'd say let them stay, but it's our bloody home Moggie, been handed down, flesh and blood, over centuries."

"OK Colonel. I have a plan. But I'd rather deal with it on my own," said Moggie. "My way."

"Really?"

"Really."

Harry sighed, aware that Moggie's scheme could be not only hair-brained but seriously dodgy. "No violence. These guys could be you and me in a few years..!."

Moggie slammed his fist across his chest like a gladiator before the Emperor.

"All above board sir!"

Harry looked sceptical. He'd heard it all before.

*

Forty-eight hours later, as the sun was setting, Moggie arrived at Harry's ancestral home, Somerby Hall, all tooled up, with two empty coaches.

He and his mates quickly and quietly set up a barbecue with beer and burgers.

Banged a gong and lured the homeless outside for a feast.

Dumped their belongings onto the wheels and padlocked the house.

When they realised they were being thrown out there was a brief scuffle - two bloody noses and a bone-crunching rabbit punch - which Moggie subdued with more booze. then coaxed them onto the coaches with promises of paradise, their very own home, and waved them off.

He'd inherited a derelict hill farm in the Brecon Beacons where these guys could start a new life, do whatever they wanted, their own commune, away from the city.

Moggie had always hated that bloody place in the middle of nowhere. Now he'd found good use for it. And was helping these guys, and Harry, at the same time.

Job done.

And just for once something made him feel good inside.

*

Harry and wife Viv, an ex-Chelsea model, had been back in their home some weeks when she got news of her father, Frank. His long-suffering housekeeper Fay had called to say he had cancer, terminal cancer, and was planning a trip to Britain sometime soon. For some childish reason father and daughter had not spoken for years, something to do with him having an affair with his television P.A. while married to Viv's mother. They had a screeching match over the phone – neither backed down - then both simply stopped communicating. Which meant he never saw Tara growing up, and Viv never got a look at his millions.

On hearing about his illness Viv promptly sent him an email and hoped she might hear back. She assumed he was coming home to see the family at long last and end his years on British soil. He never replied to the email, so she hoped he'd reverted to his old game show tricks and was going to turn up as a sudden surprise.

*

Though it was several years since university fees had been cancelled, Viv's daughter Tara could still not kick her secret habit which had helped finance her degree. She called it "social welfare", others called it escort work, albeit at the classy end.

There she was, in her usual suite in the Jumeirah Carlton Tower in Knightsbridge, being kind to a rich old Arab when her phone rang. She paused what she was doing, leant across the bed, didn't recognise the number but answered.

There on-screen was old grandpa Frank in California.

She gazed at his gaunt pallid face – he looked terrible; he gasped at her heavily made-up eyes, ruby lips, red satin gloves, and a naked old guy in the background.

Neither liked what they saw and both instantly hung up, pretending it was a wrong number and never happened.

*

Sitting in LAX waiting for the British Airways flight to London, Frank put his phone away looking a little bewildered.

"Problem Mr Gruber?" asked Sonny, plucking soulfully at his ukulele strings.

Frank shook his head. "Family stuff. And call me Frank." As he took a long whiff of oxygen from the breathing mask at his side. "Guess life's full of surprises when you least expect them…"

"So you'll be doing a bit of business and a bit of family in the old country Frank."

"That's about it Sonny. It'll be one helluva ride…" sighed Frank, beginning to wonder if returning to London with terminal cancer, this street beggar he scarcely knew, on some fantasy mission for the CIA, and meeting the daughter he'd not spoken to in years, could just be the last big fuck-up of his life.

*

Duffy was in his Fortnum's bar "office" with politician Suki Carter, the meeting she called to discuss her urgent "personal problem."

He'd ordered bubbly from Toto the barman, and knew this lady by sight – often popping up on television to attack the government – a feisty piece of work.

"What I'm about to tell you is in strict confidence Mr Duffy", she said.

"Just plain 'Duffy'..." he smiled. "And it's always in confidence."

Suki hesitated then took a large envelope from her bag.

"I'm married, but a couple of months ago I... unwisely... started an affair with a colleague. We spent a weekend in Cannes. And this week, this week, this arrived in the post."

She opened the envelope and took out the photo of Godfrey, the Prime Minister, and herself, kissing on their balcony at the Carlton Hotel.

"He must have been hiding across the Croisette. Behind the palm trees. Used a telephoto lens," she seethed, biting her lip.

Duffy's mouth dropped and slurped his bubbly over his white shirt as he stared at the photo.

"Jesus Mother of Sundays! It's you and the bloody Prime Minister!"

"Keep it quiet..!"

Duffy summoned Toto for more champagne.

"I don't have to tell you. This is dynamite! Tory girl and the Marxist!"

"It's not funny."

"I know. It's deadly serious. Anyone been in touch?"

"Nothing. But I expect it's blackmail. They'll want some huge payment from us both..."

"Or they threaten to publish."

Suki nodded.

Duffy's phone. Sheryl Crowe. "All I Wanna Do is Have Some Fun..."

"Must change that ringtone!" He took the call on voice when he saw it was Julie Slade and listened. His face fell. "OK Julie. I'm really sorry. I'll get back to you..." He hung up and turned back to Suki.

"Look. Can I keep this photo? Get it dusted for finger-prints – there won't be any – then you tell me when anyone contacts you asking for money – and we'll take it from there. For the moment sit on your hands. Try find out if Godfrey's been sent the same photo. This could take down the government – or at least the P.M. It's very very dangerous – you watch your back!"

"It's all my silly fault," said Suki. "And I'd just ended it all..."

"Love hurts. Let's just play one day at a time Mrs Carter. By the way – that call – did you know a Treasury guy called John Slade?"

Suki shook her head.

"Just found washed up in the Thames..."

*

It had been some months since Zaffy arrived in London, from her journey up through Spain with the boy soldiers Chindi and Sami. They'd gone their separate ways on entering this crowded hellhole – a mix of adrenalin-fuelled excitement and despairing loneliness.

She'd fallen on her feet getting the job in the hospital and they'd disappeared into the ether. One morn she thought she'd spotted them on the tube, another at a street market. But they'd moved on, out of her life. Least here they were safe...

Zaffy walked down a back street in Ealing and rang a doorbell.

A large African lady answered the door, wearing a hijab. She was about fifty, in a long dark dress, her eyes sad but wary.

"Yes?" she said, not recognising the visitor.

"Aunt Huda?" asked Zaffy curiously.

"I am Huda."

"It's me – Zafira – your niece from Sudan!"

Huda stood back a moment, stared long, then rushed forward and warmly hugged her.

"This is a miracle. My Zaffy! Allahu Akbar. I thought I'd never see you again – when my sister died, and your father, and brother..."

"And here I am..."

Huda led her into the house and they sat in her living room.

"I'm all alone," she said. "My boys've moved away – one's a musician, the other in IT. Their father disappeared…"

"Why you Muslim Aunt – we all Christian at home?"

"My husband… He took me to Allah. And I found Him comforting. Perhaps you..?"

"I like Christian."

"What you doing here my darling?"

"Working in a hospital", replied Zaffy. "Came up through Libya with two soldier boys who looked after me."

Huda held her hand thoughtfully.

"Hospital..? You must stay here - have fun, like old times."

"I could not …"

"Shush. I'm inviting you. Then you tell what you really doing here…"

Zaffy hesitated to show the soldier's photo who'd shot her family back home but decided to wait till she knew her better.

"Aunt Huda, I'd love to stay."

And they embraced once more.

With the glowing fire in the hearth and a photo of her mother holding her as a baby on the mantelpiece, Zaffy felt this was a home from home. An omen.

*

John Slade's funeral was on a typical London autumn day. About twelve degrees, golden leaves falling from the trees, the smell of rain in the air.

Duffy stood beside the widowed Julie in the cemetery.

As the coffin was lowered he spotted Slade's Treasury boss, Cyril Sharp, and the office receptionist. There were other suits standing po-faced as the vicar said goodbye to a very special person that he'd never met in the real world. A guy with a glass eye who'd been kidnapped for no obvious reason and dumped in the Thames, making it look like suicide.

Then further back Duffy noticed a familiar face from television and the newspapers, Chancellor Sean O'Leary, squeezed between two minders. You couldn't pin this guy down. Watch him on

"Have I Got News for You" and he was the funniest guest on the show; see him rabble-rousing at an Equalisers' gathering in Trafalgar Square and he sent shudders down your spine.

He'd been a back-bench Leftie for yonks and was generally seen as an outdated figure of fun, until the political tide turned and he and his comrades seized the chance to take the party back to its radical roots. At least he had convictions which was more than most of the Tories had. If he said he'd spend billions on the NHS, he'd do it.

If he said he'd soak the rich to save the poor, that was his mission. And he still seemed to have most people on his side.

Duffy watched Sharp turn back to O'Leary and nod. The Chancellor returned his nod, and walked away from the ceremony.

John Slade had been laid to rest and all was well with the world.

"Do you want a drink or something Julie?" asked Duffy as they walked to the car park.

"Rather be on my own thanks Duffy."

"It's not over. I'll keep digging until I find out why he died."

"You're a true friend", said Julie, holding back her tears as she got into her car and slowly drove off.

Duffy dialled a number. "Marky. You looked at that memory stick yet?"

He paused. "Encoded? Keep at it – this could be why the guy died…!"

*

In the dimly lit luxury spa deep beneath the Bulgari hotel in Knightsbridge, sipping the very best Krug, beside the bubbling vitality pool with its gold leaf glass inspired by the Byzantine mosaics of Venice and Ravenna, against a backdrop of textured Vicenza stone, lounged four whispering bodies in earnest conversation.

Saladine, the billionaire divorcee, in a shimmering deep blue satin bikini, was introducing an Arab friend to the two local politicians, Godfrey Young, the Prime Minister, and Sean O'Leary, his Chancellor.

The Brits, known in the City as "the Marx Brothers", in their beige trunks looked pale and never seen the inside of a gym, compared to the honed dark body of the Iranian. In the background three black suited body guards, obviously tooled up.

"I thought I should be intermediary between my friend Hossein Sulimann, and yourselves," smiled Saladine.

"We're flattered", said Godfrey, gripping the Arab's hand.

"Aye," chirped Sean.

"It is my humble pleasure to meet such international statesmen," smarmed Hossein.

Saladine continued. "Hossein was Commander of the Quds Force in Iran for many years. Very respected. Now, he's a consultant with the highest possible connections in the Middle East."

Godfrey knew the Quds Force alright – a special forces unit of the Revolutionary Guards. He also knew the U.S.A. outlawed them as terrorists.

"I need not give you two a history lesson, but I will." said Saladine. "These are crazy times in Islam. Iran, as you know, is Shia, while the other big nation, Saudi Arabia, is Sunni. Right now there's a power play going on in the Middle East – in Yemen and the Lebanon. America is backing the Sunni countries, led by Saudi, while Russia is friendly with Iran and their friends. We – my contacts in Iran - are getting worried as Israel – the longtime enemy - and Saudi Arabia for the first time ever are covertly talking together, turning against our Shia brothers…"

"Is very dangerous," murmured Hossein.

"And, with my British background, I realise this country - the U.K. - must soon take sides… with either us, Iran and the Shia, or Saudi and the Sunni."

Godfrey looked nonplussed. "Well, traditionally, as you know Saladine, the U.K. goes with America…"

"Not after that Kabul fiasco", snarled Sean. "We should do our own thing - assess what's best for us in this brave new world, best for the party..?"

"Iran is a very rich country," teased Hussain. "We're looking for new partners. Partners who are no longer friendly to Israel. Partners we can invest in. Partners we can share with…"

Godfrey looked seriously at Sean.

"This is interesting. But obviously we need to discuss with the party."

"Or we simply take the decision ourselves," added Sean.

Godfrey shook his head.

Saladine stood. "As George Bush said, when he illegally invaded Iraq... 'You're either with us or against us'"... she said with a serene smile.

"I hope we can work together gentlemen. You will be rewarded..." added Hossein.

And both exited, leaving Godfrey and Sean staring hard at each other.

This was probably the most important decision they'd have to make in their political lives.

CHAPTER FIVE

Duffy stood sweating at the mike: "We're up all night to get lucky..!" as he ended Daft Punk's knockout song and brought the rafters down, the crowd in this tiny Soho club showing their love for their hero. He bowed low and made his way over to a corner table where Zaffy, his hospital nurse, in a simple red dress, stood applauding him.

"Nothing you can't do Duffy!" she laughed.

He kissed her on the cheek. He found her devastatingly attractive but also awesomely vulnerable. He wanted to play it gentle, perhaps just keep her as a loving friend.

"Zaffy, I'm flattered you let me punish you.."

"No more praise. But you're good. Should turn professional..."

"Like the day job too much."

"Ain't seen you since hospital – how are the ribs?"

"All good thanks Zaffy." He paused. "Never thought I'd see you again."

"Gave me your card. So here I am."

"Like a drink?" asked Duffy.

"Just a Coke."

Duffy attracted a waiter and ordered.

"You really a detective?" asked Zaffy.

Duffy nodded, taking a swig of scotch. "Sure – right now, doing a blackmail and a murder..."

"OK. I got something," said Zaffy, hesitantly. "Personal."

"Always is sweetheart. Long lost boyfriend?"

"Not quite." She paused long. "Two years ago my family was shot in Juba, South Sudan. My mother, father, little brother. All."

"Shit, I'm so so sorry," and squeezed her hand.

"The police found this on my brother's phone." Zaffy took out a phone and showed Duffy the photo of a soldier, wearing an Arab shemagh scarf across his face. "They think he's the killer. I want you to find him. He's British."

Duffy stared hard at the soldier. Just see his eyes poking through the scarf.

"Why think he's a Brit?"

"That time only European soldiers around Juba were from here. Britain. It's him. I know it."

"OK. Zaffy – I like you and this is a terrible story. But what happens if I find this guy?"

The Sudanese nurse bit her lip and said nothing. She didn't have to.

*

In a corner of an East End pub Godfrey and Sean were gorging on meat pies and beer.

"This is more like it – I hate bloody fizz!" sighed Godfrey.

"What'd you think of that then – Saladine and the Iranian ?" mumbled Sean, his mouth full.

"Elephant in the room Sean – they're after our nuclear secrets..!"

"Bullshit. We can trust these guys - you've always backed Hezbollah, always opposed the Yanks and Israelis – we both have!" argued Sean.

"I know. But this is bigger. Like they're wanting a secret alliance."

"So? Keep it secret. We get rewarded. No-one needs to know..."

"You serious Sean?"

Sean nodded. "Got a confession Godfrey. I've known about this for months. Saladine came to me, to get you involved. I thought it sounded reasonable. Long as no-one knows officially..."

"You've known about this for months!?" roared the P.M. "You agreed behind my back!?"

"Course not Godfrey. You're the bloody boss. This is your

decision."

"Exactly. And I don't like it. Not tying us to Iran. Secretly or not secretly."

"OK OK. I'll get a message to Saladine. Not for us. Not right now." said Sean, backing off.

"Not anytime Sean. Agreeing to that would make us stooges, turn the country into a puppet state secretly run from Teheran!!"

Sean said nothing, chomping through his pie and downing his pint.

*

Duffy was leaning over Marky's shoulder, staring at her iMac computer. She looked and dressed like a tomboy, short-cropped pink hair, nose-stud, no makeup, grunge t-shirt. But her South Kensington apartment was coolly stylish with a flat screen TV along one wall, expensive oil-paintings hanging from the others, a spotlit horse's head made from driftwood in a corner.

"What you got Marky?" asked Duffy.

She turned to him smiling. "I think we caught a whopper."

"So?"

"That USB stick from John Slade's computer. It was encoded. Fucking firewall. No access. Kept me up for nights then I cracked it. And here we are..." She pointed to the screen. "Confidential bank account. Somewhere in the Caribbean. Probably Virgin Islands. Two deposits of a million in the last six months."

"I'm holding my breath here..." said Duffy.

"You'd never guess. The guy who lives and breathes to help the poor. The guy who invented the Equalisers to make sure we're dumbed down to the lowest level."

"The Chancellor!?" gasped Duffy.

Marky nodded. "The very same Sean bloody O'Leary!"

"Fuck! Who paid him?"

"No can tell. Sort of dark web transfer. Tracks well covered – across four or five different continents."

"Wow." He leant and kissed Marky on her cheek. "Mega breakthrough. He could be behind that little scrote beating me up..."

"And killing John Slade."

"Possibly." He stood back and stared anxiously at Marky. "This is suddenly serious, doll. Don't want you in danger."

"Can look after myself. Kick boxer, remember."

Duffy shrugged.

"What next?"

"Find where he got his millions. And I'll look into O'Leary... the whiter than white do-gooder who could be on the take, big time..."

Marky's blue eyes glowed into Duffy. "Wanna stay the night Duff?"

The singing detective thought deep and nodded warmly. "Your mum out of town?"

"Gone to the races in Deauville or somewhere..."

Marky got up and pulled Duffy into her arms.

*

Frank and his new street beggar buddy Sonny were deep in the bowels of the London Hilton on Park Lane hotel, sipping mai tai's in the notorious Trader Vic's French Polynesian bar.

The ailing TV producer had last been in this place in the eighties and nothing had changed. Least there was continuity but Frank was what had changed as he sat gulping air from his breathing tube.

He started uncontrollably coughing.

Sonny leant across and patted his back. "You OK Frank?"

Frank nodded and got his voice back. "Comes and goes. Sorry."

His cell rang and he answered.

"Gruber."

An American accent at the other end. "If it's breakfast time in L.A. it must be cocktails in London."

"We're having mai tai's. You following me?" spat Frank.

"Just a hunch. It's what you do this time of day in the Hilton. Rooms OK Frank?"

"Sure. Everything's dandy."

Frank looked around the bar at drinkers on their own,

wondering if any of them were CIA. There was a scruffy young guy in a baseball cap drinking Bud in a long glass; a blonde with too much makeup, smiling broadly across at him, sitting on a stool, slowly swinging one leg over the other, then repeating it; and a little old lady with a straw hat and Harrods' shopping bag, drinking tea with crumpets.

"Well, just checking in. No news yet. You guys just go shopping, enjoy London for a few days and we'll be in touch." And Mike hung up.

Frank, irritated, stared at the phone then turned to Sonny.

"Let's get outa here."

"Where to mister?" asked Sonny.

"You like old stuff?"

"Sure."

"Then we'll go visit the Natural History Museum. Not been there since I was knee-high…" and they both shuffled out of the bar. "Remind me, gotta call my daughter sometime – keep putting it off…"

Outside the Hilton, Frank trailing Sonny and his breathing gear, hailed a cab.

Behind him the little old lady dumped her straw hat and Harrods' bag in a bin, and followed in the next cab.

*

It must have been ten years since Duffy had a threesome. That cute little Greek island called Ios, across from Santorini. He'd decided to see if he could survive for a month's holiday down there just by singing in bars and he came home loaded. He couldn't get enough of those hot European chicks from France and Italy and Holland and Israel, and seemed they couldn't get enough of him.

For seven long nights he'd slept in a tiny one-bedroomed dump overlooking the fishing harbour with Sylvie from Copenhagen and Carlotta from Naples. Both spoke broken English which suited Duffy as their friendship meant not much conversation was required. But it did require a lot of drinking. With a bucket-full of retsina inside you the rest was on automatic pilot.

Each night was like being a performing acrobat, ducking and diving, always trying to make sure that you were equally attentive to each of your two lovers. The next morning no-one moved till lunchtime – everything ached - then it was more drinking, Duffy serenading in some backstreet dive, and back to business in the bedroom. By the time he'd got home he'd lost two stone.

And now here we were again.

With mother and daughter.

Seems the racing at Deauville went so badly that Marky's very attractive, very rich Mum, Davina, had unexpectedly come home a night early and was slightly worse for wear from the in-flight champagne. She'd cruised into her apartment in the dark, crawled into the same bed as Marky and Duffy, and the rest was history.

The two ladies woke at dawn and, in these liberated times, decided to take full advantage of the naked man lying between them.

Strangely Duffy was only too obliged to respond to these two impassioned creatures and ensure their every wish was indulged. By mid-morning there was a group hug and universal sigh as each of the three slammed their heads back on their pillows with exhaustion and immense satisfaction.

Over Americano and croissants the three sat unusually quiet at the kitchen table. Each wondered if what had happened had actually happened and whether they should talk about it.

"Wonder if I need a coat today?" stumbled Duffy, testing the atmosphere.

"Who knows..." grinned Marky from ear to ear and looking at her mother.

"That..." yawned Davina. "Was the most amazing fuck I've had in years!"

All three had hysterics.

"I could say we must try that again sometime, but I won't," said Duffy making for the door.

"Where you going?"

"Houses of Parliament. Got a date with a politician."

*

Suki led Duffy to the Members' tea rooms in the House of Commons, known for its occasional scurrying mice and run by the delightful Gladys. He immediately spotted faces he knew from the papers and television, those politicians who ran the ship of state, mostly onto the rocks, and had a very high opinion of themselves.

Suki leant forward into Duffy and asked, sotto voce: "Have you found anything about the photo?"

"Nothing new Mrs Carter. Obviously someone paid to take pictures that'd compromise you."

"I'm still trying to see the Prime Minister."

Duffy nodded. "We want to know if he's received the same photos. If he's been asked for money. Then we agree to pay, arrange a meeting, and try catch who's behind all this."

"This'll ruin my marriage. And I'll have to resign."

"If we contain it, none of that need happen. Tell no-one. Except the P.M."

Suki agreed, looking forlorn. "Of course, of course."

"How well do you know the Chancellor Mrs Carter?" asked Duffy.

"Sean O'Leary?"

Duffy nodded.

"Known Sean for years. Always a thorn in the side for the Tories. Always the radical revolutionary. Ban the Bomb. Visits to Cuba. Bit of a joke till they got into power and shocked the lot of us."

"No reason for him to be behind this?"

"Not that I know. He and Godfrey are really close. He'd never hurt his old Marxist mate... not like this..."

"Forget it. Obviously barking up wrong tree..." Finished his cup and stood. "Please call when you seen the P.M. and meantime, relax. We'll win this..."

Unbeknown to either, Sean O'Leary was sitting pawing over a newspaper in a far corner of the tea rooms and noted Duffy leaving with Suki Carter. He lifted his smart phone, and quickly took a photograph, grinning quietly to himself.

*

Frank was taking a selfie with Sonny beside a Tyrannosaurus Rex, one of the oldest carnivores to walk the planet, when the text arrived. The message was brief. "Holiday Inn, Kensington High Street. Room 108. 8pm sharp. Come alone." Frank's jaw tightened. The moment had come. Sooner than he'd thought. The museum was due to close and they'd be heading back to the Hilton for an early dinner.

"Problem?" asked Sonny, nodding to the phone.

Frank shook his head. "My consultant. Gotta go check in tonight. Won't be too long."

"No probs – I got the mini-bar and TV – hey, I'm on vacation thanks to you mister!" laughed Sonny.

Couple of hours later Frank arrived at the Holiday Inn. It had the feel of one of those bland South Los Angeles motels you'd drive past fast without stopping. Just the place the CIA would choose for a no-nonsense briefing.

He lugged his breathing apparatus into the lift, got to the first floor, and shuffled slowly along to room 108. What the fuck was he doing this for!? He could still be beside that pool in Beverly Hills with the girls.

Knocked on the door.

Nothing.

Checked the number on his text message.

Knocked again.

The door opened halfway. A male voice, British, invited him in, by name.

He'd expected an American. Big room with one dim lamp in far corner. Frank could hardly see anything it was so dark. He heard the chink of glasses in the gloom.

"Like a scotch Frank?" asked the Brit accent.

Frank could only see the man's silhouette against the ugly venetians.

"Sure. Thanks," answered Frank carefully, looking around him. Just him and this stranger, no-one else.

"Please sit down," said the man, coming over with a glass.

Frank sank into the sofa, breathing stuff at his side. He took a long whiff of oxygen, grabbed a slug of scotch and looked at the man standing in front of him.

Could see him clearly now. He did a double take. Been fucking years. He stared long and hard. Felt his pulse quickening. Mouth drying up.

"Harry!? Is that you?" he gasped incredibly.

Harry gave Frank a bear hug.

"You can see just fine Frank. It's me. After all this time..." And sat opposite him. "So sorry about the cancer... we'd tried to call, you never replied..."

Frank was totally confused. Speechless. "What's going on? I... I thought this was some business meeting... really important... and you're here... How's Viv – how's my lovely daughter – is something wrong - I gotta see her – was gonna call tonight, promise... she OK?" He struggled to stand.

Harry waved his hand calmly. "Calm Frank, calm. Viv is well and looking forward to seeing you." He paused dramatically. "This is business." Another long dramatic pause. "I'm the CIA's point man in London."

"You what!?" gasped Frank, slumping back on his sofa. For a moment he was gobsmacked, the past flashing in front of him. Always been hints that Harry was "something in intelligence", but it was never spelt out.

"Well. More liaison really. I was seconded from MI6. Nobody knows. Not Viv, not my own mates. Top secret."

"All this time Harry – all that army shit – you been working with Langley."

"Last ten years or so. When I was fighting in the Middle East was their eyes and ears. Then came back, out of uniform, and they asked if I'd be their London guy."

Frank could not believe what he was hearing. After all the dirty stuff he'd done for them over the years to find that Harry was working for the same lousy firm.

"Been tough keeping it quiet. But this is my last job. Then I just walk the dogs..." smiled Harry.

Frank was not impressed. To find his son-in-law suddenly giving him instructions. "What about me? I'm on death's door and been dragged over here to do what?"

"They value you Frank, you know that. We all know you're sick, we respect that, but this last job means you return home, where you belong, meet the family…"

"Die happy? Don't soften me up Harry. What's the fuckin' job!?" seethed Frank.

"We'll be there to watch your back, make sure you're safe."

"So !?" shouted Frank, wheezing desperately in frustration and anger. "Fuckin' tell me!"

Harry looked hard at his ailing father-in-law and said quietly "Sorry Frank, right now it's an 'on or off' job, depending on developments…" He pauses. "But if it's 'on'… it's so hot it's restricted to same day reveal…"

"Same day!?"

Harry nodded severely. "You won't know the job till you're bloody doing it..!"

CHAPTER SIX

Suki Carter had been leaving messages for the Prime Minister for days, trying to tell him about the Cannes blackmail photo, but he never returned her calls. He probably thought she was trying to start up their romance again. So when she accidentally bumped into him that evening in the car park she couldn't believe her luck.

"I haven't been avoiding you Suki" Godfrey whimpered. "Just frantic. And anyway I thought we agreed it was over." He was looking around to see who else was in the car park in case they were spotted together.

"There's something I must tell you. It's personal. And urgent!" hissed Suki.

Godfrey sighed, resigned to hear it out.

"Follow me." And walked urgently back into the Houses of Parliament to the lift that had once taken them to the Victoria Tower, where their secret tryst had begun weeks earlier.

Once more they were up there in the moonlight. Alone together. This time there was a frisson, an edge, between them. Both still wanted each other. But their heads told them otherwise. Too much to lose. But it was deeply tempting.

"Quickly Suki. What is it you must tell me?" snapped Godfrey, breathing heavily.

"Someone's sent a photo of us kissing in Cannes." whispered Suki, also breathing heavily.

"Bloody hell. Let me see!"

"I don't have it. They simply sent it in the post – no message – nothing."

"They're trying to blackmail us."

"Were you sent one too?"

Godfrey shook his head. "Where's it now?"

"With Duffy. He's on the case."

"Who the fuck's Duffy?" spat Godfrey.

"Detective. He's OK – wants to help me."

"You've given this bloody photo to some seedy detective!?"

Suki nodded, looking frightened.

"Do you have any idea how dangerous this is – I'd have to resign, get a divorce!"

"And me."

Godfrey grabbed Suki by the shoulders and roughly pushed her to the edge of the wall. The Thames was glistening and rippling way down there in the dark. If she fell now it'd look like suicide.

Suki was reading his mind.

"Did you ever see Francis Urquhart in 'House of Cards'!? He threw his girlfriend Mattie down from a tower like this one – made it look like suicide..."

Godfrey stepped back from her instantly.

"Have they asked for money?"

"I've heard nothing Godfrey."

"Give me this Duffy's details. And let me know if you hear anything else."

He led her back down the stairs to the lift. "I'm going to deal with this my own way. Someone's going to get hurt, and it won't be me!!"

They both got into the lift and stared silently at the walls.

The Prime Minister was outwardly furious and inwardly scared. Out there somewhere in the night was a loose cannon, determined to bring him down.

*

Zaffy had been staying with Aunt Huda for nearly a month when she thought she'd spring a surprise and take her out for a special Sudanese meal. She googled African eateries in London and found Mabola in Notting Hill.

But it was Zaffy who was destined for surprises that eve as the manager greeted them and she recognised him as Jamal, who'd worked with her at the Paradise Hotel back home in Juba.

They ordered tabikh alyoum - lamb stew, and samak magli – spicy tilapia fish, followed by khunaf – shredded pastry with stuffed nuts and syrup.

"This is the happiest night in years," said Huda, squeezing her niece's hand.

"Thank you my darling."

"Pleasure's mine Aunt - you've been so kind."

"But you are not complete," mused Huda.

"Complete?"

"You need a husband. Then you can stop work and make babies…"

Zaffy laughed. "There are other things to do."

"Like what?"

Zaffy hesitated. Not the right time to reveal the search for her family's killer. That she'd asked Duffy for help. "I want to explore London – the art, music – not get married."

Huda sighed. "I wish my sister could see you now. She'd be very proud."

"I do miss my family…"

At that moment someone came up behind her and put their hands over her eyes. She immediately stiffened, felt for the sheath knife she'd worn ever since that desperate African journey…

A familiar young voice whispered in her ear. "Za-fi- ra!!"

She tore the hands away from her eyes and was stunned to see Chindi, her boy soldier friend, standing there.

She leapt up and hugged him.

Not much more than fifteen, he stood beaming, slightly sweating, in a stained old apron. A tartan patch over his left eye.

"Chindi! Chindi! Why you here!?"

"Kitchen. Sami and I do the dishes!"

"Why the eye patch?"

"Had a fight with Sami…"

"Why?"

He squirmed slightly. "We both want to marry you."

"What!?" She laughed… "And..?"

"Toss a coin when get home…"

Zaffy, still giggling, turned to her Aunt.

"Aunt Huda – my friend Chindi who saved my life coming over."

Huda shook his hand stiffly. "Proud to meet you Chindi."

The boy soldier bowed to her and nodded to Zaffy. "Not as quiet as she looks – a fierce warrior!"

"Where's Sami?" asked Zaffy.

"Breaking dishes – as usual."

At that moment Jamal beckoned Chindi back to the kitchen.

"I'll contact you and Sami" promised Zaffy, "now I know you're here…"

And waved as the young Sudanese disappeared to the kitchen.

"I'd like to help them if I can," said Zaffy, paying the bill. "They're good boys…"

"Everybody want to marry you," mused her Aunt. Then under her breath…

"We'll find you a nice Muslim boy…"

*

Frank had had a shit of a night. Hardly slept a wink in his suffocatingly warm room at the Hilton, overlooking Park Lane. His lungs were gently burning and his stomach ached from the cancer. Every few hours he hopped out of bed, took more pain-killers, and washed them down with neat scotch.

But it was more his mental angst that kept him awake. He was still in a state of shock on two counts.

First, seeing Viv's husband Harry, after all these years only to learn that he was his CIA handler in London, and second, to be told they'd only reveal his mission on the actual day… assholes.

He tried to work the logic on why they chose him. They could have got one of their action men do the job, a super-fit ex-special forces Seal, instead of a doddery old git living out his final weeks. Then again, they knew he could be trusted. He'd never failed a mission in the past. And perhaps it was because he was dying that they now wanted him. To get up close and personal to their target.

Then he realised.

In a nano.

It wasn't Sonny who was the "disposable". It was him. He

really was a dead man walking. He was their very own kamikaze pilot, their suicide bomber. Whatever the plan, he was going to die anyway, give or take a few weeks. It was too clever.

And so CIA. Except. Except. Why did they get him find a total stranger and bring him over as the "disposable"? Someone he'd assumed would die instead of him, and no-one would miss them..? Unless Sonny was going to die in the plot too – they'd both die in a bombing or whatever. Frank felt angry that Harry had told him so much yet so little.

He said there'd be another meeting about the details. How the mission would happen. So Frank was left this morning, with a headache from no sleep and too much Scotch, an aching stomach from his cancer. Perhaps he should just vanish. Walk out of the hotel right now, get a flight somewhere and escape the hold they had over him.

But they'd still find him. Once you worked with these guys you never left. They wouldn't let you.

He remembered their veiled threats in L.A. about harming his family and wondered if Harry knew anything about this. Probably not. It was dog eat dog in this game. You could trust no-one.

And thinking of family.

His daughter Viv. Grand-daughter Tara.

Viv and he had argued years ago over his infidelity and never spoken since. It was so damned childish. His one and only. He must call her later today and make a meet.

As for little Tara, the sweet kid in Dorset who loved ponies, there was that embarrassing call few days ago when he saw her on his cell, dressed like a tart and possibly working as one.

He wondered if Viv knew about this.

And Harry, how could he face him in front of Viv, knowing he was secretly running the mission. It was all getting too much.

He took an another swig of scotch then shuffled off to collect Sonny for his sunny-side up.

*

Duffy had sat for two hours sitting astride his Harley, peering through his smoked visor across at the House of Commons car park. He was waiting for one man. Sean O'Leary. So far the only clue to John Slade's murder had been taken from his home computer, where Marky had found a hidden account revealing the Chancellor was receiving secret payments amounting to two million.

Now Duffy knew that all, or most politicians, were corrupt – remember the expenses scandal – but guessed, like everything else, there was a sliding scale where they could sink deeper and deeper into the mire.

It looked like O'Leary was in pretty deep – somewhere round his shoulders – if someone was throwing him a few mill for a few favours. Just what would that buy?

Special questions in Parliament encouraging investment in some business or another – a housing estate, motorway building, the new airport – where someone out there, high in the business world, would make a mega killing from bribing the Chancellor with a paultry two million.

But. But, if all this hidden bribery was linked to the Treasury guy's death, surely it was more than a business scam. Or was it? Could be a London mafia link. The Turkish or Roumanian gangs. People smuggling or drugs. Turning a blind eye. Dirty work, dirty times.

And then this bizarre blackmail photo of the Prime Minister bonking a bloody Tory. Couldn't look worse. If that photo got in the press could mean adios Godfrey and a new election. And that could make Sean O'Leary the new leader. So perhaps this jigsaw puzzle was coming together after all.

At that moment the Chancellor came out of the Houses of Parliament and got into his chauffeur-driven car.

Duffy started his bike and followed at a discreet distance.

They were heading into the West End.

Round Trafalgar Square. Up St. Martin's Lane. Across Charing Cross Road into Soho.

The Cleopatra Club.

Duffy knew it well. Done a singing gig there earlier that year. Bloody expensive dive with a louche rich crowd of all ages. Sort of place a top show biz talent might be eating then go take the mike after supper. You never knew who you'd bump into from Jagger to Lady Gaga...

He parked his bike and entered.

It was heaving.

Duffy went straight to the bar and ordered a chardonnay, nodding to Maurice the manager through the crowd. As usual a buzzy eclectic colourful mob standing elbow to elbow like a scene from a very precious cocktail party, which indeed it was.

He scanned the room for O'Leary who had vanished. Could be anywhere.

In this place there were hidden alcoves within alcoves for the celebrities with special guests who didn't want to be seen, and theatrical balconies overlooking the stage for the luvvies who were desperate to be seen.

The band was ending a big number and Maurice was at the mike sounding all apologetic. Tonight's special singer, all the way from New York, had lost her voice and couldn't make it.

Duffy watched the manager turn across to the bar and beckon to him.

Suddenly the crowd started chanting his name... "Duffy! Duffy! Duffy!"

Maurice on stage was still beckoning for him to join him.

Duffy loosened his tie and pushed his way through the crowd.

"Ladies and gentleman", cried Maurice. "The evening is saved by a very good friend of Cleopatra's – please give him a big hand – Duffy!"

Duffy took the mike. "I just popped in for a glass of wine..."

But the crowd roared for him to sing.

And Duffy obliged, with his usual flourish.

Kicking off with Sinatra's "All of Me"... then Queen's "Radio Gaga"... E.L.O's "Mr Blue Sky" and closing on the Bee Gee's "Stayin' Alive".

All classic fodder that had this champagne crowd whooping for more.

As Duffy wiped his brow and pushed his way back to the bar a waiter came up. "Someone would like to meet you sir..." He wouldn't say who.

Duffy followed him to a dimly-lit alcove in a far corner.

He'd seen her on television and the papers but never in the

flesh.

She oozed sex from every pore and then some. Around fifty. Bit of botox.

Carefully groomed long blonde hair. Low-cut red satin dress. And those pouting lips.

She held out her heavily diamonded hand to Duffy as if she were royalty.

"I'm Saladine," she whispered huskily. "Come and join me Mister Duffy."

From the shadows Sean O'Leary watched Duffy kiss her hand, then vanished towards the exit...

CHAPTER SEVEN

It was a reunion both were dreading for different reasons. Mother and daughter. Viv and Tara. Neither had seen Frank for years and with him on death's doorstep, it was going to be a very restrained affair.

Viv's grudge against her father dated back to when he left her and went to California with that other woman. That was the last time she ever spoke to him. She couldn't forgive him walking out on Mummy and herself, she being only a young kid. Of course he'd gone on to be ludicrously successful making his TV shows, sending her expensive presents at Christmas, but she refused them all, even the pony which she so desperately wanted. There was a constant ache inside her that cried out to talk to her father, trying to forgive and forget, then with her mother recently dying from the Covid virus in a care home, the anger returned.

She'd done well in her early London days, modelling for the best fashion houses in her twenties, flat in Chelsea, front cover of Vogue, then having a fairy tale society wedding to the dashing young cavalry officer, Harry Wickham. He'd whisked her off for a sun-drenched honeymoon in Bali, then returned to live in dreary Army quarters at Tidworth while he gallivanted across the Middle East, getting more medals, and promotion.

These days happiness for Viv was riding her faithful Flora across the Dorset hills, and listening to "The Archers" with a hefty Bombay Gin and tonic in her hand.

Punctuated of course by the ghastly episode with the Equalisers who stole their home for several weeks until Moggie miraculously got it back. But now, now she was to confront her father Frank and had to remind herself that he was on his last legs.

*

Tara had never met her grandfather. Seen videos and family photos, but never sat in the same room. She knew only too well her mother's history with Frank, or lack of it, and dreaded to think what would happen when they met. He'd seem like a total stranger who knew nothing about his grand-daughter. Nothing about her idyllic childhood, the boarding school near Shaftesbury with the nuns, and, more recently, getting a B.A. in History at Sussex. She'd have loved an older shoulder to cry on, to bounce ideas off regards her career decisions. All she got from her mother was meet a rich man and marry him, while Daddy advised her to go Down Under for a few years to find herself. As if. So instead she decided to lead a secret life.

Which was why she was dreading seeing Frank. That fucking phone call.

When he called and must have seen her on the bed with her "client." She'd blotted it from her mind and hoped he had short term memory. That was one part of her secret life. She got a kick out of dressing and acting like a tart. Loved it. And she got paid for it. A public service, she told herself. And so far no complaints.

The other secret would make her parents cut her off without a penny. Again, no-one knew. Or was going to.

*

Frank sat nervously sipping mineral water, Sonny at his side, in Viv's favourite watering hole, The Wolseley. Still one of the most chic and stylish restaurants in London where you could have Adele and Biggins, Prince William and Kate on adjoining tables, George Clooney and Brian May on others.

He and Sonny made a strange incongruous couple. An old man holding an oxygen mask grimly smiling beside a younger black companion. Frank was wearing a classic blazer with a red silk kerchief in his pocket; Sonny a slightly crumpled beige suit and yellow spotted bow tie.

There was a noisy cooing flurry at the entrance as they saw Jeremy King, the legendary and ever charming owner, gliding towards them followed by a stylish woman and glowing young girl.

Frank swallowed hard and stood to greet them.

Viv and Tara.

Frank shuffled silently around and hugged Viv. Tears in his eyes. Then without a word he turned to Tara and did the same. Two long hugs for all those wasted years.

"My girls," he wheezed. "I am so so sorry."

Viv grabbed his hands and stared at his watery eyes. "So am I Daddy. So am I."

"Please sit," mumbled Frank. "Viv, Tara… this is my travelling buddy, Sonny. He's from L.A. He's looking after me…"

"I'm watching his back," joked Sonny.

"It's wonderful seeing you… I'm sorry you're… so sick," said Viv, clutching Frank's hand across the table.

"No Harry ?" he asked carefully, wondering how Viv would react if she knew about the CIA stuff.

Viv shook her head. "Sends his apologies. Running his own security firm, now he's left the Army – hardly see him."

"Always was a busy boy – guess we'll meet sometime soon."

"Make sure you do," said Viv.

"And Tara – you are just so cute – it's our first ever meeting I think," said Frank with a knowing twinkle.

"Absolutely," agreed Tara. "About bloody time!"

After more awkward small talk they got to order.

Kedgeree. Flat Iron Steak. Coq au Vin. Steak Tartare. Bronzed Truffles. Apfel Strudel. And Sherry Trifle Roulade. Washed down with a cool Dom Perignon.

Viv asked Frank how long he was in London.

"Few weeks I guess – just wanted to catch up on my old family before it gets too late."

"How long you got Gramps?" asked Tara, never one to hold back.

"That's not fair Tara," glared Viv.

Frank stared at her a long moment.

"Not a problem Viv," Frank took a deep breath. "They say

weeks Tara. But you know, could be a whole lot longer – I get pain then take the pills and I'm fine…"

"This guy's fitter than I am," laughed Sonny. "Marathon man."

"You must come down to Dorset Dad …" said Viv, realising soon he'd be gone. "Stay as long as you like… both of you." She wondered if they were a couple…

"Love to. Got a few contacts to look up in town then we'll do that …" said Frank, coughing and grabbing his breathing mask.

"You two known each other long?" Tara asked Sonny.

"Sort of picked me up in the street," he grinned. "But we're just good friends…"

After a long rambling lunch Frank decided he'd done enough talking and promised to meet Viv again later in the week. They lingered outside on the pavement, with Frank whispering to Viv that when he goes she'll get everything, then limped sadly into the dusk dragging his breathing apparatus, Sonny at his side.

"That went well Frank," said Sonny.

Frank nodded and said nothing.

*

Mother and daughter shared a cab, with mixed feelings - elated yet sad at seeing Frank and the terrible state he was in. Viv bit back the tears, pulling herself together as she got out at Regent Street, leaving Tara to go on to Hackney.

As far as she knew, Viv thought her daughter was off to her posh publishing job. But this was Tara's other secret. Her parents would have a heart attack if they knew what she was really doing.

As her taxi neared the East End, she wiped off her makeup, popped in a nose ring, and pulled on a yellow Smiley Face tee-shirt.

*

When the sultry billionairess Saladine invited Duffy back to her luxury suite at The Dorchester, the singing detective quietly pinched himself under the tablecloth at The Cleopatra Club. Only months earlier he'd flown all the way to Shanghai to try hitch up with one of the many Chinese millionairesses who were desperately looking for love. Or so the papers had said. It had been an embarrassing disaster which he vowed never to repeat. But this was different. This was the dancer from Sheffield who found Allah, married a Qatari prince, took a mega divorce payoff, and was now the richest woman on the planet. You always knew if she was in town with her convoy of limos racing past Harrods and up Park Lane, but nobody actually knew what she did. Until now. As Duffy sat in the warm glow of those mascaraed blue eyes he got the feeling he knew exactly what she wanted to do.

"I'm having a party", breathed Saladine as she quietly devoured Duffy through her long lashes.

One hour later he lay in her giant-sized bed at The Dorchester, exhausted.

It had been a very passionate party. Just the two of them. They'd sat drinking Krug in her drawing room then moved gently to her boudoir, leaving a trail of clothes behind them.

Her body was trim with voluptuous breasts, long blonde tresses loosely hanging way down to her waist.

She quietly put ruby red lipstick on her nipples, lightly sprinkled talcum powder over her soft white skin, dabbed My Burberry Black Parfum on her chiselled cheeks at £2000 a pop, then handed Duffy the honey.

For a split second he wondered if she was about to serve an early breakfast but quickly became creative, pouring the syrup all the way down from her lips to her scarlet painted toes.

Then it started. Ever so slowly. Each body playing gently, carefully, hard to get, feeling, teasing, caressing, licking the other, touching every moist sweet cavity, until each was awake, excited, roused and rampant, all care tossed aside as they moved together as one impassioned beast, breathing lustily, riding the other, thrusting deep, louder and louder, until a shrieking explosion burst from both. A shared cry of joy. A sigh. Then silence, save for their thumping hearts.

They lay in each other's arms then began once more, with even more passion and purpose. This time more acrobatic. With Duffy spinning on her softness, topping and tailing, tailing and topping, then their mouths locked as one, an ecstatic shriek of delight. And both collapsed panting on their pillows. The smell of sex all over them. Her nails scratching bleeding into his back, staining the crisp white satin sheets.

*

Duffy woke the next morning in the same bed finding Saladine dressed and ready to leave.

"Don't get up Duffy. I like you in my bed…"

Duffy pulled himself up on one elbow. He felt drained. "Must get going – work to do my love…"

"Wait darling. When I was married to my Arabian prince he treated me like a sex slave…"

"Shit - I'm sorry." He wished he was that prince.

"He'd lock me in the bedroom for days on end…" smiled Saladine going to the door.

"What a bastard…" sighed Duffy, with envy.

"So he could ravage me whenever he wanted…" laughed Saladine, blowing him a kiss as she closed the door firmly behind her.

Duffy's head flopped back on the pillow imagining the scene. Her locked in a bedroom at the mercy of her cruel prince.. Wicked. Then a thought. He stared at the closed door. No way. Got up quickly and turned the handle. Nothing. Turned again. Wouldn't open. He was bloody locked in.

Seemed like Duffy – serial shagger of this parish – had become a sex slave for the richest girl in town.

*

As the church clock sounded noon, the priest standing in the small garden at the rear, lit his roll-up and started studying "Racing Ahead", his cell phone at his side, ready to call in today's bets. It was a special arrangement, him keeping out of the church for half an hour from twelve, rewarded by a fifty quid donation, which he'd put on the horses.

At exactly the same time an attractive middle-aged woman,

in an expensive fur coat and scarf, entered the front of the church and went straight to the confessional.

She sat and said quietly: "I'm here."

From the confessional came a male voice. "It's not good news I'm afraid."

"Tell me," said the woman patiently.

"The main man will not play the game."

"That's very disappointing," she replied, trying to hide her irritation. "Why?"

"He says he thinks we should remain 'independent'. Not be tied to a foreign power."

"You would not be tied. We would simply influence your decisions from time to time. Perhaps share some technology... This would help your country and benefit you both personally," she persevered.

"I know this, but I don't think he'll change his mind."

"Does he know we will pay him millions?" she sighed.

"It makes no difference."

The woman paused a moment. "Could we influence him in other ways..?"

"Like what?"

"A little pressure. On his family or friends..?"

The man in the confessional paused. "Let me try him again. Perhaps I can persuade him."

"That would make sense, for all of us. Otherwise..."

"Otherwise?"

"Otherwise he will have to go."

"What do you mean?"

"He goes and you become leader."

The man in the confessional paused a long time. "He's been a friend a long time. I couldn't hurt him."

"You'd do nothing. We would facilitate. Either way, we must make this deal happen. I'll give you a week, then let me know if you've changed his mind. Understand?"

"Understood. Did you deal with Duffy?" asked the man in the confessional.

"Duffy's a pussy cat. He's no danger to us. I quite like him..."

"He might become a problem."

"Leave him to me."

"If you think…"

She interrupted him: "There's another payment transferring to you tomorrow… And remember, it'd be disastrous if the newspapers found out…"

The male voice went silent.

As Saladine emerged briskly from the small church and got into a waiting limousine.

Sean O'Leary stumbled from the confessional, looking shell-shocked.

*

Duffy had spent an hour trying to get the Dorchester reception come up and unlock the bedroom door, especially as Saladine had given instructions he was not to be disturbed. As he caught a cab back to the Cleopatra Club to collect his Harley he could still feel her nails ripping into his back. It had been some night, and wondered if he'd ever see her again.

It seemed his wish had instantly come true as he approached his bike to find a black limo sidle silently up beside him. Obviously electric, no noise at all. The back door swung open and a hand beckoned. This dame was insatiable.

As he climbed inside he got the shock of a lifetime.

No Saladine. Instead two males in surgical white masks and aprons. He was thrown into a seat and tied down. Brutally, efficiently. All without a word as the car moved off on its batteries.

One of the surgeons spoke. A high squeaky voice: "Mister Duffy. We'd like you to help us."

Duffy scanned the limo. It was all white and there was a fridge freezer down one side. The surgeon had carefully taken two trays from the freezer and laid them on a table under Duffy's nose. The other robotically opened a drawer and spread out a selection of scalpels, surgical knives, axes, and several syringes alongside the trays.

Duffy almost vomited when he saw what was lying there.

On the first tray was a selection of fingers. Amputated fingers. Thumbs, forefingers, little fingers. All neatly sliced at one end.

About ten of them.

On the second were two penises. Frozen. One circumcised. One foreskin.

He didn't like this at all.

The first surgeon lowered Duffy's seat to horizontal like an operating table, and whisked off his trousers with a theatrical flourish. Like a matador flicking his cape at the about-to-die bull.

Duffy suddenly looked and felt very naked.

The second took his hand and held it firmly on a wooden chopping block.

"We don't like busybodies."

The first pushed a button and Chopin started playing. "We don't like them at all."

"Your thumb or your cock Mister Duffy?" asked the second politely, grasping a large scalpel and peering at both parts.

"I've done nothing – what do you want!?" croaked Duffy. All was silent in this purring electric car, that and the bloody poncey music.

"I think he's playing with us," whined the first.

"Ever the innocent," agreed the second.

"Shall we proceed and ask questions after?"

"It's worked before…" playing teasingly with the scalpel.

"Let me help you," pleaded Duffy. "I hate blood."

The surgeons looked at each other and deeply sighed.

"You have a photo of the Prime Minster?" asked the first.

Duffy thought then nodded furiously.

The second took his thumb, licked his lips, and looked at Duffy's groin.

"We would like it please." Laying the scalpel on his prick.

Duffy nodded furiously again. "It's back there, with my bike."

"Are you sure?"

"Bloody sure," swallowed Duffy, pulse racing.

"You wouldn't lie?"

Duffy furiously shook his head, avoiding looking at the two trays.

The first surgeon tapped to the driver who turned the car around and headed back to The Cleopatra.

They skidded to a hushed halt and Duffy was thrown from

the limo.

"The photo!" screeched the high-pitched one, now pointing an Uzi at him.

Duffy went to the bike's handlebars, unscrewed one end and pulled out the rolled up photo of Suki and Godfrey.

The shriek looked at it carefully. "No copies?"

Duffy shook his head.

"You sure?" yelled the shriek.

Duffy nodded, as the surgeon thwacked the Uzi's butt across his face, slamming him to the ground, then leapt back into the electric limo, silently gliding off.

Duffy sat rubbing his bruised cheek. What a fucking nightmare. Did I just dream all that? Guess the P.M. put the dirty brigade onto me.

He then slowly undid the laces on his left boot. Pulled it off. And, from inside, shook out a folded piece of paper. Opened it up slowly. His copy of the compromising photo. Godfrey and Suki. Game on.

CHAPTER EIGHT

When Tara entered the Equaliser "factory" down a quiet side street in Hackney, hot on the heels of lunch at The Wolseley, it was like landing on another planet.

On the outside the building looked liked a decaying warehouse, but inside it was a buzzing glossy 21st century powerhouse, in every sense of the word. For the word "power" was burnt into the DNA of each and every one of the 300 Equaliser foot soldiers manning this operations zone.

The atmosphere was that of a military HQ but even more focussed, more zealous, more deadly, more sinister. For it was from here that Sean O'Leary's dedicated youngsters in their yellow Smiley Face tee-shirts, aged mostly 16 to 21, were out there bending the minds and actions of the public and politicians. It was these "grassroots campaigners" who were really running the New Dawn Party, were really running the whole bloody country.

The building was open-plan with rows and rows of desks where the youngsters sat glued to their computers. Along the sides hung television screens covering the news in different parts of the country, while a giant flat screen sat on the main wall, from where Gonzo, the thirty-something Equaliser 'leader' from Glasgow, would instruct his troops twice daily with campaign instructions and developments. As all were meant to be of equal ranking Gonzo could not be referred to as their General or Captain, so was simply called "One".

The operations room was split into different specially defined sections.

There was the obvious 'fake news" department from where

each day the Equalisers would create false news stories honed to turn public opinion against the Tory opposition or particular individuals. These would be written in this section then spread across social media via Twitter, Facebook, all the newspapers, and their hotline to the BBC. These guys knew historically that the more you stated something over and over, repeated as often as possible through the news channels, then eventually the public would take this as gospel and believe it. Even if it was a blatant planted lie. They knew that most people outside of their building were not interested in politics, only how much they took home every month. They knew that the public were mostly pretty dumb and loved to hear emotional stories about the down-on-their-luck, about victims, about the starving poor, and that this ammunition would be used viciously and ruthlessly by the Equalisers to further their cause.

Then there was the "activist" department from where weekly demos were meticulously planned for locations across the country, covering different hot issues from higher pay for the public sector to abortion, the NHS to trans gender toilets. Some of these demonstrations would be disciplined peaceful marches, others would be deliberate anarchistic free-for-alls where shops and banks were razed to the ground. Always thoughtfully targeted but made to look like the work of a rampant mob.

Then there was the "attack" department which meant getting "up close and personal" with selected individuals, verbally and/ or physically. These mostly would be elected Tory M.P.'s who opposed New Dawn policies and were getting in the way when it came to passing Bills in Parliament. The strategy here would be low-key assaults via social media, generally threatening and highly personal messages often promoting blasphemous rumours, sexual or professional, that could mean the end of the target's political career. That was the mental war. The other was less subtle and meant abusing them in person outside their offices and homes. Shouting at them, throwing bricks through windows, shit through letterboxes. And finally, there was the death threat message which often unsettled them enough to employ bodyguards.

This same ploy was also used in marginal seats when elections – council or for Parliament - came around, as ordinary members of the public were targeted to ensure victory for the Equalisers' allies.

And finally, there was the "covert" department, which was the most secret of all as it was here that red lines were frequently crossed, the law often broken, in order to achieve their ends. It was here that they recruited long term "sleepers" in councils, charities, hospitals, unions, quangos, universities, the media, etc. who would quietly work to push through the aims and beliefs of the Equalisers. They had so many sleepers influencing stories in the BBC it seemed like a dormitory. This was the "dirty tricks" section where during elections they would encourage university students to vote more than once – which was illegal - by using both their uni address and their parents' home address, and get sympathisers on councils to create masses of fake postal voters at election time to make sure they stayed in office. Once more, consequentialism won the day – the end would always justify the means.

Coming from a comfortable middle-class family in Dorset, having a private education and romping through her degree, Tara felt a physical rush every time she entered "the factory" in Hackney. This was reality – from her cushioned upbringing, to become an Equaliser was like fucking a tattooed builder from Liverpool. It was raw, rough, and bloody sexy. You could taste and smell the adrenalin and power as you walked through the door. It was the place to be. These guys – her new family – had a unique belief in themselves - were running the whole shebang and no-one knew it.

At first she thought she'd never fit in, then the more she immersed herself in their causes, the more she saw how the rich fat fuckers were screwing up the world, the more convinced she was that she'd found her new home.

"Late again Tara," shouted Gonzo, looking at his watch. He had short carrot coloured hair, an ear-stud, spots, and a large red nose which accounted for his nickname. Always wore denim dungarees with a different daily, usually cynical, badge. Today's was "Save The Piranha."

"Sorry Gonzo – family lunch," smiled Tara, sitting at her desk in the "attack" section.

"Where you go? The Ritz?"

"Pizza parlour," lied Tara. If she'd said The Wolseley, Gonzo's chip would fall off his shoulder. She felt she still had to conceal some parts of her past without class envy getting in the way, no matter how much she loved these guys.

Gonzo doesn't believe her. "You still sure about working here?"

"I love it – you know that. Found somewhere that means something at last, instead of all that superficial shite out there…" says Tara, wondering what's coming next. She knew Gonzo liked to toy with her, to send her up. She also suspected he wanted to fuck her. Which might be fun.

"Office," he snapped. And walked off.

Tara leapt up and followed him through the rows of workers on computers, some of them looking like young kids. All of them earnest, eager, committed.

To the side of the giant flat screen was Gonzo's office. There were posters of Castro, Karl Marx, Stalin, and Marilyn Monroe with her skirt flaring up over that air vent. Classic Gonzo. You could never totally put this guy in a box.

"Sit Tara," he said, slumping on an old leather sofa.

Tara obeyed.

"We're pleased with you."

"Thanks. I'm enjoying it. Loving it."

"Are you 100% with us?" asked Gonzo, scratching his butt.

"You bloody know I am."

Gonzo's eyebrow lifted questioningly.

"Listen," said Tara, wondering what she must do to prove herself. "Remember it was me who targeted my own family in Dorset – got them thrown out of their home - just for you guys!"

"But they're back in again…" smiled Gonzo.

"That's not my fault," sighed Tara. "If they ever find out I was behind that…"

"They won't."

Tara bit her lip. "Do you want me to walk?"

Gonzo stared at her discomfort. "We love you too. But there's one last task to prove yourself – to become one of us…"

"Tell me. I'll do anything – you know that," pleaded Tara.

"OK. You know this Land Tax we're trying to push through Parliament?"

Tara nodded. Her father Harry was always harping on about

it. Worried they'd have to sell up if it came in as they could never afford the increase.

"The P.M.'s doing an enquiry into it before going to a vote. See if it'd alienate ageing voters sitting on their expensive bloody houses."

"Tough titty," smiled Tara. She was sick and tired of the baby boomers sitting on their millions having bought their homes in the eighties for a few grand, and kids these days not being able to buy anything, just throw away their savings each month on rent.

"Well. There's a Tory I want you to target. Every time this comes up in the Commons she attacks us. And right now looks like she's winning. Seems Godfrey's got a soft spot for her. Or she's got something over him."

Gonzo handed a file to Tara.

"Everything you need to know about her."

"How far you want me to go?" asked Tara.

"Whatever it takes…" sniffed Gonzo.

Tara opened the file and looked at the Tory politician.

Suki Carter.

*

"Few more days Frank, bear with…" smiled Harry, as he sat in the Aqua Shard bar, level 31 of the tallest building in the land. He was sipping a Corpse Reviver No. 2, while his father-in-law downed a White Lady. In the background Sonny was chatting up an attractive Eastern European barmaid.

"And our target's wandering around down there as we live and breathe," continued Harry, looking out over London's eclectic skyline, with its eye-catching but visually ludicrous Cheesegrater, Walkie Talkie, and Gherkin monstrosities, all looking like some futuristic scrapyard gone very wrong.

"We taking out a politician?" asked Frank, wheezing into his breathing mask.

Harry shrugged. "It's complicated Frank. Bloody complicated."

"Surprise me."

"Let me give you the backstory. Said I was seconded from M16. Wrong. This government has virtually closed down, sidelined, both MI5 and MI6 - they do their own shit – using the Equalisers."

"But they're just kids, from what I heard…" said Frank.

Harry nodded. "Everything's gone topsy-turvy since this lot got in. First cancelled Trident, then ran down the military, then the spooks." He paused. "But. I'm still doing dirty jobs for Langley."

"So it seems."

Harry paused and stared hard at Frank as if he's weighing up whether to reveal something of great portent. Then said in a 'watch my lips' mode: "We've reason to believe a foreign power's trying to take control of this country…"

"Fuck me," breathed Frank. "Don't tell me – Russia?"

Harry shook his head. "Middle East. That's where the new global power lies."

"What about Washington and Moscow running the planet, like always?"

"My guess Frank is that they'll both implode in the next twenty years, probably go bankrupt. And when you and I are well gone – in about forty years – the two giants'll be China … and Islam. China's already bought Africa and the Pacific region; Islam's furrowing deep into Europe. China doesn't do God, and Islam doesn't do Communism. Two unstoppable forces. One helluva big bang."

"If you're right Harry, glad I won't be here…"

Harry nodded silently. Seriously.

"So, back to the current op. A foreign player, from the Middle East, is planning to turn this country into a puppet state. They call it 'state capture.' Try and influence our foreign policy, especially with Israel. Possibly grab our nuclear secrets."

"Shit," breathed Frank.

"Lot of soul searching in Downing Street - they're all jostling for power… see who can get closest to the Middle East guys…"

"Heavy politics Harry. So…?"

"Yup?"

"Who we taking out – our guys or the Arabs?"

"Can't say yet Frank… too soon."

Harry stares at a text on his phone.

"Sorry – gotta go." He stood abruptly. "Viv loved seeing

you by the way. You're coming down for a weekend." He shook Frank's hand.

"So when's this kicking off Harry – my days are numbered?"

"Brief you soonest... Have another cocktail on me, you and your 'disposable'..." And he's gone.

Frank ordered more drinks, then peered out over the capital, biting his lip so hard it started to bleed.

*

Duffy, still recovering from his attack in the limo, was looking forward to meeting Zaffy's best friends, her boy soldiers from Sudan. They'd come up through Africa together and the boys had saved her life more than once. He'd promised them all a very English day out which meant boating on the Serpentine with beer and sandwiches.

Chindi and Sami were two skinny bright-eyed teenagers who'd grown up quicker than they should, simply to survive in their desperate man-eat-man war zone.

They could skin antelope in the dark, bring down a charging buffalo at fifty paces, and fire a rocket-propelled grenade before they could read.

"Hope not too cold for you guys," smiled Duffy in straw hat and shades.

"It ain't Africa," said Chindi, covering himself with a blanket.

"Don't moan – is warm for London," laughed Zaffy.

"We made right choice, coming here," added Sami.

"Sudan is beautiful, but all that blood," added Zaffy."Not good..."

"Still home... but here, here we're free," said Chindi.

"I hear you saved Zaffy's life many times on the road..." said Duffy.

"Remember the hyenas..." teased Sami.

"Me fast asleep by the river, then wake up to find twenty standing round me... getting closer and closer..." said Zaffy.

"While we was swimming with the crocodiles..." smiled Chindi.

Sami imitated shooting with a machine gun. "Boom boom. If

we hadn't got there in time you'd be supper missy!"

Zafira clinked bottles with the two. "My superheroes!"

"Then there was Libya..." mused Sami, his face darkening. "Not good."

Duffy cracked open more beers. "Tell me about it... if you want..."

*

As the trio headed towards Sabha in southwest Libya the gigantic flaming sun was slowly setting over the desert in a blood red sky.

Zaffy and her young warriors, Chindi and Sami, were driving their faithful old Jeep, despite the punctures and breakdowns, on their journey from South Sudan to London and a new life. Their plan was to shoot through Algeria to Morocco, across to Spain and Europe.

Since Gaddafi's overthrow Libya had been run by rival gangs of militias, psycho warlords all armed to the teeth, high on LSD or Tramadol, all totally ruthless, so the boys were on constant alert for danger.

Zaffy was dozing in the back of the Jeep when the engine slowed.

"We're being followed," shouted Sami who was driving.

Behind them a cloud of dust and a Humvee carrying a dozen Arab militants waving Uzi's in the air.

"Let them pass," hissed Chindi.

Zaffy woke and stared warily at the ragtag bunch of screaming zealots as they roared past them, then skidded to a halt yards ahead, blocking the road. "Shit!" she said, pulling out her knife.

"Stay still," urged Chindi. "We can deal with these fuckers..." as he cocked his machine gun.

A tall man in a long red beard and white robes approached them. He was a walking killing machine. Belts of bullets across his chest, pistols in his belt, and carried a massive bazooka.

At his side a smiling little guy, with a shaven head and black beard. He was European.

"Fuck!" whispered Sami. "They're ISIS!" They had to be, with a European amongst them, probably a Muslim convert. "How can we help guys?" he asked politely.

The red beard motioned for all three to get out of the Jeep, which they did.

"Where you from?" asked the little guy.

He was English. Had a funny accent, like the Beatles. This suddenly looked bad. Really bad. These converts were more crazy than the Arabs.

"Sudan." said Chindi quietly.

The little guy turned to Zaffy. "What's your name darlin'?" He ran his finger slowly across her lips.

Zaffy shook it off. "Don't touch me" she snapped.

Little guy smirked: "I'll do exactly what I want doll..." He turned to the red beard and nodded to Zaffy.

"What you doing ?" snapped Chindi, pointing his gun at the little guy.

The European whipped out a pistol: "Taking my girl for a ride."

The tall guy grabbed Zaffy, and tied her hands with a chain.

Two other dead-eyed grim-faced beards had joined them.

Little guy looked carefully at the boy soldiers. "You two Christians?"

Chindi and Sami looked at each other.

"Muslim," Chindi lied, holding his breath.

"Allahu Akbar," chanted Sami, with serious dedication.

The little guy approved. "Don't follow or you're dead," he smiled, dragging a struggling Zaffy back to their vehicle.

The armed men slammed Chindi and Sami to the ground with their rifle butts, and Zaffy was driven away into the red dusk, a chained prisoner of ISIS.

*

Later that night Chindi and Sami arrived on the outskirts of Sabha and spent the night in the Jeep. They feared the very worst for Zaffy but were determined to find out what ISIS had done with her.

At dawn they headed to the town market for food and any clues that could lead to where she was imprisoned. Didn't take long. All the locals knew what was happening in their town and they didn't like it. Seemed the migrant traffickers – the people smugglers – who were getting paid to transport thousands of Africans across the Mediterranean from Libya to Italy and Greece, had turned back the clock by centuries and were selling these migrants as slaves. Every week in a migrant warehouse the "merchandise" was paraded in front of interested buyers, where these impoverished Africans would be sold as farm boys, maids or whores. The boys learnt the next auction was noon that same day...

*

Chindi and Sami, their heads covered, blended into the shrieking crowd attending the slave auction in Warehouse B, central Sabha.

Along the walls on each side were bamboo cages crammed full of silent wide-eyed Africans, mostly male, in their early twenties. These were the young men who'd left their villages in the Congo, Mali, Chad, having saved for years for the price of travel to Europe. Always knew it'd be risky, always heard of the boats sinking at sea and the drownings, but they persevered as this was their one ticket to somewhere that meant hope. Never in their darkest moments did they dream they'd be standing here locked in a cage, shoulder to shoulder with many other migrants, being sold to rich Arabs.

Standing on the central stage was the auctioneer, a jet-black gimlet-eyed Arab with a hooked nose, and keffiyeh, cracking a horse whip. He made no pretence about what he was doing, referring to the young blacks standing beneath him as 'Abd'... 'slaves'.

There were two boys, the latest hot 'merchandise' from Nigeria, for sale. Each looking terrified. They'd given all their savings, travelled for weeks, to reach Europe, and now they were being sold as 'bodies' like they did in the bad old days. The whites of their eyes bulging, gulping hard as they held back the tears, each with shackles and chains cutting into their skin.

Chindi and Sami couldn't believe what they were seeing.

"Fuckin' evil," whispered Chindi.

"We must do something," agreed Sami, looking around at the

others in the crowd. All Arabs. How many would help try rescue these slaves. He saw no sympathy, no anxiety; the crowd were enjoying this stone-age circus.

The auctioneer started his bidding. "Eight hundred... here we have two good fit boys who can work on the land... or be servants in your homes..."

He looked around the crowd. There was interest from several bejewelled Arabs, who nodded at the auctioneer.

"900... 1000... 1200" A long pause, then wham, went his horsewhip as the price was settled. The two boys were sold to a large fat farm-owner for 1200 Libyan dinars, the price of a mongrel, and led off through the crowd in tears.

Chindi and Sami were aghast at what they saw next.

The little guy – the English ISIS convert – had climbed on stage and stood beside the auctioneer, with two girls in chains.

One of them was Zaffy, wearing a dirty headscarf.

The auctioneer beamed: "Gentlemen, this is a very special bargain. My friend Jazza here is selling his beautiful Yazidi wife..."

The little guy nodded enthusiastically and gave a thumbs up.

"Who is as giving in the bedroom as in the kitchen" roared the auctioneer, causing guffaws of wild laughter from the crowd.

He then turned to Zaffy. "And this lovely lady is a virgin from Sudan... who'll work as your maid or satisfy our friends in the whorehouse..." More hooting from the raucous crowd, desperately drunk or high on drugs.

Zaffy stared ahead; expressionless.

Chindi and Sami gripped each other's arms.

"We gotta stop this!" whispered Chindi.

"Not yet brother," urged Sami.

The auctioneer began to bid for the Yazidi girl. "500... 900... 1200... 2000!"

And a short sweating fat man in a red fez bought Jazza's ex-wife, the Yazidi girl.

The crowd cheered. Sweating, swaying, entranced.

"Next! The virgin!" cried the auctioneer, slapping his whip across his calf.

"What do you give for this pretty creature from Sudan – make someone here very happy..."

And the bidding commenced. "600... 1000... 1500... 2000... 2500... 3000!"

And the auctioneer cracked his whip.

The virgin from Sudan was sold for 3000 dinars to that same short man in the fez. He had bought a bargain – two girl slaves who'd make him rich from selling their bodies on the streets.

Zaffy's head slumped forward as, still shackled to the other girl, both were led out a warehouse side-door to a waiting Mercedes belonging to their new owner.

An elated Jazza, who'd made a healthy profit from the sale, accompanied them to do the hand-over.

Chindi and Sami were waiting with their Jeep engine idling.

Sami sliced Jazza across the face with a long dagger, dragging the girls from his grip.

Zaffy was numb with shock and joy.

The Yazidi confused, wondering if these were more enemies trying to harm her.

Chindi downed the new fat owner in the fez with a rabbit punch to the back of his neck.

As Jazza blindly staggered screaming down the street, face covered in blood.

Sami took an axe from the Jeep and cut through the girls' chains. They were free.

A stunned moment as Zaffy looked around her and hugged her boy soldiers.

They pulled her into the Jeep and looked around for the Yazidi, but she'd vanished, nowhere to be seen. Probably run for her life down the nearest alley rather than go off with more strangers.

Sami slammed the accelerator and the Jeep roared off from the warehouse, with Chindi holding Zaffy close at his side, and Jazza still stumbling on the street behind them.

Half an hour later they stopped at a well for water, then raced on towards the border for fear the ISIS mob might be not far behind.

But their bravery had paid off and in days were crossing into Morocco, the smell of Spain not far away across the sea.

*

"You boys are bloody heroes," said Duffy, clinking his bottle with theirs.

"If it wasn't for them I'd be trapped in Libya," mused Zafira.

"You might have liked life as a whore" smirked Sami.

"I could have been rich..." Zaffy laughed.

"What I want to know, is if that little ISIS shit has returned home," said Chindi. "I'd love to meet him again one day..."

"Who knows guys..." agreed Duffy, "he could be somewhere in London right now..."

CHAPTER NINE

If someone had told Godfrey Young as a young man he'd end up being Prime Minister of Great Britain he'd have head-butted them on the spot. His early years were on a tough Manchester council estate, followed by a politics diploma at the local Poly, and joining the Communist Party. He trained in judo, drinking ten pints of bitter a night, and Karl Marx. By twenty he knew his vocation was to rid the country of capitalism and bring in State ownership. This way the poorest of the poor had a chance in life, and the rich fuckers would pay their due.

His first proper job was with the RMT – the Rail, Maritime and Transport Workers Union - where, within three years, he'd elbowed his way to the governing council, and was just one person away from being General Secretary. Pete Wilkins, was the person standing in his way and had the age and seniority that would make Godfrey wait another ten years or so.

Until the car accident. One wet and windy night poor Pete had been out drinking with Godfrey and, driving home alone, had crashed through a bridge barrier, drowning in the river below. Rumours abounded that Godfrey had spiked his drinks or cut his brakes, but this was the nonsense of thriller fiction. For his part Godfrey was so upset he didn't attend the union office for a fortnight, grieving for his old mate, but duly accepted Pete's General Secretary post after a few month's grace.

Ironically it was always assumed that the dear cuddly Prime Minister was the more malleable and vulnerable, compared to his number two, the Chancellor, Sean O'Leary. Few realised it, but it was Godfrey who had the nerves of steel, the stealth of a cobra, and could not be trusted under any circumstances.

That night with the silly lovelorn Suki up on Victoria Tower he was seconds away from pushing her over the side into the Thames, but her timely comments about the murder in "House of Cards" had saved her life.

As for the fucking photo of her with him in Cannes, at least his boys had got the copy back from that nerd detective Duffy. But who in God's name had the original? Who paid a photographer to shadow them around Cannes then take that deadly picture of the P.M. holding a hot totty Tory in his arms.

But right now he had other matters to deal with, of more importance.

At exactly three o'clock Sean O'Leary arrived at his Number Ten office for their meeting.

The Chancellor sat and fidgeted nervously. Godfrey noticed. This was out of character for the garrulous Sean.

"What's up Sean?" asked Godfrey with slight irritation. He'd cut short an excellent lunch in Soho because of this meeting and missed out on the Baked Alaska.

"It's the deal with Iran again. Saladine wants to know your answer. If we want to do business with them?" said Sean somewhat nervously, knowing what was at stake, remembering Saladine was willing to get dangerously physical if she didn't get her way.

"I've already told you – this ain't good for us Sean. We'd be painting ourselves into a corner, and Iran'd be running the show..." sighed Godfrey.

"Shall I ask her for more time?" suggested Sean meekly. "She's getting very pushy..."

"She's only a fucking dancer from Sheffield Sean!"

"And the richest bitch on the planet..!"

Godfrey digested this a moment. Sean had a point. To alienate this powerful woman might be extremely short-sighted in these unpredictable times. One day in the future she could be a very valuable asset... and the country needed financial investment, desperately.

"You're right Sean," sighed Godfrey. "Let's buy some time. Tell her we're still discussing this offer."

Sean nodded with relief. "Catch you later for a drink," and

exited.

Godfrey stared at the closed door and wondered just what sort of a deal his old partner Sean was cooking up with Saladine behind his back...

*

Suki had had a positively exhausting day in the House of Commons and was hoarse from shouting down Labour's proposed new tax on burning coal in private homes through the country.

For years the trendy middle-classes in London and across the land had been enticed, seduced, and persuaded to buy wood-burning stoves, the epitomy of class and style, the must-have cool kitchen accessory, experiencing the purity of that true Scandinavian experience, warmth from logs fresh from the wild forests, and none of that impure polluted coal.

Then, like all those who were lured into buying diesel cars through Blair's government, black became white and white became black. Just as proud owners of diesel cars suddenly found themselves priced out of the market by new green taxes, so now the same pro-active climate cleansing warriors were urging citizens to stop using wood-burning stoves or having old-fashioned log fires in their living rooms.

The nation was stunned as suddenly they were being told just how poisonous the fumes were from burning wood and especially coal; that you could inhale cancerous bodies from lighting such fires, everyone must go electric. So the sexy had gone out of romantic adventures on that cosy shag pile rug in front of the warm glowing hearth; now it was urged to have a clinical bonk in front of an bland electric grill.

Suki had just emerged from the bath in her Gloucester Road flat, poured herself a large merlot, and was watching "The Crown" on Netflix. At the back of her mind she was still wondering who'd taken the incriminating photo of her and Godfrey in Cannes. It was dynamite for all concerned. Duffy had called to tell her that a gang of wackos in a limo had forced him to give up her copy under duress, which might or might not have been linked back to the P.M.

But still she wondered who took the picture. She did have

a brief drunken fling with Darius, a gorgeous young researcher, moons ago, but surely it wouldn't have been him. Then again he always avoided eye contact with her in the corridors these days. Silly really, she still wore the lovely silver necklace he gave her after their night together.

It was then she heard the noise in the street outside. At first she thought it was the neighbour's telly, then turned her own down to listen more clearly. It was chanting over and over.

She went to her bedroom, ripped off her dressing gown, threw on a smock and went to her front door to peer out.

There were dozens of them. A sea of yellow Smiley Face tee-shirts, shoulder to shoulder across the street outside her flat. The notorious Equalisers.

And they were angry, as they all waved their banners.

"Land Tax the Rich!" "Land Tax the Rich!" "Land Tax the Rich!" repeated over and over.

As Suki edged out of her front door the crowd went silent.

She could see it coming but did not have time to duck as the egg hit her full on the face.

The crowd did not laugh or jeer; they simply all applauded with straight faces.

Suki wiped the yolk from her eyes and wondered how to react. Whatever she did they'd win. If she shouted at them, they'd shout back louder. If she rushed inside, it would look as if they'd scared her.

They stood still silent, glaring with hate, daring her to fight back.

She faced them, raised a single middle finger, then, shaking her head with deliberate sadness, slowly went back inside.

She sighed deeply, leaning against the closed front door, as the chanting started up again.

"Fuck!" she spat, realising someone had got the Equalisers to target her at her private home, as she so openly opposed the Land Tax. So much for democracy.

She wondered if Godfrey himself was behind this, or one of his minions, or whether the out-of-control Equaliser militants had chosen her as their next Tory scapegoat. Any day social media would be buzzing with venomous messages against her, urging her to commit suicide, or others to put an end to her.

Seconds later a brick crashed through her living room window.

She ran upstairs, dialling the police, and got to her bedroom.

Through the curtains she looked down at the mob, still chanting.

At their rear was an attractive redhead who was obviously controlling the demo. She had a quiet confident smile and looked far too intelligent and classy to be mixing with this rabble. Probably a guilt-ridden privately educated wonk who was rebelling against her privileges.

The girl put her fingers to her mouth and did a loud wolf whistle.

The chanting stopped.

The rabble dispersed.

Leaving Tara alone standing looking up at Suki peering down from her bedroom.

The two locked eyes a long moment.

Suki felt a shiver down her spine as she turned away from the window.

That pretty girl out there had smiled at her, yet was so fucking scary…

*

Charlie was enjoying the interview. He was doing an exclusive for "The Evening News" with the Chancellor, Sean O'Leary. Just sitting in his office revealed much about the man's character.

He'd already been down the tick list on his childhood; father a tool-maker, mother a nurse; terraced house with outside toilet in gangland Glasgow; his apprenticeship at the Govan shipyards on the Clyde; breaking his jaw on a fight over a girl; joining the Communist party in his teens; getting married to a teacher and calling their kid Red. Textbook stuff. But the office showed a softer side. Framed photos of his family with their pet wolfhound, walking the Highlands, fishing on the lochs.

Which made this notoriously thuggish politician positively human. The only chink was the yellow Smiley Face tee-shirt hanging mounted in a frame behind his desk.

His proud followers.

"Which brings us up to the present day Sean," said Charlie, pausing before he got into more touchy subjects. "Tell me about the Equalisers. Who are they, and what are they for?"

"Glad you asked me that Charlie," smiled Sean in his most charming way.

"I founded the Equalisers well before the election. They're a grass-roots bunch of believers in our far Left ideas. Sincere, genuine, many of them teenagers, students, but also pensioners. All of life is there."

"So they were your activists who got you into power, into Downing Street, but what's the point of them now?"

"People say they're our Praetorian Guard," chuckled Sean, mischievously.

"Bodyguards to the Roman Emperors?" asked Charlie.

"Only joking," soothed Sean. "We use them for PR purposes, to keep the country's spirit up, to remind them that this party believes in democracy, nuclear disarmament, and the NHS."

"Isn't the truth that they're your enforcers, that they intimidate your enemies?" urged Charlie.

"Course not son," sighed Sean, getting tired the way the interview was suddenly going.

"Didn't they throw a brick through a female Tory's window this week, and this morning she found a bloodied coffin outside her door!? All because she opposes the Land Tax?"

"No proof my people were behind that!" Sean got to his feet and looked at his watch.

"Before I go Mr O'Leary. A treasury official was recently found in the Thames. John Slade. Was this suicide or something more sinister?"

Sean walked to the door and opened it.

"Interview over Charlie. You're crossing the line with this stuff," snapped Sean.

"Did you know this John Slade?"

Sean shook his head, waited for the reporter to leave his office. "Duffy a friend of yours?" he suddenly asked.

"Duffy? Sure – did a feature on him few weeks ago," answered Charlie curtly as he walked out.

The Chancellor leant against the closed door. All these personal questions about Slade must have come from Duffy. He had to be dealt with. Permanently.

*

As the church clock sounded noon, the priest was sitting on his toilet, trousers round his ankles, lit his roll-up and started studying "Racing Ahead", cell phone at his side, ready to call in today's bets. Once again he'd agreed to keep out of the church for half an hour from twelve, rewarded by a fifty quid donation, which he'd put on the horses. Last time he made a grand, which he decided he'd spend on a dirty weekend in Vegas.

At exactly the same time an attractive middle-aged woman, in an expensive coat and scarf, entered the front of the church and went straight to the confessional.

"I'm here. What's he decided?" said the woman.

"Nothing yet. He needs more time. Wants to think about it," said a hoarse male voice.

"You OK?"

"Sore throat, sorry."

"We haven't got for ever. I need tell Iran it's a green light or it's not!"

"Another week or so – I'll try push him."

"One week! Fucking make it work! Remember what I said, if he says no then we'll facilitate his removal."

A long pause from the confessional. "The Prime Minister? How would you do this?"

"We have ways. It'd look natural..."

"Kill him!?"

Saladine said nothing.

"Then..?"

"Then you become leader and everybody's happy," she smirked.

No response, then.

"I'll get back."

"Did you receive the latest payment?"

A pause. "Of course, thank you."

"Next week then." Saladine whipped off her black scarf and walked briskly out of the small church.

Moments later, from the confessional slowly emerged the man with the hoarse voice.

Godfrey... A deeply haunted look on his face.

Saladine, from her smoked glass limo around the corner, nodded to herself as she saw who she'd been talking to. Now at last there'd be some action from these idiots.

*

Duffy was walking up Shaftesbury Avenue towards Chinatown when the Pretenders started thumping out "Back on the Chain Gang" He'd changed his ringtone. It was Charlie checking in after his interview with Sean O'Leary. Told him how Sean threw him out of his office when he mentioned John Slade. Not that it proved anything.

Duffy hadn't told the journo what Marky found on the USB stick, merely hinted the Chancellor was behaving in a very fishy way and did turn up at Slade's funeral, though claimed he didn't know him. Also thanked Charlie for bringing up Suki's intimidation by the Equalisers. He still had the second copy of the Godfrey photo and wondered whether he could solve that jigsaw. Unless the Chancellor was behind all the shit that was happening around Whitehall – Slade's apparent murder and that telltale photo from Cannes. But why? Charlie mentioned some wedding singing gig in Dorset he might be interested in – friends of Tara's - and rang off.

Duffy was crossing the Avenue when someone from behind suddenly pulled him sideways. Probably saved his life. A motor scooter had been roaring up the road heading straight at his back and would have run him down but for the quick actions of that stranger.

Duffy stood a moment staring after the disappearing bike wondering if it was deliberate. No-one he recognised.

She was already sitting in the window of Lee Chow's café when he turned the corner into Chinatown.

Zaffy.

Any excuse to see this girl. Got ever more dazzling each time he saw her.

Duffy gave her a hug. She looked tired but pleased to see him. All those late nights working in the hospital. They looked at the menu and ordered.

"Nearly got run down just now..."

"Who?"

"God knows... prick on a scooter" shrugged the detective.

Zaffy reached across and took his hand.

"Take care Duffy... you are very special to me..."

Duffy's eyes widened. Perhaps he'd got this lovely all wrong. Perhaps she was just shy.

"I love you..." she whispered.

Duffy put his hand over hers.

"Like my brother..." she added.

Duffy quickly withdrew his hand. "Not much luck finding your killer," he said hoarsely.

"Knew it'd be tough."

"Sat all afternoon looking at Brits who worked in Juba and he's not there."

"I know it's him in the photo", insisted Zafira. "And I know he's here..."

"Many mercenaries in Sudan?"

Zafira nodded. "The bad guys. Government brought them in from South Africa and Europe. Really crazy."

"OK. Let me get Marky – my IT girl – take a look - I want find him as much as you do."

"It's important - thank you."

"Get out of London much?" asked Duffy.

"Never."

"Been invited to sing at a wedding, in Dorset. Very old England. Come along if you like. As my friend..?"

"I would..."

Zaffy froze, looking at someone across the road, watching them from an alley. On the phone, casually smoking, trying not to attract attention.

"What's the matter?"

She choked, pointing across at the figure, wearing a grey hoodie.

"He tried to sell me – in Libya – it's him - ISIS!"

She stood and stared, hands to her mouth in shock.

Duffy looked across the street, and was out the door in a flash, chasing the little guy in the hoodie. Had a beard and scar, just like the shit who beat him in that club. Was he following him? Or worse, Zaffy? Was it him nearly ran him down on that scooter?

He was fifty yards ahead, ducking and weaving through the tourist crowds wandering dozily through Chinatown, peering at the restaurants, reading the menus.

Duffy raced through them, shoving them aside.

Scanned ahead.

More tourists, stood chatting, blocking his view.

The little sod had disappeared.

Looked around him. He was deep in Chinatown. Wall to wall eateries. Scarlet dragoned Chinese lanterns swinging overhead. Oriental music caressing gently from every restaurant doorway. Dim sums and noodles from Shanghai, Hong Kong, Korea, Thailand, Malaysia, Cambodia, Vietnam. And those delicate wafting perfumed aromas floating across the lane... ginger, garlic, spring onion, Sichuan pepper, soy sauce. Hypnotic. What the fuck.

Duffy was running out of time fast.

To his left a Chinese street market, steaming and stir frying pork and chicken and fish.

To his right a health store with two smiling Asian girls sat in the window.

Duffy shot in, knocking one of the semi-naked girls over, up the stairs.

Four doors. Opened each. Couples bonking. Through door end of corridor.

Stairs back to ground level and he was back again amongst the dozy holidaymakers.

Almost impossible to get past them.

Saw him.

Hiding in a doorway hundred yards away. Not moving. Smoking. Playing cool. Trying to blend in.

Duffy put on an agonising spurt.

Closer.

Nearly there. Hadn't seen him coming.

Closer.
Smelt his rotten breath.
Grabbed the little scrote.
Spun him round.
Slammed him against the wall.
Hard.
Screamed.
Bad teeth.
Grey hoodie and beard.
He was fucking Chinese.
Wrong bastard.

CHAPTER TEN

It was a classy wedding at an ancient pile just outside Shaftesbury in Dorset. Duffy had been invited to Paris for the weekend by Saladine but decided to go for the safe option and was belting out classic oldies in a marquee crammed with posh totty from the home counties.

He'd been preceded by three gorgeous lookalike blondes in sprayed-on gold dresses who played Bach rock on their pink violins, called The Fondles, and was now closing his stint as wedding singer with Dexys Midnight Runners :

"You in that dress, my thoughts I confess
Verge on dirty
Ah, come on Eileen..!"

Duffy had flung his signature red silk bow tie into the crowd and unbuttoned his shirt. Always a bad sign. With a dramatic flourish he ended the song and stage dived into the swaying crowd to be caught in a belly flop by admiring fans. Applause ringing in his ears he made his way to the top table to join his refined hosts.

They were a weird bloody mob.

Duffy had got the invite to be wedding singer through his reporter mate Charlie, and the bride was Tara's cousin, Lucia. He'd brought along Zaffy as a platonic mate, partly because he admired her and her guts, partly because he wanted to help find her family's killer, who she swore was a Brit soldier.

But it was the rest of Tara's family who were exotic, to say the least.

Her Dad, Harry, worked in security in London, and was quite an amusing cove. Liked his drink and had an eye for the ladies. Her mother, Viv, had amazing bone structure, had worked as a model, and was still a stunning beauty for her age.

Then there was Viv's father, over from Los Angeles, a Hollywood TV producer, carrying a breathing cylinder around with him and looking pretty sick, accompanied by a shy black guy Sonny, who seemed to be his carer.

The wedding speeches were over, bride and groom had kicked off the dancing, balloons released from the ceiling, and everyone was entering that dangerous later-to-be-regretted champagne zone where whatever they said or did would not be remembered next morning. Full denials at dawn.

"I do so hate weddings," slurred Tara to Duffy. "They're so fucking artificial."

"Don't believe it – one day you and Charlie…" replied Duffy, emptying his flute.

"Bullshit – he's just an old friend – from our schooldays… Not my type."

"What is?" asked Duffy, raising an eyebrow.

Tara stared unblinkingly at him.

At the other end of the table Zaffy, who was not drinking, turned to Harry, and asked: "Did you travel much, with the Army?"

"All over m'dear – but don't talk about it. Like to dance ?"

Zaffy hesitated, realizing she'd probably have to support this man on the dance-floor, but nodded politely.

"Where you from ?"

"South Sudan."

"I know it well…"

They both stood and stumbled into the braying mass that were leaping about to the Bee Gees.

Viv leant across to Frank. "Playing your song Dad - 'Staying Alive.'"

"No joking matter kid," rasped Frank.

"Why don't you see a doctor while you're here – second opinion?"

Frank smiled. "Going this week. Old friend in Harley Street."

Tara took Duffy's hand. "Ever seen Orion?"

Duffy looked blank.

"The hunter. Come and I'll show you the brightest stars – Betelgeuse and Rigel. It's a clear night!" She stood and tried to drag Duffy outside.

"What about Charlie?" he whispered, not wanting to upset his mate.

"We're only looking at the stars Duffy!"

And she dragged him out of the marquee, across to some trees on the grassy hill.

They walked for several minutes.

"The stars?" panted Duffy, trying to dodge the cowpats in the moonlight.

Tara grasped his waist and shoved him to the ground. "You're the bloody star, stupid!"

Duffy hesitated, then let his inner appetites give in to his enthusiastic partner.

They swiftly pulled off pants and panties, and he began to lick her nipples, then navel.

She suddenly sat up abruptly, banging his nose, and cried in pain. "I'm being eaten alive – sitting on a bloody ant hill!"

They hoisted up their knickers, and limped back to the marquee, Duffy dabbing his bleeding nose, her rubbing her bum.

So much for star-gazing.

*

Duffy and Zaffy were staying the Saturday night with Tara's parents at Somerley Hall, their sprawling mansion near Semley. She felt privileged to experience a historic home where the English noble knights once dwelled, though it could not compete with the ancient Sudanese castles where Sultans lived with their voluptuous harems.

At ten the next morning they all sat in the breakfast room and devoured porridge, prunes, and kedgeree. Another strange English custom, thought Zaffy.

All were in attendance.

Duffy, Zaffy, Tara, Charlie, Harry, Viv, Frank, and Sonny.

Tara kept scratching her bottom.

"What's the matter darling?" asked Viv.

"Sat on a bloody anthill," she snapped.

"Pull the other one," laughed Charlie.

"Don't believe me then," replied Tara moodily.

Duffy rubbed his nose and avoided Tara's glance.

"I think we boys should do some exercise this morning," suggested Harry.

"Count me out ," wheezed Frank.

"Of course Frank." said Harry. "Now Duffy, I hear you not only sing, but you're a private eye?"

"I try to be..." nodded Duffy.

"Excellent. I thought we might do some trail running. I set clues and you try find your way back here fastest. Which if you're a detective Duffy, means you've got an advantage!"

"I do hope so," answered Duffy, who hated childish games.

"This is what we'll do. I'll drop you three – Charlie, Duffy, and Sonny – at the foot of Win Green. Big hill not far from here. Then it's a three-mile race through the woods, ending up back home. There'll be arrows pinned to the trees telling you which way to go... First home wins a bottle of bubbly. What do you say?"

The three males nodded grimly. Not much choice.

*

Back home in London on that sunny Sunday morn, Duffy's computer moll, Marky, was beginning to scroll down dozens of faces of U.N. British soldiers who'd fought in the Sudan over the past few years. It seemed an impossible task.

She sat, totally naked, with the photo of the soldier in his shemagh holding the rifle, that Duffy had given her, and had Springsteen pounding out in her earphones.

So far, not so good.

She paused. Made a coffee, and slumped on a sofa with "The Sunday Times" for a few moments.

Then had a brainwave and returned to her iMac.

She put "British Mercenaries Sudan" into Google and waited

to see who'd turn up.

*

Duffy might have been good in the sack but wasn't that fit. He hadn't run a mile for years – when Jo's policeman husband found him in bed with his wife and chased him across the West End with an axe. But this was different. His rivals were not much better. Charlie was younger and probably faster. Sonny was a mystery though looked too chunky to be a winner.

Harry had driven off with Tara after breakfast in his Range Rover to pin clues to the trees in the woods, while the guys changed into shorts and running shoes.

He then drove them to the foot of Win Green. It was a really steep climb up the hill, spattered with bushes and gorse, before they entered the woods which stretched for miles.

Tara had come along with their working cocker, Sirius.

Ever competitive, Harry had the trio line up at a starting line he'd marked out with branches. He then reminded them of the rules.

"There's five arrows pinned to trees in the woods. Simply follow directions and we'll see who gets back home first!"

"Why don't you take Sirius with you – he loves a good run?" suggested Tara.

"Not a good idea darling – these chaps are racing – he might get lost," said Harry.

"Come on Dad – he'd love it." She stared pleading at her father, who melted, with some irritation.

"Oh alright. Who's taking him?"

"I'll take him", offered Charlie. "He knows me."

"Duffy". Tara picked up Sirius and plonked him at his feet. "You take him."

Duffy smiled blandly back and nodded. Last thing he wanted holding him up was a bloody mutt.

"OK." said Harry impatiently. "Are we ready to go?"

The guys shuffled onto the starting line of branches.

Harry then raised his old Lee-Enfield .303 rifle to his shoulder.

"Ready, set." And fired a bullet into the air, scattering crows from the trees around them.

Charlie, Sonny, Duffy and Sirius, leapt forward and climbed up the hill as fast as their limbs and muscles and hearts could power them.

Charlie the youngest forged ahead, twenty yards in front as they neared the top.

Sonny, despite his apparent weight, was next, leaving Duffy panting with the dog in the rear.

As he reached the crest of the hill Duffy turned back to see Harry and Tara driving home in the Range Rover. Perhaps he should simply follow them back by road and beat the others. Probably get the dog run over.

Now Duffy was into the woods.

Tall majestic oaks hundreds of years old, splayed their rambling acorned branches across the sky, blocking out the sunshine.

He couldn't see either Charlie or Sonny.

Sirius was running in circles, chasing a rabbit into a burrow.

Duffy jogged round a giant tree and there was the first clue. Piece of paper with an arrow. Pointing hard right. He just hoped the others hadn't flipped it in the wrong direction as a joke.

He called Sirius who appeared from nowhere and they both raced to the right.

Three minutes later there was the second clue. Straight on.

This was easier than Duffy had thought. Except he was coming in last.

Certainly wouldn't be winning that bottle of bubbly.

The woods had darkened ever deeper as he ran through the oaks.

Dodging small thorny branches aimed at his eyes, leaping across puddles of black stinking mud.

Wind starting to howl as distant thunder boomed, a storm looming from afar.

The sky turning a velvet coal black.

Then he was startled.

Just a few feet in front of him something splintered into the nearest tree.

He stopped, panting, dog at his side.

There was a gash in the bark. Half an inch wide.

Another deafening thunder clap, nearly overhead.

Duffy raced on, puzzled.

Seconds later a whining zing past his ears.

Fucking close.

Then a gentle thud, inches into the tree beside him.

His heart pumped ever faster.

Hit him in a sickening flash.

Some fucker was shooting at him.

These were bloody bullets.

Three shots.

And they meant business.

He paced ahead now, streaking as never before.

Thunder clouds turned day to night as rain started to bucket down from the tree tops.

Sirius sensed trouble and was at Duffy's heels.

He ran faster and faster, stooping low around the oak branches, zigzagging side to side, listening for sounds behind him through the deafening thunder.

The third clue. Hard left.

Down into a little leafy valley. Ferns and pine saplings. No real cover.

Hared down, Sirius at his heels, skidding on the rain-sodden muddy slope.

Water streaming down his face, stinging his eyes.

Then climbed the far side towards another cluster of sprawling gnarled oaks.

A distant shot cut through the downpour.

The dog yelped with pain and collapsed.

Duffy stopped. Knelt beside Sirius. Bleeding from back left leg. No entry wound. Just a graze. A bullet graze.

Duffy scanned the horizon behind him. Caught fleeting movement in bushes.

Glint of glass through the sheeting rain. Then nothing.

He bound the dog's leg with a scarf, picked him up, and ran into the woods.

Fourth clue.

Straight on.

No more bullets.

Duffy had now given up on racing and was more intent to just get back alive.

Moving swiftly but silently as possible.

Fifth and final clue.

To right.

Emerged from woods onto a hill overlooking Somerby Hall.

Down below him stood Charlie and Sonny, soaked to the skin, talking with Harry and Tara. All huddled under brollies.

Duffy streaked down to the house, handed the stricken pooch to Tara, and told his story.

None of them could believe it.

"Not still hung over Duffy?" joked Harry, wondering if he was seeking attention, and finding excuses for coming last.

"This little fellow's nearly copped a bullet," said Duffy, rain trickling down his face.

Tara tearfully rushed off to bathe the shivering dog's wound.

Why would anyone want to harm Duffy, hero of the beau monde, the singing detective. He could suggest quite a few people but said nothing.

As they all headed inside for mulled wine and dry clothes, Duffy noticed Harry's .303 Lee Enfield leaning across the back door, amongst the wellies.

He paused until he was alone then went across and inspected the rifle. It was still warm, strange if it only was used to start the race an hour ago. And of its ten cartridges, just five remained. One to start the race, and four to try shoot him down.

Little doubt that someone in the house had been trying to scare, wound, even kill him, with this very rifle. Was this some kind of warning, he wondered..?

*

Marky was still naked. Still scrolling down the unsmiling faces of seasoned military vets on her iMac. Still listening to "the Boss". Now chewing on a pineapple and ham slice of pizza, washed down with "The Famous Grouse" straight from the bottle.

She looked at her watch. Nearly noon. She was getting bored. She could drop down to her gym for an hour's workout or go for a 10k run. No she couldn't.

Not after pizza and scotch. So probably have to go catch a movie. Something with a bit of noisy blood and guts, then she wouldn't fall asleep.

More of these killing machines on her screen.

This time all mercenaries.

Paid murderers.

"Soldiers of fortune", they used to call them.

Not many Brits, mostly South Africans, Russians, and French deserters from the Foreign Legion.

Some of these unshaved he-men were really really hot.

Yes, she could.

This one's sexy eyes.

She'd seen those eyes.

Quickly moved to Duffy's photo of guy in the shemagh covering most of his face.

But not the eyes.

She stared at both.

And again.

Took a long gulp of scotch from the bottle.

Squeezed her left nipple with excitement.

Bounced back and forth.

Another swig.

Another squeeze.

And dialled Duffy.

Couldn't wait to tell him.

She had a match.

*

When Duffy entered the drawing room for his mulled wine and cake, he could not believe his eyes.

His weekend partner Zaffy, the quietly innocent migrant who he'd brought down to Dorset for a taste of English country life and secretly fancied, was standing over their aristocratic host Harry, holding a glistening sharp knife to his throat. Its point pressing on his jugular, her hand shaking in anger.

All the others - Tara, Charlie, Viv, Frank, and Sonny – were standing at the far side of the room. Not exactly cowering, but keeping well out of the way of this crazed African stranger who'd decided to behave like a jihadi under their own roof.

"You did it!" seethed Zaffy.

This was a side Duffy had never seen. She'd become vicious, struggling to contain her fury.

"Got the wrong man..." choked Frank, as a pinprick of blood oozed from his neck.

Before Duffy could say a word, his phone rang.

The chain gang song.

He quickly answered.

Marky in the nude.

"Not right now Marky, sorry," he whispered and was about to switch off.

"I've a match for the killer!" she cried. And pointed her phone to the guy on her iMac screen.

It was Harry.

Duffy stared agog at the phone. "Thanks Marky", and rang off.

He turned to Zaffy.

"Put that down Zaffy!" snapped Duffy from clenched teeth.

"This is why I come here. This man killed my family in Sudan!" sobbed Zaffy, as she threw a framed picture at the floor.

The glass shattered, revealing that picture of the soldier in a shemagh Arab scarf.

"I found this upstairs – Harry!" breathed Zaffy with emotion, her knife hand shaking near Harry's throat.

"Is that you Harry?" asked Duffy softly.

Harry nodded slowly, trying to avoid the knife. "My mercenary days in South Sudan. Few years back. But I never killed your family Zaffy."

"You did!" she snapped. "The police gave me your photo – they said you must have done it!"

She suddenly pulled the knife from Harry's throat and drew her arm back calmly, as if about to plunge the blade into his chest.

In a split second Sonny hurtled through the air from the end of the room, grabbed the knife, and knocked Zaffy to the ground, pinning her arms behind her.

Duffy was impressed. This quiet little ukulele player was not so fey after all.

Harry stirred, and nodded thanks to Sonny.

"Zaffy. I was as a mercenary there – only killed rebels, never civilians."

He paused. "I couldn't shoot a family. Couldn't live with myself…"

"He'd never kill kids Zaffy…" pleaded Viv.

"Shit happens in war…" murmured Frank.

"You got the wrong bloody man, girl!" spat Tara.

Zaffy whipped out her phone and showed Harry a picture of her smiling brother.

"I remember that boy… took my photo…"

"Then you killed him," said Zaffy.

"I can say no more. I'm sorry," said Harry patiently.

"It can only be you."

A long awkward silence filled the room.

Duffy sensed it time to go. Pronto.

"C'mon Zaffy – leave these folks in peace…"

And led her to the door.

So much for a quiet weekend in the country.

CHAPTER ELEVEN

Sonny's whole life had been one big lie, and that's the way he liked it. As a black kid growing up in South Central Los Angeles you were lucky to live past twelve, what with the drugs, the gangs, and the drive-by shootings. He'd seen his school buddies stabbed in the neck and die bleeding on the sidewalk; his girlfriends dragged screaming into tinted limos by the gang leaders in their diamonds and furs and guns; his cousins beaten by the cops for crimes they never did.

After a while it affected you. Affected Sonny. You retreated into a fantasy escapist world where no-one could get you. Your very own safe space before they were invented. Except this was all in your head. Cutting off all that shit happening around you. Making like it wasn't there. That you were a hero in your own widescreen movie every day of the week. And in there you could not just do anything, you could be anyone. Which is why our Sonny liked to put up those dream barriers and got a kick out of being whoever, whenever.

Trouble was, sometimes, sometimes reality did come crashing through, and that hurt. Nowhere to run to, nowhere to hide.

In his early teens in South Central, he told his buddies he was going to be an astronaut, an assassin, a rock star, depending on the time of day. Like the others he did his share of petty pilfering, sneaking chocolate bars and beer down his jeans, or running off with some little old lady's purse. He never got thrown in jail but he nearly did. Each time he was caught he did his sob act, big time. How his mother had brought him up on his own while his Daddy was a lifer. How he had to work all day chopping animal meat, just to survive.

Always worked. Always got off. So successful he got a job parking cars on the Twentieth Century Fox lot off Pico, just so he could sneak into auditions, for he thought he could be the next big thing in the acting world. Did a dozen movies as walk-on cowboys or crowd stuff, but never got any lines.

It was one late night on the parking lot when he spotted a guy with a flat tyre and went to assist. Seems he was a military consultant on some war film, and for a crazy reason they seemed to hit it off, ending up in a bar off Sunset till the early morn. His name was Mike, had been with the Marines in most places, and was helping out on action movies. For his part Mike was impressed by Sonny's vivid imagination and creative energy; at first he was taken in by Sonny's story about doing the parking job for a buddy down on his luck, and that his Daddy was a beer billionaire. Then, as the evening and drinks got longer, he realised Sonny was trying to impress him, and that this guy lived in a fantasy world. By dawn Mike had told him to cut through the crap and suggested they meet for lunch to discuss a possible new job that could interest him. On one condition. Sonny must never lie to Mike. He needed absolute trust. Nothing less.

Over omelettes and hash browns in Mel's Diner on Wiltshire, Mike asked what he wanted out of life. Sonny was ready for this and told him about repaying society, about giving back what he'd been taking all these years, struggling as a poor black kid in the slums of South Central. Mike said nothing, threw down his napkin, and stood as if to leave.

"Don't bullshit me boy!" he muttered, his eyes burning into Sonny's.

"Gimme a chance. Please!"

Mike hesitated, standing by the table. "Tell me what you fucking really want out of life!"

Sonny breathed heavily. "I wanna be me. The real me. I wanna stop pretending. I wanna feel good about myself!"

"And just what would you do – how far would you go – to be you?"

Sonny looked him in the eye. "Depends."

"On money?"

Sonny nodded. "And the job."

Mike sat again, and took a mouthful of omelette. "Everything I tell you now Sonny is off the record, understand?"

Sonny did a little nod, wondering what's coming.

"It's confidential." Mike paused again. "I like you. I love your mind. The crazy inventive way your brain spins. Not many people out there like that. Which makes you special."

Sonny wiped his mouth nervously with a napkin.

Mike sat back and stared a long moment at Sonny, weighing him up and wondering if he'd made the right decision. Took a tooth pick and played with it, twisting it over and over between thumb and forefinger. Then suddenly sat up, military stiff, inhaled, exhaled, deeply.

"I work for the CIA."

Sonny nearly choked and grabbed a glass of water.

*

Sonny had now been working for "the Firm" for about ten years. For once he had the most exciting glamorous dangerous job on earth and couldn't tell a soul. Thing was, if he bumped into any of his old South Central buddies and told them he was a CIA agent they wouldn't believe a word. Just another of Sonny's lies, living in that fantasy world of his.

So far he hadn't done anything too violent which he was happy about. Just snooping, following, getting information. Though he'd been in a few car chases, could handle a Glock 22 handgun like a professional, and had shoved that Commie bastard off a bridge onto a freeway, which he deserved.

This latest assignment had appealed to his sense of humour.

He remembered standing on the sidewalk outside the television store, watching "American Families" through the window. He was in his early teens and they'd just had their condo burgled so they had no set of their own. He'd stand there shivering in the cool winter eves, balaclava over his face to keep warm, sipping Jack Daniel's through a straw, trying to guess what they were saying on screen, as he couldn't hear anything from outside.

He'd never forget that name from the credits.

"Produced by Frank Gruber."

And now, this guy was part of an international operation, organised by Mike.

But Frank was dying of cancer, and the Firm saw a way of making use of him. He'd been doing covert stuff for them for years around the world and was seen as a safe pair of hands.

Shit was, his illness was terminal so he and Mike had cooked up something very special between them. If the old guy's days were numbered, then very soon he'd be dust, so why not craft an operation where his death was seen as an inherent advantage. Why not turn him into a walking, talking suicide bomber, without him knowing? Especially with that breathing cylinder he took everywhere.

It was a fucking cool idea.

The bosses at Langley were wetting themselves.

He just had to be approached by Mike who'd set the ball rolling.

The possible target was known to only a handful of key agents, Sonny included.

Mike would meet and activate Frank. He'd also suggest he found a "disposable" to take with him on his mission to London. Someone who might need to die during the operation, no questions asked.

Knowing Frank as he did, Mike suspected he'd head to Hollywood Boulevard, the arsehole of L.A., to find his "disposable" amongst the sleazeballs crawling around there. Which he did. Sonny followed him there and watched him collect the first guy, a young Army vet begging on the sidewalk, then a girl druggie.

Quick as a flash Sonny got ahead of Frank, came across a third beggar with a ukulele, paid him fifty dollars for the instrument, and told him to scram. Sonny took his place which is where Frank found him.

After that it was easy. Frank took all three beggars to Dan Tana's for a meal and had to choose which would be his "disposable."

Sonny loved risk-taking and living on the edge.

He knew Frank might not go for him; he might choose one of the others; but he had a one in three chance. Good odds. He also knew that if he wasn't chosen then he'd deal with that person in his own way, and make sure Frank went with him in the end.

So that's how it all happened.

And right now he was standing beside the producer of "American Families", Frank Gruber, in the Visitors' Gallery of the House of Commons in England, staring down into the political chamber where the Prime Minster of Great Britain, Godfrey Young was speaking about a Land Tax.

He was interrupted by an angry female from the opposition party – Suki someone – who said if he passed the Bill, he'd turn the middle-aged into paupers.

He shouted back that she wouldn't know poverty if she slept with it.

"This is like a circus Frank," mused Sonny.

"More entertaining..."

"Why we here?" asked Sonny innocently.

Frank smiled at Sonny. "Curiosity. I wanted to see the Prime Minister in action. See if he's sleazier than our President..."

"And?" asked Sonny.

"Just as bad..." and limped off, aware that one of those lying bastards in the chamber could be his target in the coming days... Or not.

*

Godfrey sat in his office following a very robust PMQ's – Prime Minister's Questions. His throat was hoarse from all that shouting, and his hands shaking with rage from Suki's persistent badgering. He felt that she was crossing the line over his bloody Land Tax, that it was getting personal. If this feud continued, onlookers might start thinking the passion was a little too real, that they were, or had been, lovers.

But now he had another anxiety. Following the clandestine confessional meet with the chameleonic Saladine, he had proof that she and Sean were planning to get rid of him if he refused the secret Iranian deal. He'd also found out that Sean would become P.M., and, that he was still taking bloody bribes from the Arabs.

He sent a brief text on his phone, and within minutes there was a knock on his door.

"Come," he said, sitting up in his chair to appear more prime ministerial.

A well-built guy around thirty entered. This was one of the "doctors" who'd abducted Duffy in their limo, wearing surgical masks and white aprons.

"Sit down Simon."

"Prime Minister," nodded Simon with professional efficiency.

"First, thanks for roughing up that little toad Duffy, and destroying the bloody photo."

Simon smiled, quite pleased with himself. "Our pleasure. Almost shitting himself. Thought we were going to cut off his prick. Worked a treat."

Godfrey sniggered. "Would you really have done that?"

"Don't ask. But we did show him trays of amputated fingers…"

"No…"

"Made of wax," reassured Simon. "All just a wind-up sir."

"You're a hard man Simon," laughed the Prime Minister. Then cleared his throat. "Now. Something rather worrying's cropped up."

Simon leant forward on the edge of his chair, listening with intent.

"Our ears only."

Simon nodded.

"I believe… I believe I might be in danger - there are people out there, plotting to get rid of me. For real."

"Shit!" spat Simon.

"Bit of a shock, I can tell you."

"What can we do for you?"

Godfrey sighed deeply. "As you know, we've wound up the Tory fuckers at MI5, so all our security depends on the Equalisers, and, oddballs like you two."

Simon smiled.

"But. This is a fucking wakeup call, I can tell you." said Godfrey, deadly serious. "You're great fixers you guys – you make things happen, or, not happen. Right now I need a 24/7 bodyguard. Someone always near, looking out for me, who I can trust, who could stop a bullet. You with me?"

"Sure boss. We've close contacts with sympathetic army vets. Twenty-four hours and I'll find you the best bodyguard in town!"

"Thanks Simon. Funny old world, politics. Every day you get death threats on Twitter and dog shit in the mail, but when you really believe you're a target... everything changes," whispered Godfrey, looking into the middle distance.

Simon stood and shook his hand.

"I'll bring you the best. An assassin's assassin. You take care sir," and exited.

Godfrey stared at the closed door, the words ringing in his ears. "An assassin's assassin." He liked that.

Then peered into his desk drawers looking for something to protect himself.

He found a hammer – for hanging paintings on the walls, and a long metal dagger, for opening envelopes.

The hammer he placed behind the Roget's Thesaurus in his bookcase, and slid the dagger inside his jacket.

For a moment he shadow boxed viciously at the air, skipping around the floor like he's in the ring, southpaw leading with right jabs, then hitting with a left cross right hook.

He slumped back at his desk, looking quietly satisfied.

At least he was prepared for whatever might be coming his way.

*

In a basement health club in Battersea two men were on the running machines. Each trying to outpace the other. Going from speed 12 to 13 to 14. These guys were flying.

The older guy was ahead of the other one.

Harry raised an arm and Sonny slowed down. "Jacuzzi?"

Moments later they were sitting in bubbling warm water up to their necks.

"Where are we on 'the op' boss? Frank's slowing up every day – might run out of time..." said Sonny, looking serious for once.

"I know Sonny. Anytime soon. Need more intelligence, then once confirmed, we'll move fast."

"Understood."

"What's Frank doing while you're here?"

"Harley Street. Looking up some old doctor buddy from school. Probably getting viagra."

"Whatever he's doing, he's on borrowed time," says Harry. "I feel sorry for him...after all, he is family..."

*

Frank stopped at the gleaming crimson door of the stunning Georgian terraced house in Harley Street. This place was steeped in history, with its first surgeons practising here in the 1860's – all twenty of them; now there were thousands of medical centres around the area. Winston Churchill's personal physician worked from this street, Lionel Logue, the Australian speech therapist who helped King George VI lose his stammer had a home, along with impressionist painter Turner.

It was decades since Frank had last seen Paul Swithers, now Sir Paul, and one of the country's top consultants.

The receptionist showed him into a room that looked like a museum.

Strikingly bold oil paintings of sea battles and military campaigns on the walls, busts of Hippocrates and Plato, a long groaning bookcase lined with leather-bound tomes of Sir Walter Scott, Byron, Pepys, and Albinoni's Adagio in G Minor quietly playing in the background.

Frank stood open-mouthed, breathing cylinder at his side, surveying the art, the literature, feasting on the rich crisp aura of civility, smelling deep the class and crystal glass sophistication. Something the Brits did well, the past, whereas in L.A. everything was now, cheap, and tacky.

A small grey-haired man in specs waddled into the room with the energy of a baby penguin let loose for the first time.

"Frankie Gruber!" he yelped, grabbing his guest to his pinstriped waistcoat.

Frank steadied himself and wheezed back. "Paul, you old bugger! Haven't changed in all these years!"

"Now, you're fibbing Frankie. I think we've both aged. Least the bodies have... Sit down!"

Frank sank into a creaky Victorian armchair, almost lost for words in seeing his old mucker for the first time since they were kids. "You're my oldest friend in the world Paul."

"Ditto Frank. Where have all the years gone? Coffee?"

Frank nodded.

Paul poured two coffees from a gleaming silver pot on his desk, handing a cup to his old friend.

"That bloody boarding school in Salisbury."

"Chafyn Grove."

"Both about ten. Rugby in the snow, cricket in a heatwave, even if you hated sport," remembered Paul.

His skin was lined but tanned, probably from tropical five star holidays in the Caribbean. His eyes radiant blue and sharp.

"You nearly drowned in the swimming pool..."

"Holding your breath longest contest. I passed out under water," mused Paul.

"Saw you lying on the bottom." Frank started to giggle.

Paul raised his cup in salute. "Saved my life Frankie, you really did."

Frank shrugged it off. "Then I buggered off to the States...

"And I went to medical school," sighed Paul. He looks whimsically across to Frank. "What would you change if you could do it all over again?"

"More wives, more fun, who knows?" laughed Frank. "You?"

"Loved every minute. Still do. Wouldn't change a thing."

Frank nodded. Probably he wouldn't either. Life had been generous.

"And is Hollywood the fake paradise everyone says it is? La-La Land?"

"It's what you make it Paul. I can't complain. Travelled the world doing my own shows, and made a lot of cash. I'm happy."

Both looked at each other silently, weighing up how each had changed, how they looked now, each experiencing a tinge of sadness and regret. Time could be fucking cruel.

"Why you here, apart from seeing me?"

"Family stuff," paused Frank. "I haven't got long."

"Cancer I'm guessing?" asked Paul, looking across at the

breathing gear.

Frank nodded. "Terminal. Few weeks to go. Or so they say."

"Where?" asked Paul very matter-of-factly, getting up and crossing to his old friend with a stethoscope.

"Lungs and liver" stammered Frank, taking a puff from his breathing mask as Paul held the icy cold stethoscope to his chest.

"L.A. hospital?"

"Cedars-Sinai Medical Center. Beverly Hills. Best in the land."

Paul stepped back from Frank. "Doctor?"

"Dr Chang. Female. Asian. She's good. I trust her," said Frank, almost defensively.

"Not on chemo?"

Frank shook his head vigorously. "Just pain-killers."

Paul sat back in his desk. "More coffee?"

Frank shook his head. "I better get back. I'm here with a friend. Be wondering where I am."

"I know it was a lifetime ago Frankie. But I still remember you pulling me out of that bloody swimming pool. I remember the vomit. The sore stomach. I remember nearly dying." He looked grimly at Frank. "I owe you."

Frank shuffled to his feet and grabbed his breathing cylinder. "Been great Paul – to see you again." He was quietly welling up.

Paul came over and held Frank's arm.

"I want you back here in a few days. We're going to run some tests. I want to make absolutely sure there's no hope with the cancer. OK?"

Frank sighed. "Haven't got much time here Paul. With family. And they already told me. Month at the most."

Paul nodded reassuringly. "And they're probably right. I'd just like to do a double check. Perhaps give you a more accurate time. Perhaps it's not as bad as they say, perhaps it is…"

"Don't give me false hopes Paul."

"I promise nothing. I'll call in a couple of days and we'll do the tests. For free." He held out his hand and they shake.

Frank walked out into the London dusk.

This was an unsettling bolt from the blue. What if Paul found that he had more time. That there was some remission. He couldn't bare think of it.

If he was not dying there was no point in following through the fucking CIA operation.

For now he'd wait. Wait to see what unravelled.

He just wished he'd never clapped eyes on Paul. Never really liked the pompous little asshole anyways.

He found a shady bar just off Oxford Street and ordered a double gin martini.

Suddenly felt like his life was spinning out of control.

*

The Prime Minister had just returned to his Number Ten office after wandering through Parliament Square. The sun had gone down and the lights come on. There were the usual groups of demonstrators, mostly against the Land Tax, watched by huddles of tourists with flashing iPhones.

It always inspired Godfrey to see the real world like this. It made him feel so bloody proud that he was now leader of the country, that these were his people, whether they liked it or not. But. But it also worried him that out there right now in the darkened shadows could be some crazy with a sniper's rifle, following his every move.

He'd thought of warning the police except he couldn't reveal that it was Saladine and his Chancellor who might be plotting his execution.

A quiet knock on his door.

"Who is it?" he cried hesitantly.

"Simon Holloway."

"Come in Simon," cried the Prime Minister with relief.

Simon entered, leaving the door open behind him.

"Got a moment sir. Sorry it's so late."

"Always for you Simon," smiled Godfrey.

"I think I've found your man," he said quietly.

"The assassin's assassin?" beamed Godfrey.

Simon nodded and gestured to someone standing outside, to enter the office.

In came a little guy, hardened, fit, smiling, dressed in a suit with a regimental striped tie and shiny black shoes.

Had a scar across his eye, but gone was the beard and grey hoodie.

He put his hand out to the Prime Minister.

"Dave Chubb sir. Pleasure to be of service," he said briskly.

Seemed that Jazza Al Britani, the Muslim convert who only months earlier was ruthlessly executing British forces in the Middle East, was now back using his original name, and could be working as the Prime Minister's personal bodyguard.

"Military service?" asked Godfrey, impressed by his stiff back and shiny shoes.

Dave nodded. "Iraq and Syria sir."

"Welcome Dave." smiled Godfrey, firmly gripping the soldier's hand. "Suddenly I feel safe again…"

CHAPTER TWELVE

Duffy lay drifting in and out of sleep on Suki's sofa. When he heard the Equalisers were intimidating her day and night because of her hostility to the Land Tax, he felt it his duty to come around and show she wasn't on her own. What with the personal insults and the unconnected blackmail photo with the PM, our Suki was certainly becoming a person of singular importance.

He wondered if they were getting into her head, with their threats, and the physical presence outside the house. Right now all was quiet out there – it was two in the morning – but she'd had this obsession about them putting a giant spider through her letterbox, a tarantula. Of course everybody knew how big these things could grow – the size of a dinner plate – and one landing on your naked chest in the middle of the night could probably kick off a heart attack, but they rarely killed you.

Just made you ache for a few days from their poison. Anyway, Duffy had scanned her house and found nothing. He suspected she was getting neurotic.

He tossed and turned on the sofa, wishing he'd not had those three scotches, which were beginning to make his head swirl. And every time he moved, that bloody great lump on his belt stuck into him. He hadn't carried for years, but in the light of the last few weeks, he thought he'd better resurrect his Heckler and Koch P30 to let him sleep at night, and here now it was bloody keeping him awake.

He drifted off, thinking back on the Dorset trip where so much had happened, where there'd been so many questions and so few answers. Why was he targeted in those woods and nearly shot, who was the shooter – could it have been Tara, who he'd dallied with on an ant-heap the night before, or her illustrious father Harry who'd been the perfect host? As for Zaffy's quest for her family killer, she'd at last found the guy in the photo – again Harry – who'd vehemently denied everything. Duffy's instincts made him believe Harry, but still felt there was something not quite right with father and daughter, Tara and Harry. Time would out. And that final unsolved dilemma. Who murdered John Slade and why? He knew the Chancellor was somehow involved, perhaps, who knows, even the PM.

He drifted deeper into a whisky-sodden mist. Saladine, in a snow-white silk turban with an enormous diamond, and nothing else, was whispering to him, trying to make him follow her into a candle-lit cave with animal skins on the ground and Toytown uniformed soldiers lining the walls; Godfrey and his Chancellor in Equaliser Smiley Face tee-shirts, were tiptoeing through behind her, fingers to their lips; Tara covered in black feathers, was swaying to and fro in a swing hung high from the roof of the cave; and way at the back, in the shadows, sat an enormous tarantula, on either side a man in a surgical mask and apron, and astride its back was Harry dressed as a Celtic warrior in woad.

Duffy cautiously, tentatively followed the naked Saladine into the daunting cave. She turned away from him to light a fire beside the skins, then lay back gesturing him to lay beside her.

He drew closer, unable to reject her, feeling that animal attraction again.

As she ripped the turban from her head, revealing a writhing mass of black serpents, emerging from her empty skull.

Duffy suddenly felt sick.

And smelt smoke.

Not the smoke from the fire in the cave.

He sniffed hard and sat bolt upright on Suki's sofa.

Smoke.

He looked around and put on a lamp.

Smoke in the room.

Ran to the front door.

Mat inside was roaring with flames.

They'd poured petrol through her letter box then shoved through a burning rag.

Whoosh.

Duffy grabbed the duvet from the sofa and threw it over the blaze.

It worked. He suffocated the flames and they died out in seconds.

Suki was at his side in striped pyjamas.

"Christ Duffy – if you hadn't been here…"

"Just luck darlin' – go back to bed – we'll clean up in the morning…"

"It's worse than a police state." Suki shook her head in despair and went back upstairs.

Duffy took out his pistol, cocked it, opened the front door and stared into the darkness.

Nothing. An urban fox trotting along the street, minding its business.

He slumped back on the sofa. Three o'clock. These fuckers'd stop at nothing.

He closed his eyes, carefully. Didn't want to return to that nightmare.

On the walled bookcase opposite him, quietly reclining on David Attenborough's massive tome, "Life in the Undergrowth", sat an equally massive tarantula, patiently watching Duffy slowly fall asleep.

*

"I got a bad feeling about this." Addie Asher had flown in from Tel Aviv only an hour ago and already was in Harry's Mayfair office. She was about thirty-five, a chiseled jawline, sleek short curly dark hair, and dangerously icy green eyes.

The office was all heroic oil-paintings - Churchill, Thatcher, David Stirling.

"Go on Addie," said Harry, knowing when Mossad felt bad this could be cataclysmic.

"I'm thinking 'state capture'."

Harry nodded. He knew only too well where she was going but wasn't letting on. "Like South Africa?"

"Where the very rich Gupta family sank their teeth into every government department, secretly paying Zuma a second salary…"

"And ran the country through their puppet President," added Harry.

Addie stroked her hair and leant back looking long at Harry, waiting for his response.

"And you think this is happening here under our noses?" asked Harry.

"I think it's very likely, considering the assholes in charge. But then, you probably know that already ."

"We have our suspicions Addie. Let's say we're on the case. Thanks."

"You and your Langley buddies can always rely on us. We have the same enemies."

"I do hope so." Harry hesitated. He didn't want to give the Israelis too much, too soon.

"Course you do Harry. And you know the ex-Commander of Iran's Quds Force is here in town…"

"Hussain Sulimann. I do. Acting as our old friend Saladine's walker. We're keeping a close eye," assured Harry, wondering how closely his own movements were being monitored by Mossad.

"I'd hate this government to hand them nuclear secrets…"

"Heaven forbid."

"And there's something else…" said Addie.

"The cyber threat?"

Addie nodded. "Getting worse daily. They're fucking clever. Too clever. A group called APT 37 – Advanced Persistent Threat 37 - coming from somewhere around Teheran. They're targeting regional aerospace, defence, petrochemical industries…"

"And doing what?" asked Harry.

"Spying and sabotage. Been attacking our military for months – Haifa naval base, Yitzhak on the Golan Heights, Hatzor Airbase - but no chinks in our armour. They think we're vulnerable then when they come calling we crush 'em dead."

"Nothing new there."

"It starts out real gentle with the hackers sending spear phishing emails to bait targets with job offers; then they get inside their computers and plant malware…"

"Whoa Addie. I'm a soldier not a bloody geek – what the

hell's 'spear phishing'?" asked Harry with a wry smile.

"Sending fake emails to targets to try steal their sensitive info... or plant corrupted software..."

"Just testing..."

"The worry is these bastards have already got through our computer defences and planted their malware bombs, ready to detonate, without us knowing."

Harry sighed and stood. He reckoned Addie had been sent on her own phishing expedition to see what he knew. "Let's hope we're ready for them."

Addie took the hint and stood too.

"Fancy dinner?" asked Harry. He'd always wanted to break through that razor-wire protective barrier that Addie hid behind.

"Thanks Harry - straight back on a military. Just wanted a face-to-face."

Harry held out his hand. No breaking down that barrier anytime soon.

"Always my sincere pleasure. Big respect for you guys."

They firmly shook hands. Business-like eye contact. Addie went to the door and turned.

"Harry. What the fuck's Operation Red Czar?"

Harry imperceptibly flinched a second then smiled. "I'll look into it."

"Same old Harry," said Addie wryly as she exited.

"Safe journey Major." replied Harry with clipped precision.

As the door closed behind the Mossad agent Harry peered out of his window, saw her climb into a black cab, and drive off. It was all so mundane, so ordinary, you could almost forget these two were international killing machines.

*

Not many people knew, but deep in the bowels of the Palace of Westminster, in a basement beneath the House of Lords, was a 25-yard rifle range. There you could grab a .22 calibre rifle, ear defenders, and shoot away to your heart's content.

This damp dark drizzling morn the Prime Minister stood beside his Chancellor as both leant into their weapons and peered at their targets.

"I've got Saladine on my back again, wanting your decision." said Sean O'Leary.

"An admirable position I'd say," replied Godfrey coolly, "if not a trifle uncomfortable."

The Prime Minister squeezed his rifle's trigger and narrowly missed the bullseye.

In the background of the rifle range where deep shadows nudged into the flickering fluorescents, lurked Dave Chubb, the P.M.'s new bodyguard. He'd been briefed to keep a low profile, stay in the hinterland, out of the media, but always three steps away from protecting his new boss. Dave was in his element, never been so close to power in his life, never been so close to snuffing it, in a heartbeat.

"This is fucking serious – you don't mess with these bastards!" Sean turned from the range and eyeballed Godfrey. "I'm worried about you – about us – if we turn them down…"

Godfrey's face turned bright puce.

"Sean. You're forgetting who we are. We're democratically voted leaders of the U.K. – these foreigners can't come here and threaten us!"

Sean stared at the Prime Minister and said nothing. Both knew bloody well that Saladine and her Iranian masters could do just that, and were doing so. He was torn two ways. If Godfrey turned down their suggested deal – taking secret payments and letting them influence foreign policy, perhaps even more – then the next move could be the P.M.'s elimination. And Sean would then replace him. He'd give anything for that job, but not like that.

"In the end it has to be your decision Godfrey." He put his hand reassuringly on his old mate's shoulder. They went back a long way. It mustn't end in bloodshed.

"Whatever, I'm here at your side. Remember that."

Godfrey peered down the sights of his rifle.

"How could I possibly forget, my dear old comrade," he smiled. Ever since the confessional meet with Saladine, Godfrey knew he could no longer trust his Chancellor. He knew that Sean was still getting bribe payments from Teheran, and was most certainly involved in a plot to kill him, if he rejected the Iranian deal.

Godfrey squeezed the trigger and hit the bullseye dead centre.

He turned back to Sean with a rictus grin. "Game over Sean, don't you think..?"

*

Suki stared out of her window at the street outside. No sign of the Equalisers today.

Perhaps Duffy's presence had scared them off. Perhaps not. Thank Christ he'd been there when they shoved that petrol rag through her letter box. She could be sitting in ashes right now. She could be dead. She was beginning to think that opposing the Land Tax bill was not that important. Not worth dying for.

Her stomach gurgled. Lack of sleep. She slumped on her bed a moment. Lay back. All this angst was catching up on her. No work today. Stay home. Her stomach belched with a stabbing pain. Sat up quickly. Her breasts felt swollen. Sudden nausea.

Vomit in her mouth. Slid off bed and ran to the bathroom. On knees in front of toilet.

Head over cistern. Retched painfully for what seemed like minutes. Then leant back.

Her brow sweating. Head thumping. Stomach aching. Throbbing. Not food poisoning.

Not booze – hadn't drunk for days. Not that. Surely not that. It'd been weeks since she'd seen Godfrey. But. She had missed her period.

She opened her bathroom cupboard and took out a pregnancy tester. Sat on the loo and, with a shaking hand, peed on the stick. Waited and waited. Then the result.

She took out her phone and quickly dialled.

"Wiz? It's Suki Carter. I urgently need to speak to the Prime Minister. Tell him it's personal... Tell him it's really important. Really."

Then slumped back on her bed.

"Fuck bloody fuck..." and began to quietly sob.

CHAPTER THIRTEEN

As usual the Prime Minister was awakened each weekday at 6am sharp by the start of BBC Radio Four's "Today" programme. But the news headlines this morning made him sit up so hard he bruised his head on the bedpost. It seemed that the House of Commons was in lockdown. Minutes earlier there'd been a massive cyber attack across all computer systems and everything had gone dead.

Godfrey summoned Chubby – as he now called him – and both raced into his offices as the sun was slowly rising over a dank London town.

Already the security wizards were crawling all over the Palace of Westminster, trying to crack the malware that had attacked the most important networks in the land.

A pattern was emerging across the computer systems.

It was beginning to look like blackmail.

A cyber weapon or hacking group identifying themselves as Wannabuy was responsible.

Like all ransomware, it took over infected computers, encrypted the contents of their hard drives, then demanded a payment in Bitcoin in order to decrypt them.

But it was the amount demanded that made Godfrey wonder if this attack was merely a marker of what could get much much worse.

Wannabuy was demanding a one-off payment of ten Bitcoins – amounting to about £250,000 – from the British government.

This was derisory, insignificant. They were taking the piss, having brought the UK political machine to its knees. It was both a sinister gesture, and a threat.

Within an hour the P.M. and his computer geeks had paid the ten Bitcoins as demanded, and the computers hummed back to life.

Godfrey looked at his watch. Just past eight. She'd be having breakfast in her suite at The Dorchester. Probably just ejected the toy boy.

He dialed a number from his desk.

"Saladine? Godfrey Young. I'd like to talk…"

*

The richest woman on the planet was draped loosely in a black Chinese gown, lounging on a Louis XV pink chaise longue, sipping a mimosa cocktail. Her Iranian consultant, Hossein Sulimann, ex-commander of the Quds Force, sucked black tea through a gold straw from a yellow velvet armchair opposite.

They were both watching the television news with some amusement when Godfrey entered.

"It seems someone closed down your government Prime Minister?" said Saladine with a saccharine smile.

"Not for long Saladine. All sorted now. Back up and running…" laughed Godfrey, well aware he was probably talking with the masterminds behind the malware attack.

He sat across from the coffee table, from where he could see the faces of both the Sheffield dancer and her Iranian commander at once. He knew full well this was to be the most important negotiation of his life, of his career, and wanted to be on top of everything going on in the room. He wanted to catch every eye flicker, every nervous twitch, every half wink.

"So who was behind this cyber attack?" asked Hussein, with a knowing glint.

Godfrey paused. "Has all the hallmarks of North Korea," he lied.

"Ah…" nodded the Iranian. "This is probably correct. You have very good intelligence Prime Minister."

"So?" asked Saladine. "You've come for breakfast?"

Godfrey locked eyes with her. A deadly glance then softened. "I want to do that deal."

Saladine slowly put down her mimosa and sighed deep as she leant back into the chaise.

"At last, you see the benefits for both countries," she said.

"What made you decide, after all this time?" asked Hussein curiously.

"You could say that cyber attack made me realize how vulnerable we all are."

Saladine leant intimately towards him. "You've made the right decision Godfrey. We all need partners, friends. I am so pleased. From now on we're two great nations working together."

"Secretly," added Godfrey.

"Of course," nodded Hussein.

"And you'll be richly rewarded for your wisdom, each month," said Saladine.

"Appreciate that. Thank you." Godfrey paused. "We've never discussed the nitty gritty, the fine details of this deal..."

Saladine looked at her Iranian consultant and nodded.

Hussein cleared his throat. He'd been waiting weeks for this moment. Now his patience had been rewarded. "The agreement will take two paths. Foreign policy and business investment. We guarantee both these areas will be enriched by your nation working more closely with Iran."

"OK," said Godfrey. "Tell me about foreign policy."

"Israel," chipped in Saladine. "We want to isolate the Zionists from every other country in the Middle East, and then Europe."

"We want to close down her trade routes, to make her shrivel up and die," added Hussein.

"This could upset our American friends," sighed Godfrey.

"As a Marxist you have no American friends," spat Saladine.

Godfrey shrugged, but knew this was going to be a very touchy policy to follow through without alerting the CIA and associates.

"And business?" he asked.

"Ah. This is even more interesting and more profitable. The U.K. provides most of the weapons to our enemy Saudia Arabia. We'd like this to slow down, eventually stop, diverting those same shipments to Teheran," said Hussein, getting excited at the enormity of this deal.

"Shit, you're asking a lot here," said Godfrey, beginning to wonder if he could pull any of this off.

"And finally my dear," soothed Saladine, "we'd like to work closely with some of the U.K. companies in the nuclear physics industries…"

"What!? Not to make a bomb!?" gasped Godfrey.

"Of course not," hissed Hussein, "purely research and development."

Godfrey went quiet. His fears were proving correct but he had little choice.

"I can see you're getting worried but each month you'll find a million sterling paid into your personal offshore bank account. Good insurance for the future. For that rainy day," said Saladine, sensing the P.M. was about to chicken out.

"I… I'm not sure about this after all," stuttered Godfrey.

"You have no choice my dear. Today you are the hero that stopped this terrible cyber attack. Think how bad that could be if it went on for a week, a month… The country would collapse, and so would you…" smiled Saladine.

"We are at your side brother, you are now family," consoled Hussein like a sledge hammer blow on the head.

Godfrey nodded quietly with resignation. They had him. Gagged, trussed, and skewered.

"Only one loose end. Your Chancellor. He's knows everything. He could talk to the press anytime and that would be the end," whispered Saladine.

"We cannot pay both of you all these secret millions," added Hussein flippantly.

"Sean. What do you mean? He can be trusted," said Godfrey.

"He was ready to take your place," laughed Saladine.

Godfrey said nothing but swallowed hard. She was right. He'd lost trust in him himself. But kill him..?

"What do you suggest?" asked the Prime Minister.

From where he was sitting he could observe every facial expression from both Saladine and her Iranian consultant. Neither betrayed their thoughts. Except Godfrey knew they were leaving him to deal with his old comrade Sean on his own terms.

*

Frank sat staring from his bedroom at the Hilton at the tourists wandering through Hyde Park below. Harry, legs astride in military stand easy position, was at his shoulder. Each was sipping tea from china cups, balancing the saucers in the other hand.

"This bloody cyber attack's changed everything Frank. Changed the priorities." said Harry.

"How so?" asked Frank, leaning forward to catch an open-topped Morgan driven by a flashy blonde racing down Park Lane.

"I can reveal... it's the Iranians putting pressure on the government."

"Iran? So they're the 'state capture' guys..."

"Yup. Blackmail pure and simple. Do a secret deal with us or we close you down."

"Clever," smiled Frank.

"I reckon right now Downing Street's shitting itself, wondering which way to turn..."

"What sort of deal?"

"Shafting Israel and an arms deal with Teheran."

"Very tidy."

"How's the cancer ?" asked Harry suddenly.

"Do you care?"

"Course I bloody care. We're family, and, doing a job together..."

Frank thought a moment. "I'm coping. Must be the pain killers. Probably should have died last week, but still got a bit of life in me Harry... just."

Harry squeezed Frank's shoulder.

"Good man. Almost ready to go..."

"So who's the target - us or them?" asked Frank.

"Who do you think?" shrugged Harry.

*

Downstairs in the Hilton bar Sonny was swigging a vodka and coke, and reading the L.A. Times. Beside him an exotically made-up girl, looking very much like a geisha, had started chatting him up. Great cheekbones, probably a wig, too much powder, scarlet lips, and deep blue eyes.

"Flown in from L.A. last week," said Sonny.

The girl fluttered her languorous lashes. "And what do you do?"

"International finance. We sell airplanes around the world."

"That's cool," simpered the girl, with a foreign accent.

A man exited the elevator and headed to the main entrance, waving to Sonny.

Sonny waved back at Harry, wondering how the debrief with Frank had gone.

He was getting itchy feet and wanted a bit of action. Perhaps this cyber attack would activate Operation Red Czar sooner than later.

The girl turned to see who Sonny was waving to, but just missed him.

She turned back to Sonny.

Her left hand brushed across Sonny's, while her right found the diazepam in her handbag.

"Can I get you a drink?" she asked seductively.

Sonny was a little taken aback. Fast worker.

He looked at her with a wide smile.

Almost a work of art. Studied but a trop excessive.

Analysed her accent. German. Though could have Russian FSB connections.

She had one hand in her bag. A gun. A drug. Mouth spray. Or simply cash.

He'd love to fuck her.

Her eyes glowed. Her hand squeezed his.

He exhaled long and slow and looked at his watch. "Thank you. Another time."

And left the bar.

*

Godfrey sat alone in his office, nervously playing with a letter opener. He'd summoned his Chancellor Sean O'Leary to see him urgently.

The desk phone rang.

"Tell her I'm busy – I really don't want to talk with this bloody woman!" seethed the P.M. He was about to slam down the phone when he hesitated. "What does she mean 'personal'?" He paused. "Put her through."

Suki came on the line.

"I thought we'd agreed never to talk again!" He stopped, stunned at her response. "What!?"

As Sean O'Leary tapped briefly on the door and entered.

Godfrey gestured for him to sit down and desperately tried to continue the conversation without revealing too much to his Chancellor.

"You're sure? No-one else?" he listened, growing pale. "Understood. I'm in a meeting right now – call you later." He listened another moment.

"Later," and gently replaced the phone.

"Trouble?" asked a beaming Sean.

"Nothing I can't handle," sighed Godfrey, trying to contain his fury, bending and rebending the letter opener.

"So you're today's hero – sorting that cyber attack."

"Praise the geeks bearing gifts. But I digress." The P.M. cleared his throat.

"Sean. We've known each other a long time."

The Chancellor sat on the edge of his seat. Every instinct on full alert. He knew shit was about to be thrown. Big dollops. "You've agreed the deal with Iran."

Godfrey nodded quietly.

"And they think I'm a loose cannon," added Sean.

Godfrey stared at his desk, fiddled again with his letter opener. "It was you Sean who encouraged me, begged me, to do their bidding. And I knew if I'd said no, they'd have got rid of me and put you in my place!"

"So now the knuckleduster's on the other bloody fist..." said Sean bitterly.

"They want me to 'deal' with you," said Godfrey in a whisper.

"Why not call in your bodyguard to do it right here and now!" spat Sean.

"I've no choice. It was always going to be you or me..."

"How you going to do it? Without getting blood on your hands?"

"I'm so sorry Sean but. You got twenty-four hours to disappear. Just jump on a plane and go anywhere. Change your name. Retire in the sun. I'll give you ten year's salary. They'll never find you. Just keep your head down."

"You fucking bastard Godfrey. I made you. It's me who should be in that chair. It's my bloody Equalisers who got you into power, who're keeping you in power..!"

"I know, I know. But right now Sean, your life's at stake." said Godfrey.

Sean leapt to his feet.

"Fuckwit!"

And headed to the door.

"I'll transfer that salary. Twenty-four hours mate," cried Godfrey.

Sean gave him a hefty two fingers and was gone.

Godfrey shrugged his shoulders and grabbed his phone.

"Wiz. Get me Suki Carter."

*

Gonzo was sitting at his desk in the Equaliser H.Q., playing "Resident Evil 7: Biohazard" on his wall screen, when Tara entered.

"Just wait!" he snapped, until he'd finished the game. He was dressed in his denim dungaree uniform with today's badge saying: "Skin a Tory Alive!"

Ever subtle.

"Sit," he said and spun around to face Tara.

"You failed."

"What?"

"I told you to target that Tory bitch Suki Carter, stop her attacking the Land Tax..."

"I did target her. Day and night. Nearly burnt her home down."

"But you didn't. She's still out there. Still in our face."

"Gimme more time," said Tara, trying to appeal to carrot-top.

"Just had a message from on high. Leave her alone."

"From Sean?"

"From the Prime Minister."

"Shit."

"Exactly."

"What does Sean say – he wouldn't stop it?" asked Tara, wondering what the fuck was going on.

"Radio silence. Not answering his phone."

"OK," said Tara.

"But. We don't work for that Godfrey prat – we work for Sean. And until I hear direct from him, Suki Carter's still our target..!"

"So?"

"So Tara, this time we gotta mean it. This time we really gotta put that bitch out of action. Forever. Understood?"

Tara bit her lip. Her reputation was on the line here. She was going to have to sort out Suki Carter so there'd be no comeback ever again.

*

Duffy and Marky were both sipping Buds from cans, he reclining on her sofa with his shoes off, she hunched over her large iMac.

"It's still a mystery but I have a hunch," smiled Marky.

"About what sunshine?"

"Where the bloody cyber storm came from..." sighed Marky.

"Thought it was North Korea."

"That's what we're meant to think, what the press are telling us..."

"Your theory?"

"Take a look at this." She spun her computer to face Duffy. On the screen was a map of the northern hemisphere and a slow moving dot connecting certain capitals – Moscow, Beijing, Pyongyang, Paris, New York, London. But just occasionally it pinged off to another capital – Teheran. "It's boomeranging all over, but I reckon the source was Iran."

Duffy sat up. "Shit. So why would Teheran close down the government?"

"Blackmail. Like they wanted something in return? Some favour?"

"Some trade. Some deal. Marky – think you're onto something. A trail halfway round the world leads straight to Downing Street..."

"To a Chancellor getting paid millions from an unknown country..."

"Who'd do anything to keep it quiet. Beat me up in a club toilet..." surmised Duffy. "And murder a civil servant!"

The Bee Gees burst their conversation with "Tragedy".

"What's that – you gone gay?"

"New ringtone. Big mistake." He answered his phone. "Zaffy! You OK?." He paused. " Listen - I'd love to see you and the soldier boys – lemme arrange a surprise outing - this weekend." And hung up. "Marky. I gotta meet this head on."

He leapt off the sofa.

"What you doing Duffy?"

"Going to confront the Chancellor."

He pulled on a long leather coat and checked his pistol in his hip pocket.

"I'm coming with you..." said Marky, closing down her computer.

Duffy's phone suddenly bleeped.

"News alert." He read the text. "We're not going anywhere. Sean O'Leary's just been knocked over in a hit and run. He's in hospital fighting for his life."

CHAPTER FOURTEEN

The clays soared high above them in the crisp morning sky. Duffy and Zaffy watched with mild amusement as Chindi and Sami, the Sudanese soldier boys, aimed their double-barrelled shotguns at the orange discs flying across the horizon, shattering them with lead pellets, in this very classic English country sport. The clay pigeons were released into the air by a remote control thrower operated by Duffy.

Duffy looked at his watch. "Gotta go soon – visit a sick friend."

"The boys are having a great time Duffy ," said Zaffy.

"Saved your life – must be special…" as he sent more clays into the air. "What you decide about Harry – still think he's your killer?" he asked.

Zaffy looked away.

"It all fits. The last photo my brother took before he died."

"I don't think he did it Zaffy – I think he told the truth."

Zaffy shrugged. "That's why I came all this way – to find that man. To get justice."

"Yer yer - you need closure…" agreed Duffy. "But…"

"I don't know what to do. I like nursing, I like London. But perhaps. Perhaps I should just go home, go back where I belong… Put this Harry behind me ..?"

Duffy squeezed her arm. "Tough choice Zaffy, tough choice."

Chindi stopped shooting and turned to Duffy. "Mister Duffy. We want try something new…"

"Sure Chindi. Different angle? Different clays? Dozen at a time?"

Sami shook his head and smiled broadly.

The boys put down the shotguns and opened their khaki carrier bag. Inside was something covered in a towel. Sami yanked it free to reveal two gleaming Uzi machine guns.

Duffy recoiled with horror.

"Shit ! No way guys, this is a gents' sport not a war zone !"

The boys said nothing. They didn't have to. Their eyes begged Duffy.

The singing detective looked around him. The course captain was busy on the phone in his office shed a hundred yards away.

Duffy weighed up the distance from where they stood to the car. He turned back to the boys.

"Ten seconds. Then we bloody run for it!"

They nodded eagerly, grabbed their Uzis, and stood alert waiting for Duffy to push the release button.

Duffy did a final look around him then released wave after wave of clays spiraling high into the sky.

The boys raised their Uzis, took aim, and in ten seconds fired 100 rounds.

Clays were exploding all over the heavens, raining down on them like orange hail stones. The noise was thunderous, the boys ecstatic; they had their very own firestorm.

Duffy saw the course captain slam down his phone and emerge open-mouthed from his office.

"Time to go boys!" shouted Duffy.

The duo released a final burst of bullets into the air, grabbed their bag and all four raced to the rusting Range Rover Duffy had borrowed for the day.

The course captain saw it disappear in a cloud of blue exhaust smoke, as he bent over and picked up the Uzi bullet casings off the ground, totally flummoxed.

As they reached the motorway back to London Duffy was sure he glimpsed a police helicopter heading towards the clay shoot...

*

Frank lay in the MRI scanner listening to that old 1983 Randy Newman favourite, "I Love L.A." Took him back to the mellow yellow hazy days of Hollywood. Getting high on Venice Beach, when a gin martini was the only drink to have, when chicks could show their legs roller-blading down Sunset and not be ashamed, when even the guys had gold jewelry, make-up, shoulder pads, and big hair.

"How much longer in this shit-hole Paul?" yelled Frank to his surgeon friend.

"Another thirty minutes or so Frank," replied Sir Paul politely, from an adjacent room where he was viewing the imaging process with his radiologist.

Frank sighed. He was flat on his back on a bed in this large cylinder. From time to time there were loud noises as his body images were processed. He'd been told how safe it was as there was no radiation, just a giant magnet. The lights were bright and they were playing his favourite songs. Least he could talk direct with his consultant whenever he liked.

"I still think about those Salisbury schooldays Paul," mused Frank.

"Best of our lives..."

"Wouldn't say that." said Frank. "Remember Jeanie?"

"Jeanie? Can't say I do. It was a boys' school Frank."

"Jeanie was a local girl we met in the square. Used to hang out there weekends. Like we did. Very pretty blonde. Must remember her."

"Can't say I do," replied Sir Paul.

"You got her pregnant."

"What? Sorry Frank, this is not the time or place..."

"Like they say, what happens in Vegas, stays in Vegas... What happens in a scanner..." teased Frank.

"Nearly finished now Frank. Stay calm."

"They said her parents made her have an abortion."

Sir Paul said nothing.

"Thought you'd like to know," said Frank. He'd always wanted to bring Jeanie up – they both had dated her in their teens, and it was Paul who put her up the duff, then shrugged his way out of it. Least he knew now. And knew that Frank knew.

"You're coming out now Frank. Be still."

Frank felt his bed slowly moving out from the scanner. He was unplugged by a nurse and Sir Paul was at his side with an icy smile.

"Well done my old friend. I'll have news for you very soon. Your L.A. medics might sadly have diagnosed you correctly, and you have a short time to go. Or, perhaps, just perhaps, you're in remission and have years to live..."

Frank sat up slowly and swung off the bed.

He shook Sir Paul's hand.

"Appreciate it Doc."

"My pleasure. And Frank, I always thought you were the father of Jeanie's child..."

Frank sniggered in disbelief.

"Couldn't have been me," continued Paul, "I was into boys..."

*

Suki woke late and stared at her bedroom ceiling. At least Godfrey knew now she was having his baby. He hadn't sounded ecstatic but he'd tried to be enthusiastic. Neither could predict the future – both had partners, both had professional lives. This unexpected surprise could change everything. He wanted a meeting to discuss what they should do. Which could mean anything. Living together. An adoption. An abortion. Him saying goodbye.

She didn't know herself what she wanted. She loved babies. But not one with Godfrey. When she saw that photo of them embracing in Cannes, that was bad enough. But if the Labour P.M. sired a child with one of his most outspoken Tories, it'd certainly make front-page news. Even a movie. Who'd play her she pondered? That girl from "The Crown" perhaps. Too snobby. As for him, who'd play a Commie P.M ? Tom Hardy, he could do it. She liked a bit of rough.

Suki pulled on her clothes, showered, grabbed her bag and headed to her car.

It was another day to hammer out the Land Tax. So far she had the Labour party on the run. The Tory press were turning her into a goddess.

At last it was peaceful in her close. Seemed that Duffy had scared off the last of the dreaded Equalisers. She heard the early spring chaffinches singing from the old oak at the end of the street.

Dahlias and lilies were blooming in the gardens.

The smell of freshly cut grass. She suddenly felt good about the world. A neighbour emerged from his home down the road, carrying briefcase and brolly, and gave a friendly wave. She waved back. Life felt bloody normal again.

She took out her car-keys and beeped open the door to her Audi TT Coupe.

Put in the key and turned on the radio. Was it a Classic FM morn – Brahms or Chopin; was it BBC Radio 2 – bit of fun pop she could sing along to; or the more cerebral BBC 4 "Today" news programme where Godfrey would be over every story, especially now his Chancellor was hospitalized.

She plumped for Radio 2 and got Morrissey singing "First of the Gang to Die."

She adored the lyrics to this. Something after a few glasses of chardonnay she'd love to sing on a mike in front of a large crowd. It was so fucking sexy.

"Where Hector was the first of the gang,
With a gun in his hand
And the first to do time
The first of the gang to die. Oh my."

She was about to turn the key further to ignite the engine when Suki saw her.

In her rear mirror.

Standing astride an electric scooter, behind a lamp-post four or five cars behind hers.

It was that pretty redhead from the Equalisers.

Suki looked up and down the close.

No-one else around.

She didn't start the car.

Turned off Morrissey.

Sat a long moment thinking.

What had started as a fresh positive morning now was clouding over. Fast.

She got out of the car and stared hard at the girl.

The girl stared back. Then glided silently past her on her

Bonza scooter, down the street, out of sight.

Suki was worried.

She very slowly got down on her knees and looked under the car, as the protection squad had told her.

Nothing.

Went round the other side and peered under again.

Nothing.

Unless. That little red box. Like a torch battery. Two wires poking out.

Suki shot to her feet and called Duffy.

Fifteen minutes later he was there on his bike in a long black leather coat.

He looked under the car, then at Suki.

"Your lucky day Suki." He embraced her hard. "I think we'd better call the bomb squad."

*

Harry sat in his car across from the luxury Jumeirah Carlton Tower Hotel in Knightsbridge, talking on his cell.

"Mikie! How are my friends at Langley?"

"We're all counting the days when you bring the U.K. back on line and get rid of that Commie Prime Minister!" shouted Mike.

"Someone's tried to take out his Chancellor and failed – he's still alive in hospital…"

"Damn - who fucked up – was that you guys?" asked Mike.

"We don't fuck up Mike. Na – that was either Teheran or the Prime Minister playing dirty…"

"Shit."

"Meanwhile got old Frank waiting for the green – if he lives long enough – and right now tracking an Iranian POI who's screwing some expensive tart in a swanky hotel..!"

"What if Frank drops before he does the job?" asked Mike.

"We use Sonny – our 'disposable'…"

"Good thinking Harry."

Harry saw Hussein Sulimann exit the main entrance of the hotel and climb into a limo. He was wearing an expensive Burberry camel hair coat and looked quite pleased with himself.

"Gotta go Mike. Enemy on the move."

"Good luck buddy!" And phone went dead.

Harry started his car to follow Hussein, then had second thoughts. He might learn more about his plans if he found the bitch who'd been sharing his pillow.

He jogged across to the Carlton Tower and went straight to the tenth floor.

He'd been here before, very pissed, after an all night party. And wondered if Mrs Godwin was still running the girls. They were all very high class hookers, very hot, very attractive, mostly county. None of your Eastern Europeans here. These were fresh young English roses.

Harry went to Room 102.

The door was ajar.

He knew Mrs Godwin would be sitting on her sofa, sipping tea.

He also knew that there were adjacent joining suites from where the girls worked. That as madam, she was always a scream away, always ready to protect her properties. Her and her pearl-handled pistol hidden in her thigh holster.

Harry entered and there she was.

Late sixties, a subtle botoxed face, long blue grey hair, clear sharp powder hazel eyes. She wore a black velvet choker, and a refined red dress. Someone you could meet over champers at any cocktail party in Sloane Street.

"Welcome my dear, have you booked?" Her voice was fruity, and had that slight wheezing charm of someone who'd smoked too much in the past.

Harry smiled and shook his head. "Not today Mrs Godwin, but a friend of mine, Mr Sulimann, highly recommended one of your girls…"

"Ah," sighed Mrs Godwin. "That'll be Natasha… I'm sure you'll like her. Follow me."

She rose elegantly and walked with a gentle swagger towards a door to the right.

A girl had been listening to the conversation from within.

Heavily made-up, long tawny hair, red satin gloves, and draped in a scarlet silk kimono.

She stared through her door's peephole as a smiling Mrs

Godwin led Harry over to meet her.

"Fuck!" screeched Tara in desperate shock, and scampered out another door just as her father was entering...

*

Tara lay back on the shrink's couch staring at the ceiling. It was a precise clean tidy room, painted white. There were no spiders' webs, no dead flies on the window sill, not a speck of dust on the psychiatrist's desk. All was pristine.

Like Mr Kramer. He had a well scrubbed bald head, a tiny grey Poirot moustache, whiter than white shirt, and a purple bowtie. There was only tiny defect in his perfect appearance.

That large brown mole above his lips.

You couldn't take your eyes off it. It was really ugly. The sort of spot that someone on his salary could easily have removed at a walk-in surgery. Local anaesthetic. A quick slice. And it'd be gone. Then Mr Kramer would be truly a work of clean art. Then again perhaps he wanted that mole, as a talking point. Something for his patients to look at, then try to avoid looking at. Like it would take their mind off their own problems, seeing this poor guy had some hideous lump on his face.

Living there. Perhaps it made them return another day and another, to see if this thing had grown any bigger.

"Yesterday I nearly killed a Tory. Today I nearly fucked my father," said Tara blandly, waiting for Mr Kramer's reaction. She wore no makeup, and was wearing a simple skirt and blouse. Impressions, dear boy.

He shrugged. "Go on."

She sighed. "Week ago I made love to a guy on an anthill, then took pot-shots at him..."

"It must have been very painful."

"I missed him, but yer, I had stings all over my bum."

"What exactly do you do my dear?"

She stared at that mole beside his lips. "Don't call me 'my dear'."

Kramer nods. "Well..?"

"I'm an activist. And I work as a hooker, in Knightsbridge.

Near Harrods," she added, as if to give herself special classy credence.

"You must be very rich. Do your parents know what you do?"

She shook her head. "They think I'm in publishing – they're very proud."

"Do you enjoy your work?"

Tara thought. "I did. But. I'm starting to hurt people. Even hurt my own family. Got them thrown out of their home. So homeless guys could move in…"

"What did they say?" asked the shrink.

"They didn't know I was behind it."

"Do you feel guilt?

"I never feel guilt. Perhaps I should."

"Why are you here?"

"I wanted to talk to a stranger. Someone who can say if I'm bonkers or not…"

"I'd say you're really rather sane. But your actions are sounding a little excessive. You should pull back. Start thinking more of others. Being helpful. A little charity work perhaps."

"Sounds boring," sighed Tara.

"Do you believe?"

"Not in God. I believe in something out there. That made us all happen. Don't know what."

"Have you ever loved anyone Tara?" asked the shrink.

She thought a long moment. "Just Sirius."

"Sirius?"

"My cocker."

"No-one special in your life?"

"They're all special."

Mr Kramer stood from behind his desk. "We need a break. Time for you to think about your future. About what's important to you. About your self-esteem."

"You think I hate myself?"

Mr Kramer shook his head. "I think you have amazing talents and you're wasting your life. You need some challenges. Real challenges." He walked to the door. "Let's meet again in two weeks."

Tara heaved herself off the couch. "Why don't you get rid of that fucking mole?"

The shrink broadly smiled back at her. "I never knew I had one…"

As his patient left the room, Mr Kramer took her file and circled the word "sociopath" with a question mark.

*

Duffy parked his Harley outside the private clinic, with Marky riding pillion.

They both stood, took off their helmets, and looked up at the gleaming hospital.

"Trust the Stalinist Chancellor to go bloody private," said Duffy.

"Like the rich Russians and their secret country dachas – once they're in power they forget that equality crap…" added Marky.

They walked to the entrance of the building.

"How we going to play this – there's bound to be a guard in the corridor?" asked Marky.

"You're not looking well Marky – get the feeling you might faint any moment…" suggested Duffy. And walked inside.

They took the lift to the first floor. Didn't want to draw attention to themselves by asking which room Sean O'Leary was in.

No guards on the first floor.

Nor the second.

But on the third. At the far end of the long corridor sat a guy in uniform reading a newspaper.

Duffy nodded to Marky who ambled towards the security guard then collapsed on the floor feet away.

He jumped up and rushed to her aid, bending over her.

Marky was giving a West End performance, with every fibre twitching convulsively as if she'd had a stroke.

In those split seconds Duffy had hared down the corridor, past the guard, now giving Marky mouth to mouth, and into the private room where the Chancellor, Sean O'Leary was lying in bed.

The singing detective leant a chair against the door knob.

He only wanted a couple of minutes and a couple of answers from this shit.

Sean lay with one leg in plaster, and an infusion pump dripping pain killers into his arm. He looked pale and in a state of shock. He knew the hit and run was no accident. He knew whoever tried to kill him might try again. He knew Godfrey had tried to protect him and failed. Unless he was behind it.

He was dozing when Duffy burst in.

He sat up, flinching with pain.

"Who the fuck are you!?"

"You know me Sean. Duffy. Saw me sing at the Cleopatra. Had me beaten up in the Chelsea Barn. And you just tried to kill Suki Carter with a bloody bomb under her car!"

"Dunno what you're talking about," swore the Chancellor.

"The Equalisers do. And you run them. It was your call to murder a Tory politician!"

"You got it wrong sunshine."

"And John Slade. Remember him? In the Treasury. You made it look like suicide when he discovered you been taking bribes from Iran. They're trying to run the country through you and you're going along with it!" shouted Duffy.

"Not any more. That's over, I swear!" spat Sean.

"So who's dealing with them now – gimme a name!" seethed Duffy.

"I...I..." Sean's face drained white as he struggled to breathe, gulping for air.

Duffy saw he was in trouble and leant over him.

The Chancellor frantically pointed to the drug infuser, pumping pain killers into his arm. He tried to pull it free then gave up.

A moment. And his head flopped back, mouth open. No breathing.

Duffy listened to his chest then ran into the corridor where Marky was sat on the guard's chair with him standing over her.

"Get a doctor quick – I think he's had a heart attack!"

The guard did a double take at Duffy and ran off for help.

Marky and he went back into the room where Sean lay motionless.

The computer expert looked carefully at the infusion pump. Then at his arm.

"No heart attack Duff," cried Marky. "Someone's given him

a lethal dose of pain killers."

"How?" said Duffy.

"He's been hacked to death!" sighed Marky.

CHAPTER FIFTEEN

Godfrey and Suki sat huddled in a dark corner cubicle of the recently re-opened Gay Hussar in Greek Street. It had been a hotbed of Socialist plotting and gossip for decades, reminding them of the pleasures of old Russia as they chomped through Resztelt Máj - duck livers sautéed with onions, bacon and paprika, and Bécsi Szelet – veal Wiener Schnitzel, washed down with a bottle of György Villa Merlot.

The restaurant had been cleared, for security reasons.

Dave Chubb, the P.M.'s vegan bodyguard, sat alone near the doorway, chewing Házi Lecsó - vegetable stew. He was beside himself with inner joy. As Jazza Al Britani, the Muslim convert who'd killed for ISIS in the Middle East, he'd had a mission. To help bring the West to its knees, blowing up Brit soldiers, cutting the heads off Americans.

Now. Now he'd arrived where it really mattered. Working for the most powerful man in Britain. Knowing most, but not all, of his secrets. His ISIS handler, "13", had passed him across to Teheran, their new allies, so all his orders now came from Iran. It mattered not to Dave, still got paid twice, and still always feet away from assassinating the Prime Minister of the United Kingdom. He hoped that day would come soon. His life was in his hands. He nodded with a comforting smile across to his boss.

"I don't know where to start Suki – the baby or the bomb..." whispered the Prime Minister earnestly.

"The bomb I survived. The baby's still ticking," smiled Suki through gritted teeth.

"I warned Sean to get those Equaliser bastards off your back," he lied.

"And now he's dead."

"We still don't know what happened."

"Someone tried to run him over and missed. Then they got him in hospital."

"We think it was a heart attack."

"Rumours he was hacked to death."

Godfrey shrugged in disbelief. "By whom?"

Suki looked long at her ex-lover. Took another mouthful. "So, do you want it?" asked Suki impersonally.

"What?"

"The bloody baby."

Godfrey looked at Suki with studied care. "Do you my darling?"

"Truth is, it's a lose lose. If I keep it, it'll destroy my marriage and wreck your relationship. If I don't, it means a ghastly abortion. And, if any of this gets on Twitter, we're both doomed."

"How soon..." paused Godfrey... "would you need an abortion?"

"Sooner the better, obviously," snapped Suki.

"I suppose it could unite our parties – a child of the Left and the Right..."

"Hand on heart, would your activists support us being together?" asked Suki.

"Would yours?"

Both sat in silence. They knew the answer.

"I'm so sorry Suki," said Godfrey. "I'll pay for it."

Suki threw down her napkin and stood.

"Let's call it a day. Right now. I'll see you in the Commons, but nowhere else."

"Finish the meal my dear. Let's stay friends at least..."

"As an American senator once said to me... 'enjoy the rest of your life'".

And she was out the door.

*

Zaffy and her soldier boys sat in "The Grenadier Arms", an olde worlde pub in Battersea, drinking beer.

"I thought Sudan beer was shit, but this is real shit!" moaned Chindi, screwing up his face.

"Getting homesick brother?" asked Zaffy.

"Just a bit, but if I go back I'll be dead by twenty."

"I'm pulled both ways – go home and work for peace, stay here and help the sick."

"You given up finding the killer?" asked Sami.

Zaffy sat silent a moment. "I have a plan."

"Like what?" asked Sami.

"When the time is right. Coming all this way. I want blood."

"That Harry?"

Zaffy nodded.

"But you not sure it's him," said Chindi.

"His photo. It must be ..."

The boys look at each other.

"We'll help you Zaffy."

"Make him disappear..." added Sami, pretending to slit his throat.

"A few days then we'll do it..." She raises her glass. "To revenge..."

The boys raise theirs. "Revenge..."

Zaffy peered into the distance. Deep deep down she was still not sure...

*

Duffy sat up to his neck in warm foaming water, sharing a hot-tub in Charlie's backyard. He hadn't seen him since that fateful weekend in Dorset where they indulged Harry in his race through the woods, Duffy got shot at, and returned home to find Zaffy about to cut their host's throat. Happy days.

"Seen Tara since?" asked Duffy.

Charlie shook his head. "That was some weird weekend."

"Best forgotten Charlie, but enjoyed playing wedding singer."

"You should turn pro..!"

"Too busy being Sherlock."

"Anything for me?"

Duffy looked at him thoughtfully, climbed from the tub, and dried himself down.

"Off the record. Plenty. Some very hot potato stuff."

"Wow. Any clues?"

"The Prime Minister. A Tory in danger. A foreign power. Murder. Bribery…"

"Fuck!" gasped Charlie. "Who knows about this?"

"Fewer the better. For once that old cliché rings true – lives really are at stake."

"OK," sighed Charlie, realising Duffy was not giving anything away. Not yet.

"I know I'm being targeted, but so far just a few bruises. Once I've concrete proof - what's going on and who's doing it – you'll get it Charlie – front page news."

"Shit," said Charlie. "You watch your back my friend. I hate wearing black."

"Before I die I'm gonna nail these bastards", rasped Duffy, pulling on his long leather coat, patting his pistol in the hip pocket, and heading for his Harley, "and you're gonna help me…"

Charlie nodded from his tub, realising Duffy was walking a very dangerous line, without a safety net.

*

Peter Forrester could scarcely believe his ears when he got a call from a friend of a friend. He'd been running his company Bracknell Physics Enterprises for nearly twenty years when suddenly found his markets closing down around him. Much was due to international sanctions on his products in the nuclear research and development areas, especially if those clients were based in the Middle East.

As far as Peter was concerned he'd always traded within the law so to find that his business was slowly going under, seemed excessively unfair. Thus when an ex-colleague phoned, saying there was a rich Qatari in town looking for investment, Peter immediately suggested they meet at his factory, then, if all went well, a round or two of golf.

The business meeting could not have been better. Peter showed his Arab guest around his facilities, including how, through his research reactors, he was able to enrich tiny amounts of uranium.

After much tea drinking and mutual stories of living, loving, and working in the tropics, Peter drove his new friend to the nearby Downshire Golf Club, where they commenced a game.

Hussein Sulimann was calling himself Mohammed El Bari of Qatar, and already saw the nuclear potential of Peter Forrester's facilities. With his new connections with the U.K. government he saw no problems in making a large investment in this company and quietly building it up to meet Iran's requirements when the time was right.

Peter teed up and sent his ball flying.

Hussein followed, not too far behind.

"I think we could do some very profitable business together Mr Forrester," said Hussein, picking up his ball.

"Early days Mohammed, but I'd bite your hand off to get back into that Middle Eastern market," replied Forrester.

"You must visit Qatar – come for a week – and see what we're doing in our physics industries…"

"Name the day Mohammed…"

"I will come and visit in two weeks. Then we can discuss a contract that makes us both happy."

They shook hands over the third hole.

A hundred yards behind, Harry and Moggie were waiting for them to play on.

"Think he's taken the bait Moggie."

"Hope he doesn't choke on it sir," chuckled his old sergeant.

And they followed through.

*

The dull suburban crematorium was packed with Sean O'Leary's fans and followers.

Standing room only. Many wore those yellow Smiley Face tee-shirts that showed they were his children, his brethren, his Equalisers. Amazingly their age range went from late teens to old codgers in their seventies.

Whatever you thought about the Chancellor, he'd

manufactured a thought process, a cult, a cry for help social media mafia, that appealed to many in today's over emotive victimised society. Through Twitter and Facebook he could raise an army in minutes; destroy a career in seconds; it was both impressive and bloody terrifying.

His coffin, draped in a red flag, sat to the right, ready to be cindered, while that carrot-topped Glaswegian, Sean's top disciple, Gonzo, was addressing the troops.

"Sean was like my Dad. He was a pain in the arse too."

Titters from the reverential soldiers in the room.

"But really. I loved this guy. He stood for... everything. Justice. Humanity. He cared for the poor and hated the rich. He was today's Robin Hood. He was a thoroughly good good man. And I will miss him." Gonzo choked up.

A gentle hand clap started across the crematorium.

From where he stood near the exit door at the rear, Duffy looked around, wondering who he'd recognise.

At his side stood Julie Slade, the widow of John who the singing detective swore was slain by Sean's men, and Suki Carter, who was nearly bombed by them.

Duffy spotted the Prime Minister, in the front row, and John Slade's old Treasury boss, Cyril Sharp.

What he didn't notice was, across the room at another exit, stood his old enemy Dave Chubb, now Godfrey's bodyguard, and wearing a bizarre blonde toupee, in case he bumped into one of his past assailants and got recognised.

Gonzo raised his hand and stopped the clapping.

"Finally. There've been rumours that Sean did not die naturally in his hospital bed. If that is true, if anyone knows anything, then tell me and I'll rip that fucker's head off!" And he walked back to his seat midst raucous cheering and stomping on the floor.

Godfrey took the microphone.

"Thanks Gonzo. I think you've said it all. Sean might've been like your Dad. To me he was a brother. And also a pain in the arse." Audience tittered.

"But we grew up as comrades in the cause. We stood up in Parliament year after year being laughed at, jeered, ignored. Trying to ban the bomb. Bring our troops back home. Stop the

Iraq invasion. Then something happened. We both won the jackpot. People got angry. They got tired of paying university fees and having no homes. Tired of trains that didn't run on time. Tired of nearly dying in the NHS. Tired of being treated by the rich like animals. Tired of incompetence and idiots running the country. Tired of the virus cock-ups. What happened? They started listening to Sean and myself. And they voted us in!" Mega cheers. "It was the energy and faith that Sean O'Leary showed in loving this country and its people that made him one of the most important politicians of this century, of all time! Sean, my old comrade, we salute you!"

Godfrey turned to look at the coffin and bowed low.

The crowd knew what was coming.

So did Duffy as he got ready to edge quietly out the door.

Godfrey took a deep breath then started the anthem...

"The people's flag is deepest red
It shrouded oft our martyred dead..."

Duffy whispered farewells to Julie and Suki and slipped out the door into the yellow dusk. He had his own singing appointment that day, channeling Neil Diamond to a middle-aged crowd in dockland. Much more to his taste.

As he rode off on his Harley, he wondered if Sean's killer had had the gall to attend his funeral, and was somewhere in that room behind him.

*

Zaffy could smell her favourite stew cooking as she came through Aunt Huda's front door from her nurse's shift at the hospital.. Spicy odours wafting towards her, of ginger, honey, garlic, onion, and chicken. Perhaps a drop of soya sauce and mixed herbs. This dear woman certainly knew how to seduce her, through her stomach.

But tonight Zaffy was in no mood for small talk; she still couldn't get Harry out of her head. What if she took revenge and it wasn't him...

As she dumped her nurse's bag on the chair in the corridor

behind the front door, her aunt emerged beaming from the living room. She'd made an effort to look good tonight. A new yellow hijab; her face was scrubbed and teeth gleaming; a new long spotless white dress; and she smelt of musk.

"Zafira, my dearest darling," she cooed.

Zaffy was instantly suspicious – her aunt was up to something.

"I... I have a surprise for you." whispered her aunt, very gently.

Aunt Huda backed into her living room and gestured for Zaffy to follow.

There sitting on the sofa were two guests.

One was in his fifties, bearded, hooked nose, gold tooth, long black robe.

The other half his age, quite handsome, also bearded.

Zaffy's hand flew to her mouth in deep shock.

She'd come to London for two reasons.

First find her family's killer.

Second, to escape her fanatical uncle who'd forcefully tried to make her become a Muslim and marry his son.

It had been a nightmare of nightmares.

For many months back home she'd been visited by her very creepy uncle who was desperate for her to turn Muslim and marry her cousin. He'd never take no for an answer, until that fateful night when Zaffy was kidnapped and driven to his home.

There was no way out. They planned to take her to a mosque the next day where she would marry the son. She was locked in a bedroom, but managed to escape onto the rooftops, chased by their trusty manservant, who'd caught her in an alley. Zaffy had then stabbed him, and raced to the main highway where she hitched a lift out of town with two soldier boys...

And now there they were... in the same room.

Breathing the same air.

Her uncle Ibrahim and son Shaker.

The two men stood and bowed to Zaffy. All smiles.

"A pleasure to see you again Zafira," smiled her uncle.

"I am glad too," echoed Shaker.

Zaffy was speechless, biting her trembling hand.

Her aunt was bewildered by this response. She'd expected something more welcoming. But Zaffy had never revealed the ordeal she'd been through; never told how they'd imprisoned her.

"This is my surprise Zafira," said Aunt Huda... "I been saying for weeks find a nice young man to start a family with. Then I remember Shaker..."

Zaffy could hardly get a word out. "You called them? You brought these people back into my life?"

"We'll turn you into a good Muslim and you two can have many happy babies," smiled Ibrahim.

Zaffy had heard this shit before and had to think very clearly, very quickly.

Her poor Aunt had walked into a trap, not knowing what she was doing. The next move would have to be rapid and get her out onto the street.

Zaffy took a deep breath, smiled deeply at the two men, turned, and ran.

Straight into the vast arms of the giant Nubian Yusuf who'd been standing behind her all this time. The last time Zaffy had seen this bastard she'd slammed her knife into his stomach and he'd collapsed, assumed dead in that alley in Sudan.. Now he was laughing, holding her tight in his arms as she kicked and hit his face, trying to break free.

"Hello Zafira!" he boomed, throwing her to the ground and tying her wrists with rope.

The front door bell rang.

"Don't answer Huda!" snapped Ibrahim.

"I must," cried Huda as she left the room.

Yusuf stuffed a towel into Zaffy's mouth so she couldn't scream.

In the corridor Huda opened the front door carefully to find the soldier boys Sami and Chindi on the doorstep.

"Hi – we thought Zaffy might like come out for coffee?" said Sami.

Huda shook her head. "Sorry boys - gone to bed early – headache."

From inside Zaffy uttered a stifled scream, barely heard out in the street.

"Everything alright in there Aunt Huda?" asked Chindi, thinking he heard something.

"All fine – watching James Bond – very noisy," said Huda, closing the door.

"Tell her we hope she gets better," said Chindi.

"We'll come back tomorrow," added Sami, as they waved to Huda and walked off down the street.

"Something wrong Sami –in her eyes – she was scared…" said Chindi.

"Terrified."

The two climbed over a garden railing into the grounds of the house opposite, nestled under a row of hydrangeas, took a swig of scotch from their hip flask, zipped up their jackets, lit up fags, and settled down for a long night.

CHAPTER SIXTEEN

The dawn chorus woke a shivering Chindi and Sami, still hiding in the garden opposite the house belonging to Zaffy's Aunt Huda. The zombie commuters with their earphones were already drudging down the street to the tube station while young kids in school uniform skipped innocently past, eyes glued to their smart phones.

"Fuckin' freezing man," groaned Sami, straightening out his numb legs.

"What we doing here?" sighed Chindi.

"Looking out for the princess – making sure she's OK."

"We shoulda gone home – come back this morning and banged on the door... Huda said she was sick in bed..."

"But we didn't believe her bro..."

At that very moment Aunt Huda's front door opened and Ibrahim, Zaffy's uncle, came out, looked up and down the street, and motioned to people inside.

The giant Nubian Yusuf came out with Zaffy. She was in a long white dress, her head covered with a white hijab.

"Shit!" cried Sami. "What they doing to her?"

She staggered slightly, as they led her into a parked Volvo SUV with smoked windows.

"Fuckin' drugged her man..." seethed Chindi.

Behind them hesitantly came Shaker, her cousin, dressed smartly in a suit and tie, followed by Aunt Huda, pale, looking tearful.

They all climbed into the Volvo.

Sami had a sudden realisation. "These are the bloody cuzzies from Sudan. Remember she told us they locked her in a room..."

Chindi nodded. "She escaped and knifed that big guy... shit."

"Where they going?"

The SUV pulled out and drove off down the road.

The soldier boys leapt over the garden railing and raced to their 1971 Triumph 250cc Trophy they'd picked up for a thousand quid weeks earlier. Helmets on and they soon were sitting one hundred yards behind Zaffy's Volvo.

They drove through suburban streets for five minutes and turned into a deadend.

There it was. A domed white building with a minaret.

The local mosque.

"Fuck," muttered Sami into his helmet.

The SUV parked and Ibrahim led the others into the mosque. Again, Zaffy seemed unsteady on her feet, still gripped firmly by Yusuf.

The boys dumped their bike and walked to the mosque entrance.

"But we're Christians," whispered Chindi.

"They won't know. Come on..." And Sami walked confidently inside.

In a far corner they could see a bearded imam talking earnestly to Ibrahim.

Zaffy sat amongst the group on a chair.

Sami and Chindi edged closer and stood behind a column out of sight.

On the floor near them a dozen males were praying over and over.

The imam's voice drifted towards the soldier boys.

"Becoming a Muslim is very simple Zafira. All you need do is repeat the words of the Shahada after me: 'La ilaha illallah Muhammadur rasulullah' - I testify that there is no other god but Allah, and Muhammad is God's messenger."

"Very simple Zafira," repeated Ibrahim. "Now say the Shahada. Please."

Her uncle handed Zaffy the words to read aloud.

Sudddenly a hand brusquely gripped Sami's neck from behind.

He turned to see three hulking guys towering over him and Chindi.

"We don't like strangers here," said the largest, scowling through his long beard.

"We come to pray," said Chindi with a benign smile.

"I don't think so."

The three picked up the struggling boys and threw them out onto the street.

They tried to look back inside to see what Zaffy was doing.

All they could see was her standing reading from a book.

She finished, the imam took the book, and beamed at her.

"Now my child, you are a Muslim."

Zaffy smiled serenely back.

Chindi looked at Sami. They were too late. They'd lost her.

*

Frank lay sizzling in his hotel bath, a gin martini at his side. He'd been listening to a radio show about The Beach Boys, reminiscing about palm trees, white sands, and the Paradise Cove Beach Cafe in Malibu where you could sit on the balcony with a beer and burger, and peer down looking at those gorgeous chicks in bikinis. Made him remember there was a heaven, but it was in California.

Why was it that when you lived some place you were bored to death, the grass was always greener somewheres else, but when you got there you always looked over your shoulder and wished you were back home again. Always the mind and emotions playing bloody-minded tricks, showing you could never get it right.

The pain stabbed near his stomach, making him drop his glass, which smashed on the side of the bath.

For a moment he couldn't move. This was a new little fucker. Not felt this before. And came again. Like a needle ripping into his guts. He didn't move an inch, hoping it might just go away. He reached for his pain killer bottle and swallowed three quickly. All that shit about remission from high falutin' Sir Paul was hokum.

This little beauty was here to say, thought Frank bitterly.

Another burning kick inside as his cell rang.

He slowly reached his phone and answered.

"Gruber."

"Frank. This is Mike, your friendly CIA buddy from L.A." he

drawled.

"Mike? Surprise surprise. I'm in the bath. Should I get dressed?' Frank joshed.

"You stay wet my friend. I hear from Harry we're going any day now."

"If I last that long."

"How you feeling?"

"Right now, bad. Got a new pain."

"Shit, I'm sorry Frank."

"Not your fault. If I'm on the way, might as well do a last job for you guys…"

"You got a daughter and a grand-daughter?" asked Mike.

"You got them hostage Mike?"

The CIA agent laughed. "You've been good for us Frank. I wanna give you a "thank you" bonus."

"A kiss off?"

"A million bucks," said Mike.

"You kidding."

"For your daughter and grand-daughter."

"They don't need it Mike – when I go, they'll inherit the earth."

"Listen, I've written this off, it's happening. Who'd you like to leave a million bucks to?"

Frank thought a long moment. "Sonny."

"You what? That disposable piece of shit you found on the street?" rasped Mike.

"He's been good for me over here. I like him."

"Frank. You really sure about this?"

"Certain. Would give him a start…"

"You are one helluva nice guy, and I thought you were a dick."

"Takes one to know one old buddy…" Frank's stomach pain returned with a vengeance. "Sorry, feel like shit… gotta go…"

"Be safe Frank." And Mike knew it was his last goodbye.

*

In the House of Commons the vote had just concluded for the passing of the Land Tax and the New Dawn Party had won by twenty. All those months of Suki's emotional and reasoned argument had been washed away in a trice. She'd have to put their home on the market as the council fees increase meant they could no longer live there. Trouble was, no-one buying new houses would touch anywhere with a dot of garden, otherwise they'd walk into Godfrey's well-laid trap, and have to pay those extra land taxes towards his wage increases in the public sector.

Parliament was abuzz with rumours that Suki's leader, Nigel Warrington, the Ex-Army officer turned Tory boss, would throw in his resignation, having lost the Land Tax vote. That would cause chaos amongst the Conservatives who'd have to find themselves a new champion.

Life couldn't be worse for Suki. Pregnant against her wishes, her career in a tailspin through this latest vote. She was already beginning to think of finding something new outside politics. Perhaps divorce Henry, and the hens, and the dog.

Perhaps jump on a plane and reinvent herself somewhere in the middle of nowhere.

They said New Zealand was God's own country, except they had a Labour Prime Minister. A female who'd worked for Blair. Then again, then again, it was tempting.

If she went down there and led their National Party, the Tory equivalent, it could be two females breast-feeding it out across the House. Probably the first time anywhere on the planet. Baby wars.

She went to the Strangers' Bar after the vote and sank three scotches in a row.

Her friends kept coming up to commiserate with her, but she didn't feel like talking.

Then in he walked, and tried to avoid her.

The Prime Minister.

"Godfrey," she cried sweetly, pursing her lips as if to look pleased to see him.

"Suki Carter," he droned formally, his hackles on full alert least she go for his jugular.

"Can I buy you a drink?"

"No thanks dear – I'm with my team," said nodding to a corner, where Dave Chubb sat in the shadows.

"I just wanted to congratulate you..." continued Suki.

"Thank you – it was a brilliant campaign, well fought," he huffed and puffed.

"Congratulate you… on totally alienating the entire British middle class with your immature mean-minded mealy-mouthed pygmy-priggish class warfare Land Tax!"

She threw her glass of scotch full in Godfrey's face, strode to the exit, and shouted back across the bar, "And I'm going to have your fucking baby!"

And out, leaving a deadly hushed bar, with scotch and soda dripping down the Prime Minister's scarlet quivering cheeks.

*

Gonzo and Tara were sipping spinach soup through straws in his Equaliser office.

There was a slight tension between the two, both concentrating on their frugal company lunch, both avoiding eye contact and conversation.

He noisily sucked his carton dry, tossed it aggressively into a bin, then lay on the floor on his stomach. Still in silence he efficiently did fifty push-ups. His breath totally in control, his peak fitness apparent to both Tara and himself.

She wondered what he was trying to prove but said nothing, looking at her watch instead. Was this the moment he'd finally sack her as he'd threatened in the past. Or was this simply a physical posture and wank, trying to impress her sexually.

She took a deep breath and waited for him to land on planet earth.

"I dunno what the fuck's going on Tara," he muttered in that streetwise Gorbals guttural. "I've had the bloody bomb squad crawling all over me for the past week after your failed attempt on Suki Carter. And now the Prime Minister's playing games with me…"

"Like how?" soothed Tara, giving him a softish forced smile. Deep down she loathed this tosser. He was such a thick upstart, such a waste of space. She'd gone out on a limb so many times, against all her basic instincts, and all she got back was shit.

"Godfrey. Can't make him out. After Sean's funeral I quite liked him. We got on well I thought, got pissed together. Then. Couple of days back he calls really fired up and says he wants to close us down. Sean's baby. The fucking Equalisers. I told him go screw yourself – it was us that got him into power; it was us that are keeping him there. And slammed down the phone."

"Wow..." sighed Tara, suddenly impressed. Perhaps she'd been wrong about this arsehole.

"Then just now I get another call from him."

"No..."

"Telling me he want's Suki Carter 'taken care of', and don't call him till it's done!"

"Oh fuck," said Tara. She'd hoped that this little gig was behind her. Way behind her.

Gonzo rubbed his hands together feverishly. "So wee Tara. You're on stage again. But this time, this time my lovie, will ye go make it the final curtain..!"

*

Zaffy sat on her Aunt Huda's sofa in her living room, still wearing a white hijab and robe. Shaker was beside her with a wide smile. Ibrahim and Yusuf were on chairs opposite, her aunt carrying a tray of teas which she placed on a table between them.

Ibrahim took a cup of tea and sipped carefully.

"This is a very special day for my family. A very special day for my son," and nodded to Shaker.

"Inshallah. Thank you father," smiled Shaker. He was still dressed in a smart suit and tie, still looking scrubbed and clean for the most important day ever.

"I'm sure Zafira knows this is the happiest day of her life," said Huda.

Zaffy glared at her aunt. The drugs, whatever they'd given her, were beginning to wear off. Her head throbbed, her eyes ached. Everything had been a blur, but now was becoming clear.

The terrifying reality hit home hard. She gasped at the audacity of her relatives, all of them complicit, working against her, believing they were doing the right thing.

Closing her down. Making her a slave. Right here. Right now.

She looked around the room. Yusuf was nearest the door. The only escape was the window behind her. She made the pretence of a smile at them then leapt to her feet and jumped towards the window.

The leather belt tied around her ankles brought her crashing to the floor, her head hitting the coffee table. She had no idea her feet had been bound.

None of the others moved. They didn't have to. She was trapped. They knew it, and now, so did she.

Blood trickled from her lips as she leant against the table.

"What've you done to me?" she spat.

"You're now a Muslim Zafira. Welcome to the family," beamed Ibrahim, turning and nodding to his son.

"And Zafira. Now, at last, you are my wife," added Shaker.

"As we always promised," nodded his father.

"What!?" cried Zaffy.

"I'm sure you'll be happy my dear. When you get home," pleaded her Aunt Huda.

"Home?" asked Zaffy, fearing there was worse to come in this living nightmare.

"When we finish our tea, we're taking you back," sniggered Ibrahim. "The newlyweds are coming home... to South Sudan."

*

It was described as "half biblical, half pornographic", a blood-soaked, sex-crazed spectacle, a decadent, fascist dictatorship, where the louche men of power dined upstairs while sexual excesses festered in the basement.

It just needed a mike and Duffy would have felt totally at home, like any other dodgy Soho nightclub.

But this was the Royal Opera House and he was sitting trussed in a tux in a private box overlooking the stage, watching Oscar Wilde's outrageous "Salome."

He was alone but for his female partner, who tonight looked a mix between Monte Carlo royalty and a wealthy courtesan. Dressed in shimmering silk and a black bejewelled turban, Saladine was attracting just as much attention as Salome on stage.

She placed a diamond encrusted hand on Duffy's.

"My darling. You are a superb singer. You are a superb lover. Why don't we make music together... I want you to work for me..."

Duffy looked into those smouldering eyes of this bewitching goddess. It was bloody tempting. Except she'd probably lock him in a cage. Even more tempting.

"Please?" she whispered, fluttering those massive false eyelashes, that looked like the wings of a giant black flamingo flying high above the Okavango Delta.

Suddenly, just as Salome was about to kiss John the Baptist's severed head in front of a cowed hushed audience, Billy Joel's "Uptown Girl" ripped through the theatre.

"Fuck!" hissed Duffy. He'd changed his ringtone again. And hadn't turned it off.

He listened to the call and turned to Saladine.

"Gotta go love – friend in trouble..." He kissed her on the cheek, waved to the irritated poncey audience, still staring at his box, and exited fast.

From the front stalls, peering up through his opera glasses, Harry watched Duffy's departure with interest. Saladine was on her cell, and, moments later, was joined in her box by another exotic person of interest, Hussein Sulimann.

*

Aunt Huda was washing up the tea cups in her kitchen sink wondering if she'd made a terrible mistake calling Ibrahim in Juba, making Zafira turn Muslim and marry her cousin Shaker. She decided she'd go to the mosque and pray for her happiness. Surely her own family would make sure this girl enjoyed her new life. She and Shaker would have children, find fulfillment with Allah.

She looked in the mirror, pulled on her hijab, and grabbed her coat.

A bang on the front door.

Surely they've not come back. Perhaps Zafira refused to go home.

More banging.

Huda opened the door.

The two boy soldiers. Chindi and Sami. And an older man she'd not met but heard about. Duffy, the singing detective.

"We want to see Zaffy" said Duffy with polite urgency.

"Is she here?" asked Chindi.

"It's too late," said Huda simply with a shrug. "Sorry."

"Where is she?" snapped Duffy.

"You just missed them. They gone."

"Where?"

"Home. To Sudan…"

"Shit!" Duffy kicked the doorstep. "Sudan..!"

"When they leave?" cried Sami.

"Fifteen minutes," said Huda.

Duffy ran to his Harley and started the engine.

The boys jumped onto their Triumph.

And the trio roared off on their bikes, heading south, hoping to reach the kidnapped Zaffy before she got to Africa and a life of slavery.

CHAPTER SEVENTEEN

In the back of the Volvo SUV slumped Zaffy with Yusuf closely guarding her. Now, for the first time in her life, she was draped in a black burka, covering her entire body from head to toe. Ibrahim was driving, Shaker at his side, as the car raced from London to the channel ferry. They'd already acquired a forged passport for the new bride, so getting through Customs would be a doddle.

Zaffy quietly felt under her burka for the knife she carried everywhere, for her phone, but both had gone.

"Dover in one hour," said Ibrahim. "Then Europe."

"And home," nodded Shaker with a serene smile.

"You'll all be arrested," spat Zaffy from under her face veil.

"What for? Being a nice Muslim girl married to my son?" said her gold-toothed uncle with a snigger.

"This is abduction!" seethed Zaffy. "You can't do this!"

Yusuf laughed deeply. "You sound just like your mother…"

There was a frozen silence in the car.

Zaffy held her breath, turned to the Nubian, and said, with trembling anger, "You've never met my mother."

Yusuf looked back at her glowering eyes in the burka and shrugged.

More silence.

Ibrahim putting his foot down. They were now racing down the M20 at over 100 miles an hour.

Then it dawned on Zaffy. Like being branded with red-hot coals on your bare skin. Searingly painful. Breathtakingly shocking.

"It was you," she whispered hoarsely. "You and my uncle –

you killed my family!"

No-one in the car said a word.

She kicked hard at Ibrahim's driver's seat from behind and the SUV swerved to the right, glancing off the motorway central barrier, narrowly missing a massive car transporter with German number plates, whose driver firmly gave them the finger.

"They were Christians," said Ibrahim slowly in a cold measured tone. "Haram. I tried to make my sister understand – become Muslims like us – but she refused. She could not see sense. So…"

"So you shot my mother, my father, and my brother…" gasped Zaffy in disbelief. "Because of your God?"

Her uncle did not reply. Shaker shot an embarrassed nervous glance her way.

Yusuf glowered at her side.

"You uncle – all of you – have wrecked my life!" Zaffy struggled to find the right words. "Everything precious to me – you've taken. And now… this!" She ripped off the burka, and, dressed only in underwear, grabbed the door handle, pushed quickly, and tried to leap from the car.

But Yusuf was too fast for her, grabbing her hair, as the SUV zigzagged across the motorway.

Ibrahim locked all the doors.

Yusuf firmly pinned the semi-naked Zaffy down on the backseat like a struggling wild animal, as she surrendered and started to sob uncontrollably.

*

Suki stood with her back to the Aga in her country house kitchen. She was holding that morning's "Daily Mail" with the front page story – photos of her and Godfrey – telling the story of her shouting in the Strangers' Bar at the House of Commons – "I'm having your fucking baby!"

You couldn't make it up – this was tabloid fodder of the very best quality.

There was even an online contest thinking of the best names for a baby born to a Tory mother and Labour father, who also happened to be the Prime Minister.

Apart from the entertainment value, there was another tiny catch. Suki's husband Henry, who, within minutes, would be coming down for his fresh scrambled eggs only to learn about this historic love affair. But she'd taken necessary precautions. Hidden every kitchen knife in the drawers, was wearing gym shoes in case of a rapid exit, and had left the back door into the garden ajar.

She heard the creak of the stairs and drew her breath as her husband entered.

He took in the scene at one glance, his anxious wife holding the newspaper, and sat at the table, looking calm and unruffled.

"Don't fret darling. I've known for months. Not the baby. But you and Godfrey. Had my spies onto you." mused Henry. He leant towards Suki. "Come and sit. I'm not going to bite you..."

Suki inwardly breathed relief and served eggs on toast from the Aga.

"I'm so so sorry darling. It all got out of hand. I stopped it, then found I was pregnant," croaked Suki, biting her lip.

"Suspected as much," munched Henry.

"I can get rid of the baby."

"No need. I'll treat it as our own – we been trying for years..."

"Why aren't you furious with me – wanting a divorce or something?" asks a puzzled Suki.

Henry paused. "Been on manoeuvres myself."

Suki stared at him wondering what he was talking about, though guessed.

"Meaning?" asked Suki suspiciously.

"Asuka. Our Japanese consultant. Pretty little thing. Had a fling. Nothing important. When I heard about you. Went a bit wild meself."

"Fuck," sighed Suki with a smile.

"So. Fresh start and all that perhaps?" suggested Henry, spreading his marmalade.

"You sure about the baby?"

Henry nods. "Just hope it doesn't look like that tosser Godfrey..."

Suki took his hand. "We'll make it work. Together."

He nodded with a smile. "You staying in London this week?"

Suki got up. "Nope. This week I'm working from home. With you."

"Pub lunch then?"

"Perfect. I'll do the hens, bit of work, then get pissed with you!" She kissed Henry on his cheek and went out into the backyard to clean out their hens and collect the eggs.

What a weight off her chest, she thought. All that angst and the two-timing bastard knew all along. Not only that, he was bonking that bloody consultant girl half his age. Bitch.

Their garden was all very "The Good Life", with a rambling shed, double garage, henhouse, vegetable garden, and a long rough lawn bordered by hedge.

There were six hens – Warrens – a hybrid of Rhode Island Red and Light Sussex cross – ginger colour and like pets, named Maeve, Dee, Dozy, Beaky, Meek, and Titch, each laying a fresh egg a day.

Suki had put on her wellies and was bending over, clearing out the hen shit from the straw in the back of the coop, when she was startled by the dull thud, inches from her head.

There, stuck in the wooden wall of the henhouse, was a crossbow bolt, about sixteen inches long, with a lethal expandable broadhead, that would rip you to bits if it hit your guts.

Suki spun round to face her aggressor.

There was movement from the hedge but no-one to be seen.

Seconds later, another bolt, this time pinning her sleeve to the henhouse.

She ripped it free and was running toward the kitchen when Henry yelled from the direction of the hedge.

"Suki! Quick!."

She ran towards his voice and found him, spade in hand, standing over a tawny haired girl, dressed in black, lying motionless on the grass, crossbow at her side.

Henry had smashed her hard, her face covered in blood.

Suki recognized her as the Equaliser girl who'd been haunting her for weeks, who'd put the bomb under her car.

"Christ!" cried Suki and dropped to the girl's body to see if she was breathing.

Felt her pulse.

"She alive?"

"Only just. You nearly killed her Henry," said Suki.

"Let's call the police."

The assassin was still not moving. Looked critical.

"And an ambulance..."

Both ran into the house.

"I'll get a blanket and water..." cried Suki. "You call emergencies!"

As she ran the tap for warm water, Suki watched her trembling hands. This fucking girl had been stalking her, trying to kill her, and now they have her, caught in their very own backyard.

"They're on their way," shouted Henry, joining Suki as they raced back to the hedge with a blanket and a bucket of water.

But the crossbow killer had gone.

Not a trace.

Tara had vanished, just in time.

*

Peter Forrester poured the champagne and clinked glasses with his new Qatari business partner, Mohammed El Bari, at their board room table. Minutes earlier they'd signed the contract making the Qatari, in reality the Iranian Hussein Sulimann, the majority owner of Bracknell Physics Enterprises. Both had reason to celebrate.

Forrester as he'd found a rich Middle East invester who'd rescued his company from going bankrupt and now could open up massive new markets worldwide; Sulimann as he'd effectively bought a British company that enriched uranium, allowing him to smuggle this valuable component back to Iran and circumvent the international sanctions preventing them from developing their very own nuclear bomb.

"Inshallah," smiled the Iranian. "You have made my country very very happy. Thank you Peter..."

"And you've saved my company from destruction – I owe you everything Mohammed."

They clinked glasses again.

Hussein looked at his watch. "I must leave. My plane flies

back to Qatar in two hours." And stood, firmly shaking Forrester's hand.

"I'll see you there next week."

"We'll have a special banquet for you," grinned Hussein, bowed, and briskly exited.

Outside the offices of Bracknell Physics Enterprises a large black limousine sat with its engine idling.

Hussein sank into the lush soft black leather back seat.

Waiting beside him was Dave Chubb, the P.M.'s bodyguard. It was his day off, and he was working for his new real allies, the Iranians. He knew they were covertly rearming ISIS in a secret desert base deep in the Syrian desert. Perhaps, just perhaps one day he'd get to return to his brothers out where it really mattered.

"All done sir?" asked Chubb.

Hussein nodded. "We now own the company." He handed Chubb a small flat briefcase. "I forgot the contract. Could you..?"

"Course sir." Chubb took the briefcase and walked quickly into the offices.

Peter was sat finishing the bottle of champagne, dreaming of how he could once again expand the company. Even buy himself a new car. He liked that new top-of-the-range Mercedes.

Chubb suddenly walked in.

"Sorry to interrupt sir. Mohammed forgot the contract." He quickly placed the briefcase on the board table beside the contract papers and opened it.

"Not a problem," said Peter. "Help yourself," nodding to the signed paperwork.

Inside the briefcase lay a state-of-the-art suppressed 9mm handgun.

It had a futuristic look about it like you'd see in a Star Wars movie. Made in Utah, SilencerCo's Maxim 9, just nine inches long, was the latest pistol with a built-in silencer on the market. Trust Hussein to have one of these beauties, thought Chubb, as he slowly raised the gun and fondly squeezed the trigger, shooting through the lid of the briefcase.

An almost inaudible "whock".

Peter slipped silently from his chair onto the floor.

The champagne made a fizzing stain on the carpet.

And he never got to order that new Mercedes.

*

Harry had just had a warning phone call from Mike at Langley, telling how he'd spoken with Frank, and his cancer sounded like it was getting worse. They should get going soonest on activating Operation Red Czar before the old geezer croaked.

They'd been gifted with him and his breathing cylinder, a walking suicide bomber, who was going to die any day anyway. It had to happen in the next week. Harry was making a call to one of informants, chasing their target's commitments when he had an expected visit.

Into his office limped Tara, looking like she'd been run over by a bus.

"Shit darling – what's happened?" yelled Harry, leaping from his chair, grabbing his daughter in his arms.

She collapsed into a chair. Across her face was a long scar, her left eye bulging and bruised.

"Tell me and I'll kill the bastard!" seethed Harry.

"Personal Dad," she said carefully, trying not to move her jaw because of the pain.

"Please Tara – what happened – I want to help you?"

"You can help me."

"How?" asked Harry, feeling her pain, just by looking at her.

"I have a friend..."

Harry nodded. "Go on..."

She stared at her father and paused. "He wants to know the best way to kill someone."

"You're joking darling." After spending his entire life shooting, knifing, and strangling people, the last thing in the world he wanted to do was to help his beloved daughter do the same. He looked at her. It disturbed him. But she meant it.

"Why?" he asked simply.

"Can't say."

Harry knew he couldn't get around this. "OK. You. Your friend... wants to know the best way to kill someone."

Tara nodded.

"Surprise. Best way in the world is always take your enemy by surprise. Do your homework. Find out their habits, where they go, what they do each day. Then surprise them. Could be a plastic bag, a rope, a knitting needle. You don't need a gun or knife to kill. You can grab a rock, a hammer, an umbrella. Just do your planning. Choose your time and place so you're in control. Then do it. When they least expect it. Usually works…"

"Surprise. Thanks Dad." She stood. "I'll tell him."

"Not going already darling?"

"Got what I wanted." She went to the door. "Don't worry about me Dad. I'll call next week and take you to lunch – promise."

"Go see a doctor!" yelled her father.

And she was gone.

Harry collapsed in his chair, wondering what the fuck his daughter's gotten into. Here he was in undercover intelligence and still thought she had a nice cosy job in publishing.

*

The moment Marky got Duffy's frantic call she accessed the live eastbound CCTV traffic cameras on the M20 from London to the channel ferry at Dover. There were twenty-one positions from Junction 2 at Tonbridge right down to the coast; each one showed a live picture of the traffic passing that camera at that very second.

She had the number plate and description of the Volvo SUV she was tracking, provided by Zaffy's two soldier boys, and had already spotted it racing past Junction 10 at Ashford. They were just thirty-five minutes from Dover and that tunnel or sea crossing to Europe and Africa.

Marky was probably Duffy's greatest fan, but he didn't know it. What he saw was this tomboy rebel with pink hair, no makeup, and a nose-stud, who could find anything you wanted on the internet; what he might have missed was this deeply sensitive, very bright creature, who could mix equally with a street busker and royalty, speak seven languages including Xhosa, dating back to her art college days in Pretoria, sail single-handedly around Majorca, and cook the best chicken biryani outside Kolkata. She'd played DJ at some of the best Ibiza clubs, slept rough for a month in

Moscow, and secretly hacked the Ritz kitchens to find their recipe for Tournedos Rossini to impress a date.

Her phone rang.

The main man.

She told Duffy the SUV was half an hour from the ferry, was following a red lorry from Holland called Karsfood, and a yellow Porsche Cayman.

Then sat back in her South Kensington flat to watch the action.

*

Duffy on his Harley saw them about two hundred yards ahead on the motorway.

Ibrahim in the Volvo had pulled out to overtake the Porsche, who put his foot down, and refused to let him past. The singing detective gestured to the soldier boys on their Triumph riding at his side. They could all see their target now and throttled up.

Ibrahim didn't see them coming.

Nor did the driver of the sparkling new yellow Porsche Cayman.

Duffy raced up behind the SUV, and scraped along the inside, on the hard shoulder, overtaking the Porsche, then cutting across in front of Ibrahim.

Meanwhile Chindi and Sami on their Triumph overtook on the outside, so both bikes were now in front of the SUV, slowing him down.

The surprise appearance of the bikes made the Porsche driver slam into the side of Ibrahim's Volvo, sending both careering across the motorway, narrowly missing the other cars, and crashing into the bank on the hard shoulder. Smoke and steam billowed from the SUV's bonnet, while the gleaming Porsche's engine burst into flames.

Duffy and the soldier boys leapt off their bikes and ran to the Volvo.

Tried to open the doors. Locked.

Duffy pulled out his pistol, shot his way into the back door, and pulled Zaffy free. He took off his leather coat and threw it over her semi-naked body.

She was in tears and grabbed at Duffy.

"They made me Muslim and married me!" she sobbed.

"Then we'll get you unmarried!" said Duffy. He points his Heckler and Kock P30 at Ibrahim. "Out fucker, and get this girl unmarried!"

"I cannot. Now she is married and Muslim."

Yusuf lurched from behind Duffy but he saw him coming and shot his left knee. The giant Nubian shrieked in pain and collapsed beside the car.

"Now. Divorce Zaffy!" said Duffy, waving his pistol at Ibrahim.

"Shaker. Triple talaq. Do it." cried his father.

Shaker got out of the car trembling and looked at Zaffy. "You are haram to me; you are haram to me; you are haram to me. Talaq, talaq, talaq..."

Ibrahim turned to Duffy. "She is now divorced."

"And we'll make you Christian again sister," said Chindi squeezing Zaffy's arm.

Duffy climbed on his Harley with Zafira on pillion.

"Go back to Sudan. You're not bloody welcome here!" and rode off back to London, followed by the soldier boys.

Yusuf staggered to his feet, blood gushing from his knee.

"I will not rest until I have his head," he choked.

"Inshallah!" said Ibrahim with venom. "His days are short."

As the burly tattooed owner of the burnt-out brand new Porsche Cayman swaggered towards them, brandishing a large monkey wrench, his shaven-haired muscle-bound partner swinging a whirring chainsaw.

CHAPTER EIGHTEEN

Harry was fixed to the television news. On screen, in a community centre off the Edgware Road in London, Godfrey Young, Prime Minister of Great Britain, was giving a speech to the Iranian community, celebrating the birth of the revolutionary Islamic Republic in Teheran.

The audience was segregated with women, mostly in hijabs, sitting at the back.

Around the edges were stationed Equalisers in their Smiley Face yellow tee-shirts, acting as security guards. Dave Chubb stood near the entrance, just out of sight from the cameras, as usual. He'd had fresh revised orders from Hussein Sulimann. The Prime Minister had become a valuable asset to the regime and their cause; his life was to be protected at all costs.

"It gives me humble pleasure to salute the birth of the great Islamic Republic in Iran so many years ago. It has given us all hope. Hope to lead our peoples out of the darkness into the light. And to lead a peaceful revolution in our country against the capitalists and the Tories," raged Godfrey.

"But we should also look abroad. How in the past, British and American foreign policy has been manipulated by the Zionists, so Israel could expand into neighbouring countries, like our friends, Iran."

"So from this day on, I declare that the U.K. will no longer regard the Jewish State as allies, and will increase our trade with our new partners in Teheran. My Foreign Secretary will be flying there next week to sign a landmark new agreement to show our radical, but sincere, change of attitude to our Muslim comrades in the Middle East!"

Roars of approval from the hall.

"And finally, looking around this hall, I give my sincere thanks to the Equalisers who've made this Party what it is today…"

More hoots and thumping of studded boots on the floor in the hall.

Harry flicked off the television in disgust.

"Fucking traitor!"

As the red phone on his desk buzzed.

It was Mike from the CIA at Langley.

"I'm watching Mike," said Harry.

"This arsehole's crossed the line. Already had Israel chasing me."

"You can see who's pulling the strings now Mike. He's Iran's puppet."

"State fuckin' capture, buddy."

Harry paused. "We found a body this morning – guy who runs a business enriching uranium – just sold out to Iran."

"Jeez – they're trying to smuggle stuff in for their bomb!" seethed Mike.

"I think it's time Mike."

"Red Czar?"

"Next three or four days."

"Do it Harry," said Mike, and hung up.

Harry dialed a number.

"Frank? It's Harry. Got a green light. We're counting down… next few days…."

*

Gonzo had closed down his desk computer and was about to leave the office when Tara walked in, carrying two cups of Americano. She handed one to the Glaswegian who today was wearing a badge saying "Hug a Mugger", and slumped down on his sofa.

"Was just going home bitch," sighed Gonzo. "Thanks," taking a swig of the coffee.

"Glad I caught you. See Godfrey's speech?" asked Tara.

"Heroic. At last he's coming out and saying what Sean'd be

proud of – real Socialist ideas – and kicking bloody Israel where it hurts!"

"Very pro-Iran..?"

"Gotta be pro someone Tara – least they can throw money at us – get us out of this shit," smiled Gonzo.

"How long you been running the Equalisers Gonzo?"

"About ten years – proudest thing I ever done."

"All that rape, murder, intimidation..." smiled Tara sweetly.

Gonzo sat up straight in his chair. "Hey! Enough of that. We did what the Party wanted, to get them into power, and it worked."

"End justifies ..."

"Talking of which. Am I about to fire you, or have you silenced that Tory cow?"

"You mean the Prime Minister's lover who's having his baby?"

"OK, so I read the papers too. Is she still breathing?" spat Gonzo, with a slight slur.

Tara paused. "I shot her with a crossbow."

Gonzo's mouth dropped open. "Good girl."

"But I missed."

"Fuck."

"Thank God," whispered Tara.

"What?" asked Gonzo, swaying a little in his seat.

"I hate that poncy word 'epiphany', but that's what happened." Tara walked over and sat on the edge of Gonzo's desk. "I know you've never liked me – thought I was a stuck-up snobby bitch. Which I realize, I am. Guess I been acting like an immature kid for years, not knowing what really mattered, what didn't..."

"Till you found us..." grinned Gonzo, looking like he was falling asleep.

"That's what I stupidly thought. Then in a flash I grew up. Saw the shit and hurt I was doing to others. I should be in jail. And you. We don't need to attack and hate and kill. We can simply sort stuff out by talking, listening, being grown up."

"Ah... And now you've grown up Tara. Too late kid. You were given a job and you failed. Over and over. So." He tried hard to focus on her face which had become a blur.. "You're fired..." And slumped off his chair onto the floor.

Tara looks long at the crumpled heap.

"Should've done this long ago…"

She stood and listened. They are alone in the offices, everyone gone home.

Taking a deep breath she bent over and dragged the carrot-topped Glaswegian into his private kitchen with its sink, washer, oven.

Opened the cooker and shoved Gonzo's head and shoulders inside.

Patted him on his back.

Turned on the gas.

From her bag took a fat red candle, placed it on the sink, lit the wick, and walked out, to a fresh new world, and a fresh new Tara.

She was two blocks away on her electric scooter when she heard the booming blast, a kaleidoscope of flames lighting up the sky, a shock wave nearly blowing her off her saddle. A weight had been truly lifted; she suddenly felt free.

She pulled over and made a call.

To Suki Carter.

Who she'd been trying to kill for weeks.

*

Duffy, Zaffy, and the soldier boys Sami and Chindi were all sitting on the floor in Marky's flat reading the newspapers.

"Looks like that's the end of the Equalisers," nodded Duffy with solemn satisfaction. He'd never liked these activist crazies and their cruel behaviour.

"Suki Carter'll be celebrating, that's for sure."

"Wonder who did this? Who was brave enough?" asked Marky.

"Probably never know…" sniffed Duffy.

Zaffy let out a stifled scream.

"What Zaffy?" cried Duffy.

She was pointing to something she'd seen in the paper.

"It's them. They were attacked!" cries Zaffy.

She showed Duffy.

A burnt out SUV had been found on the hard shoulder of the M20 near Dover.

The bodies of two unidentified Muslims were found nearby.

"Shit," said Sami. "Must've been the owner of that Porsche beat them up."

"And to think those bastards killed your family Zaffy," said Duffy.

Zaffy nodded, biting back the tears.

"I must write to Harry. I was convinced… that photo. Lucky I never did anything…"

"But," added Chindi, reading the story. "Big problem. There's only two of them. One escaped…"

"That big bastard..!" said Sami.

Zaffy drew her breath.

"Yusuf. He'll be heading back here. For us…"

*

Godfrey sat in his office with his trusted security consultants, his "off the grid" enforcers. Dave Chubb, his personal bodyguard, with the terrible twins, Simon and Jason Holloway, who tortured Duffy in their limo with the prosthetic prick, over the Cannes photo.

He slammed a newspaper down on his desk, showing lurid photos of the burnt-out Equaliser building.

"I want to know who did this! How they did it?" raged Godfrey. "We lost a good patriot, a loyal fighter – Gonzo – who died for the cause."

"Not a gas leak?" asked Simon.

"This was deliberate," wheezed the P.M.

"We'll find them chief," nodded Chubb seriously.

"And we'll roast them very slowly…" added Jason with a fixed smile.

"Checked the security cams?" asked the P.M.

"Melted away," shrugged Simon.

"No witnesses. Everyone gone home." added Chubb.

"Except Gonzo,' sighed Godfrey. "I wonder? I wonder if that snoop Duffy's involved in this?"

"Duffy? Our singing dick..?" sniggered Simon. "I'd love to meet him again… he was cute."

Godfrey cleared his throat.

"Gents. I'm going through a very sensitive period right now, highly confidential deals with Iran."

They all nodded.

"I wouldn't want anything upsetting this relationship."

"What about Suki Carter?" asked Simon.

"Do nothing. Now the world knows she's having my baby, I'm getting fan mail on Twitter."

"So... Duffy?" asked Simon.

Godfrey thought a moment. "Let's really get him singing..."

*

Sir Paul Swithers had brought Frank for lunch to London's oldest restaurant, Rules.

Founded as an oyster bar in the Covent Garden of 1798, this establishment reeked of class and history. The walls were adorned with cartoons and paintings and photos dating back decades, showing off its most famous and infamous clients from Dickens to Thackeray, Clark Gable to Charlie Chaplin. He'd ordered a simple red wine – Chateauneuf-du-Pape Cuvee de Mon Aieul Pierre Usseglio [Rhone] 2009 at £110 the first bottle, to accompany the splendidly refined main dishes of Loin and Braised Haunch of Hare with port glazed chicory, lentils and pickled pear for himself, and Wild Boar Pie with red wine, tomato and parsley, for his Hollywood producer guest.

"I fear this is the last supper Paul," joked Frank limply.

"Don't be so churlish dear boy," smiled his doctor friend.

"I nearly called you but in last few days I've had more pain. Think the cancer's spread."

"Taking those pills I gave you?"

Frank nodded and munched on his wild boar. "Not doing much. Sorry Paul."

He chewed further and sipped the red plonk. "Real sore stomach pains, ripping through my gut."

"Sounds like you're allergic to the pills – I'll give you some new ones."

"What's the point doc – let me go quietly – I really appreciate this lunch, and the place… a great memory…" sighed Frank.

"I've got the results from your MRI scan," he said soberly. "So sorry it's taken so long."

Frank knew this was why his old buddy had brought him to this enchanting old place. Fill him with good food and wine and let him down gently. Way to go.

Frank slowly put down his knife and fork, took a long sip of wine, then said: "Go on Paul."

Paul did likewise, wiped his mouth pensively with the serviette, and looked Frank straight in the eye.

"We've known each other for a lifetime. Go back years. So I take this very seriously and know what it means to you Frank."

"Spit it out man!"

Paul reached inside his jacket and pulled out a brown envelope.

"The results of your scan are in here. I want you to take this and open it later. In your own time. In privacy…"

"Why not just bloody tell me now!?"

"It's better to read alone."

"You're playing mind games Paul, and loving it. Why not tell me I'm dying and there's no remission…!"

Paul stood. "This is your life Frank. Your future." He squeezed his friend's arm. "Give me a call when you've read it and considered the results…"

And he's gone.

Frank stared at the envelope and felt numb.

He feared the worst.

But what if he was in remission, that his L.A. doctors had got it wrong…

He'd committed to Mike and Harry at the CIA that he'd be part of a kill plot on some mystery target.. He knew he was an integral part of the murder, that they saw him as a walking time bomb as he was about to die anyway. Least he was. If he was in remission then everything changed. Or did it. Just hours earlier Harry had confirmed a green light for the operation so the hit would take place anytime soon, and Frank was in the midst of it. He needed time to think and plan.

If he ran, they could still hurt his daughter and granddaughter and make it look accidental, as they threatened earlier. But that was Yankee bullshit. These were Harry's family too. He wouldn't hurt them. So, yes, he could run, escape overnight.

But Mike's U.S. agents would track him down and punish him, fatally, for backing out. Or, he didn't tell anyone, not even family, about the remission, and went ahead as planned. Whatever, it was a lose lose...

He stared long at the brown envelope.

Looked around at the braying crowd enjoying themselves at the other tables.

They all had sunlit uplands ahead of them. Bastards.

Then tore the envelope in half.

And half again.

And again.

And walked out.

*

Tara was sat on a bench on the Thames Embankment outside the Festival Hall, as arranged. The river looked grey and hostile, as little boats full of tourists chugged past taking photos of Big Ben and Waterloo Bridge.

She could see Suki approaching, accompanied by two tall men. Tara wondered if she'd be arrested any moment.

Suki was suddenly at her side.

"Don't try anything silly – these men are my protection officers – they're armed."

Tara nodded and said nothing. Her face and eye still bore the scars from Henry's spade.

Suki sat tentatively on the end of the bench, leaving a gap of two metres, like that social distancing from the virus a few years back.

The security guys stood twelve paces behind them in case she was attacked.

"What's this about?" said Suki through gritted teeth. She clutched a Mace spray within her handbag.

Tara looked her in the eyes.

"Christ, your face is a fucking mess," said Suki. "But you deserved it. You bloody tried to kill me three times. Three! Setting my house on fire. Putting a bomb under my car. Shooting me with a crossbow. I can put you in jail right now."

Tara raised an eyebrow.

"But. I wanted to meet the monster who stalked me day and night. Who terrified me. Made my life hell for months. And here you are, a silly little girl!"

"I'm truly very very sorry," said Tara, her voice going dry.

"You fucking should be. I could rip you to pieces right now, but I won't."

"What I did was unforgiveable. You should arrest me."

Suki calmed and looked again at the girl.

"What's your name?"

"Tara."

Suki remembered how she felt when she first saw her standing with the Equaliser mob outside her house. That tawny hair, green eyes. She was striking, almost beautiful. But lethal.

"Have you killed before?" asked Suki.

Tara sighed and paused. "That Equaliser gas explosion."

"That was you?"

Tara nodded.

Suki was quietly impressed. "But they were your friends. Why?" she asked.

"Guess I realized too late I'd been a prick. Damaged lives, hurt people. Thought I was being clever. It was all shit."

"What do you want from me Tara?" asked Suki, feeling confused.

Tara's hand crawled along the bench and touched Suki's gently.

"Absolution."

"Why should I forgive you?"

"At your hen house. I could have killed you. But you're having a baby. That changed my mind. About everything. Taking lives for no real reason. Just fucking politics. It was crazy."

Suki moved her hand away from Tara's.

"Who was behind all that ? Trying to kill me?"

"Someone at the top – I've no idea."

Suki nodded slowly and thoughtfully.

"I hope you turn your life around." She stood. "I won't see

you again." Then touched Tara's shoulder. "But I do forgive you. It took guts to meet…"

And walked slowly off, followed by her protection officers.

Tara looked after her, then crossed to the wall and stared deep at the murky Thames relentlessly rolling on down to the sea. Life kept trudging on, whether you're part of it or not. Was it worth it? Would anybody care if you went missing?

A laughing couple walking past her broke her depressive trance.

She took out her phone and texted her reporter mate Charlie.

"It's Tara. Must meet again soon… Know anyone in publishing?"

*

Aunt Huda had been phoning Ibrahim and Shaker for over a day but was getting no reply. She'd not seen the newspaper story so guessed they were well on their way to Africa. Her conscience had been playing tricks. Had she done the right thing for Zafira, or created a disaster…

She was dozing on her sofa when there was a thumping on the front door.

It could be them back again. Changed their minds.

She opened the door and Yusuf shoved past her.

The Nubian giant had a blood soaked leg and limped into her kitchen.

"Gimme a knife and boiling water!" he shouted.

Huda stared, stunned, for a moment, then ran and did his bidding.

Yusuf ripped off his trouser leg, exposing a gaping wound where the bullet had gone in. He gritted his teeth and dabbed his the blood away. Then, grabbing the carving knife from Huda, dug deep into the gaping hole.

He stifled his shrieks, as more blood flowed onto the lino floor, then a tinkle as the bullet fell out, and Yusuf lost consciousness.

Huda silently cleaned up the mess and put his leg in a bandage.

An hour later he'd recovered and was drinking mint tea with her.

"They both died – Ibrahim and Shaker?" she asked trembling.

Yusuf nodded. "There was a car crash and a fight."

"Why are you here Yusuf?" asked Huda, fearing the answer.

"To find Zafira… and her friends."

Huda shook her head. "I cannot help…"

Yusuf held the knife to Huda's throat, warm blood trickling down her neck.

*

Harry turned back to Frank who was sitting there in his office, hugging that bloody breathing cylinder.

"Mike tells me you're getting more pain?"

Frank nodded. He nearly told him about the scan but decided not to. He'd thrown away the result. Still dying or longer to live. Most likely still dying.

"Ripping through my guts. Guess my days are getting shorter Harry…"

"Shit."

"Got some news?" asked Frank with a resigned smile.

Harry nodded and sat at his desk. "We got a location…"

"At last…"

"On a need-to-know basis, it's a hospital, but we'll make sure we shield any doctors and nurses nearby…"

"Me at a hospital. Ironic. Great choice…" sighed Frank.

"You'll have your 'disposable' Sonny with you… final details soonest."

"Less I know, the less pain."

"Sorry Frank." Harry took a long look at his father-in-law. "Drink, for old time's sake?"

Frank nodded. Least they had a date at last. He touched his jaw. Aching tooth.

Must find a dentist. Felt like his whole body was falling apart…

"And the target Harry?"

"Wait and see…"

CHAPTER NINETEEN

Duffy had dragged Marky to Watch My Hips, a gay club in Brighton so they could spend the night together in a new state-of-the-art boutique hotel overlooking the sea.

Big booze, big bath, big bed. He felt he owed her a favour in tracking down those Sudanese monsters, and it was a good excuse to get up close and excessively personal with his number one hacker.

Right now he was sitting looking radiantly cool in a dazzling Hawaiian shirt and shorts, perched on a stool on stage, going through the outrageous classics his audience craved, from his campy Freddy Mercury hits, through "Go West" to "Y.M.C.A." The place was heaving with shouty beehive wigs, flamboyant make-up, more glitter than a bent Christmas Tree, more boas than the Reptile Room at London Zoo. He had them in the palm of his hand, swaying, rocking, cooing, then changed the mood to something whispering soft and sultry...

"Me and Mrs Jones...
We got a thing goin' on..."

Marky sat at a front row table sipping Bombay gin, and melting before the ace seducer. Why the fuck didn't this darling go professional, she mused. She could see him filling the O2, all those knickers being thrown, many by girls. Tonight she was wearing a hold-your-breath floral silk dress, sparkling eye-shadow, and, with her spicy pink hair, was getting a little too much attention from some of the leather-clad butch girls in the club. Not that it mattered. Marky couldn't take her eyes off her date.

Which was just as well, as she might have noticed the two guys who'd entered at the rear. The terrible twins, Simon and Jason. As they nodded at various guys in the club, you realised for the first time that these two ruthless enforcers were themselves gay, and totally at ease in their apricot suits and bleached blonde surfer hair styles. Except Marky had never come across this deadly duo, and hopefully never would.

Duffy looked around the club as he lost himself in his music. He thought of poor Zaffy and what she'd been through, nearly kidnapped for ever, off the face of the earth, and all the time it was her own Uncle who'd killed her family. Shit happens, and it certainly had with her. But least she was safe now. He looked across at Marky.

She looked so bloody serene, this girl. He ended his gig, bowed low to his shrieking fans, and motioned to Marky he was going for a pee.

A drag act took the mike, and Marky ordered two more drinks while Duffy was in the bog. The guy on stage was stunning – too gorgeous to be a girl – and looked more Dolly than Parton herself. After two thigh-whacking numbers Marky wondered what Duffy was up to. Knowing him he was probably on the phone chasing a new P.I. job – there was no holding him down when it came to a challenge. But then, she knew that.

She sat through two more raucous songs, then headed for the men's toilet.

It was full of women. Or so it seemed. Most of them standing in front of the long mirror touching up their makeup, adjusting their bras.

Marky dropped to her knees and peered under the cubicles. No Duffy. Strange.

How could he disappear like that.

Then she noticed another door at the far end. Slightly ajar. And suddenly got worried. Duffy was always a possible target – he'd been beaten up in Chelsea, shot at in Dorset, and was the last to see Sean O'Leary alive.

Marky pushed open the door and looked up and down the street.

No-one. Except a teen on roller-blades, couple of guys in apricot suits snogging in a doorway beside a rubbish bag, and someone pushing a woman in a wheel chair.

She took out her phone and dialed Duffy's number, then looked at a map of Brighton on her iPad. The number was ringing and ringing.

A red dot appeared on her screen.

About a hundred yards from the club, going east. It was gently moving away from her.

Marky took off her high heels and ran down the promenade beside the beach in bare feet.

Could still see the GPS location of Duffy's phone. Still gently moving.

Getting closer.

Now only fifty yards away.

In the late night dusk she could see nothing.

Except. The phone position was to her right.

Over the sea wall.

Down the beach.

Duffy was in the bloody sea.

She raced across the glistening pebbles to the water's edge.

Rang his number again.

Her heart sank.

He'd changed that fucking ringtone again.

"Bring me sunshine,
in your smile..."

Bloody Morecambe and Wise, at a moment like this.

Marky waded deep into the freezing sea.

Still that song.

"In this world where we live..."

She started swimming.

Pitch dark.

The song got louder.

"So much joy you can give..."

Then she saw it.

"To each brand new bright tomorrow..."

Duffy's phone had been tied to an inflatable teddy bear and thrown out to sea. Would have been in Calais by dawn.
Marky dragged herself back up the beach and collapsed.
Someone was taking the piss.
And that someone had Duffy.

*

Frank Gruber hated dentists. When you live in Los Angeles everybody has to have perfect teeth. Whiter than white, and beautifully arranged in very straight crisp lines across your jaw. Anything less and you don't get a job, a date, or invited to parties.

So in his younger years our Frankie had spent zillions on getting it right. All his upper and lowers were replaced at immense cost and personal pain to make him look like everyone else on Sunset Boulevard. After that he discovered his very rich dentist gave the best pool parties in Bel Air, where everyone's teeth looked exactly the same and spent most of the time talking to each other.

But today that investment in his gnashers had let him sorely down.

He'd sent Sonny out on a shopping trip to find a special bottle of single malt to consume over his final days, while he found a dentist to cope with his seering tooth ache.

He ended up visiting a swish practitioner in Knightsbridge, near Harrods, and told him to fix his back left molar, which was making life unbearable.

The dentist did an x-ray, and examined the tooth carefully.

"OK. Mr Gruber. I can fill it or pull it..?"

The mind-numbing muzak had almost lulled Frank off to sleep.

He sat up with a start, for a moment wondering where he was.

"Pull it."

Half an hour later he was in the street again, minus his left back molar, but feeling a whole lot happier, looking forward to a wee dram of Glenfiddich.

*

It was one of those very inner sanctums, an exclusive private dining room, within an exclusive private dining room. Saladine languorously voluptuous, was draped along a chaise longue at one end of the room, while Godfrey Young, the P.M., and Hussein Sulimann, the consultant to Iran's Islamic Republic, sat more formally at a table.

"I think my work is done with you two," smiled Saladine. "I've brought you together and you're making beautiful music…"

Godfrey nodded. "Our agreement's working very very well Saladine. I thank you."

"The payments are getting through to your account?" she asked.

"Of course," said the P.M.

"And next month we begin the first shipment of arms from London to Teheran," grinned Hussein. "This indeed is historic."

"I heard only this morning that Israel's closing its embassy here," said Godfrey.

"Bravo. Everything going to plan." nodded Hussein.

"And following the Syrian War, Iran now occupies two borders with Israel, another first, so, with our tanks and guns, who knows what might happen..?" added Godfrey.

"You've no opposition in your party with the new policy?" asked Saladine.

Godfrey shook his head. "Every red-blooded Socialist has wanted rid of the Zionists for years – now we have power, and money…"

They each raised a glass of champagne to toast their success.

"To New Dawn…" said Hussain.

"And Iran…" smiled the P.M.

Saladine gave a gentle smile. She had weaved her magic as international broker once more… She quietly opened her address book. The next challenge would be uniting North and South Korea.

*

Watch My Hips was a favourite haunt of Simon and Justin's, so with their target Duffy performing there, that night was a double bonus. Their instructions had been to make this boy sing, so they looked forward to a solo performance. In private.

Once he'd gone to the loo it was a no-brainer.

Pistol in his ribs and out the back door onto the street.

Hang about in a doorway waiting for the girl to come looking.

Knock Duffy out, and cover in a rubbish bag.

Snog each other as the girl looks their way.

Then chase after the wheelchair couple.

Moments later Duffy had his head covered by a scarf and was being pushed away down the beach promenade by Simon in the wheelchair, while Justin sought inspiration for his phone. An inflatable teddy bear provided the answer.

Now all was quiet.

The threesome were in a dusty cellar.

Duffy, head slumped forward, was tied to a chair.

Simon and Justin stood over him with a vicious looking power drill.

Justin eased off Duffy's left shoe and sock.

"Takes me back," sighed Justin. "Used to sell ladies' shoes in the Kings Road, years ago. Never with a drill though…"

Simon lifts Duffy's chin. "You've got a lovely foot there dear boy. We'd hate to fill it full of holes…"

"What's this fuckin' about?" grunted the detective.

"Language," sighed Justin with mock effront.

"Did you kill Sean O'Leary?"

"Course I didn't – I was talking to him when he died. He was bloody hacked – someone got into the system and killed him," spat Duffy. "Nothing to do with me mate!"

"And Gonzo?" asked Simon.

"Who?"

"The Equaliser boss who went up in smoke…" added Justin.

"That was a gas leak."

The twins looked at each other. Either Duffy was telling it straight, or he was hiding something.

"You knew John Slade, who committed suicide, didn't you?"

"Never met him. His wife asked me to investigate. Found nothing."

"And Suki Carter?" asked Simon. "You know her?"

"Course I bloody do – you took that photo off me – threatened to chop me up!"

"Just checking..." Simon looked at Duffy's hands. "Perhaps your hands might be better than your foot, that way you can't hide it..."

Duffy glared at him. "I've nothing to tell you."

And Simon started up the power drill, Justin holding out Duffy's hand...

*

Harry was in pensive mood. The big job they'd been planning for months was only forty-eight hours away. Tomorrow he'd run over logistics with Sonny and Moggie, but meanwhile he was wrestling with his own conscience about Frank. With his terminal cancer, and unblemished covert CIA background, he was the absolute perfect choice for the hit job.

So far Harry had not actually spelt out the truth to his father-in-law, that he was a walking suicide bomber with the explosives hidden in his breathing canister, though he might have guessed as much. He hoped dear Viv would understand, that her father was dying for a patriotic cause, though she must never ever know.

Frank would be told on the day that he'd be sacrificed in action. There was no way round this. He was dying anyway, in obvious pain. This way it'd all be over in a flash.

And the sting in the tail would be the media spin. The fake news about the attack. He was lining up Tara's reporter friend Charlie for a big political scoop in the coming days, a front-page barnstormer when it broke.

The steam hissed around Harry's head.

He was sitting in one of London's best Turkish baths, in the

Camberwell Road.

It was men only, and several pot-bellied hairy-bodied gents wrapped in white towels, sat alone, or in couples in the intense heat.

Harry lay back and let his tensions flow away. He knew the heat dilated the blood vessels improving circulation, giving a positive tonic effect, that the pores also opened, leading to a deep cleansing of the skin.

They said it stimulated both body and mind.

Body, certainly. He could feel it working.

As for mind. His eyes, ears, and brain were straining.

Lying across from him were two foreigners talking with each other. The language was Farsi, that spoken in Iran. And one of the men was Hussein Sulimann.

The last time Harry had seen him was playing golf on that Bracknell course with the guy whose company was enriching uranium. And was now dead.

The other was thirties, leaner and fitter, probably ex-military, one of the Quds Force, Revolutionary Guards. Named Hassan.

Harry had been tailing them all day and now hoped he might get his reward.

He closed his eyes as if asleep and heard certain key words from their conversation. He knew a smattering of Farsi from his intelligence training. They were talking about a shipment arriving, and the lorry now being in place. There were ten items in the shipment and would be only used in a crisis. Codename "Surena." The Iranians shook hands, and exited the steam room.

Harry grabbed his phone and googled "Surena."

"An Iranian commander during the 1st century BC who won the Battle of Carrhae, the first major victory over the Romans.

Plutarch said about him: 'If he went on an excursion into the country, he had a thousand camels to carry his baggage and two hundred carriages for his concubines.

He was attended by a thousand heavy-armed horse, and many more of the light-armed rode before him. Indeed his vassals and slaves made up a body of cavalry little less than ten thousand.'"

So. This guy was an epic warrior... a historic legend... a Persian god.

Which meant whatever operation they had on ice could be a biggie.

Suddenly it seemed Harry might have another little problem on his hands.

*

When Marky realized Duffy had been taken, she went straight to the Brighton cops.

She knew more than enough about CCTV operation systems that, with their help, they might just track down his current location. She stood with the local plods viewing five or six different security cams at a time. Saw Duffy being dragged from the gay club into the street by two guys. Then watched as they mugged a guy with a wheelchair and pushed Duffy down the sea front towards the pier. Down a side street and they had an address. Dingy little shop opposite a launderette.

Minutes later Marky was in a police car, siren blaring, racing to where Duffy had been taken.

She followed the guys as they smashed down the front door of a terraced house and ran upstairs. Place was empty.

Then they found a cellar door.

Down the steps.

They'd just gone. On the floor was an electric drill. Duffy's shoes. And an old rope that had tied him to a chair.

No blood. Perhaps they'd just stopped him being damaged.

Marky went back to their HQ and looked again at the CCTV outside the place.

The kidnappers had been too clever.

Three cabs pulled up at once.

Two men came out with a guy in a hoodie and got into the first.

Then they swopped cabs. One getting into the second. Two getting into the third.

And all drove off in different directions.

These guys were too clever for their own good.

After all this double bluffing they might simply have taken Duffy out a back exit into the night.

One thing was certain.

This time Duffy was well and truly gone.

*

After the most traumatic terrifying week of her life Zaffy needed to party.

It seemed like she'd been to hell and back. It had all been so otherworldly. The drugging, forcing her to become a Muslim, and the fake marriage. She felt soiled inside and out, as if she'd lost control of mind and body.

Then to learn that they – her relatives - were the murderers of her family; not Harry. And desperate relief she'd discovered just in time before taking out revenge on the wrong man.

Least friends had been there for her. Duffy, her hero and confidante, always a shoulder to cry on through good times and bad; Marky who'd insisted she stay in her flat a few days; and her new blood brothers, the soldier boys, Chindi and Sami.

Sadly she'd never ever see Aunt Huda again. Not after her fateful call to Juba.

But tonight, tonight was a special occasion, as the boys had invited her to celebrate her birthday at Mabola in Notting Hill. She'd been sat in the window by Jamal, while the boys cooked up a fasulia dish in the kitchen.

While Sami was warming the bean stew, Chindi was trying something more western, creating an ice-cream and meringue pudding, a bit like baked Alaska, though in his case, baked Sudan.

Wearing a crocodile paper hat – a massive bright green toothy jaw jutting out from his head - for Zaffy's birthday, he took a large pan and danced and sang his way into the back storeroom to get the ice-cream.

He pulled at the door of the long chest freezer and found it sticking.

Sometimes after a recent opening, the suction sucked extra hard like that.

Gave the door an extra heave.

And froze with shock.

The big bastard.

Yusuf.

In his face.

Out of the freezer leapt the massive bearded Nubian brandishing a long gleaming scimitar that glinted bright in the flickering neon lighting.

Chindi dropped his pan and fled.

Yusuf was on his heels, hate burning in his fiery crimson eyes.

Chindi turned the corner into the kitchen as Sami was serving the burning hot stew onto plates. He saw Yusuf towering in the doorway and thought quickly, hurling the pot of stew at the Nubian's face.

Yusuf ducked and kept coming at Chindi, his blade slicing the long toothy jaw off his crocodile paper hat.

The boys were shouting at each other, trying to distract the giant, to stop him crashing into the restaurant and finding Zaffy.

Each had grabbed a weapon.

Sami held a large lid as a shield and was lunging at Yusuf with a meat cleaver.

Chindi had a broom stick and was trying to spear his smouldering eyes.

But Yusuf stood his ground. He knew he was invincible, that he had no trouble with these kids.

He suddenly spun on Chindi. Snapped the broom stick. Squeezed his neck in his massive paw and spat: "Where's the fuckin' girl!?"

Chindi could hardly talk with Yusuf's hand on his windpipe, shook his head rapidly from side to side. The Nubian flung him to the ground and advanced on Sami. He knocked away the meat cleaver and pushed the point of his scimitar into Sami's brow.

"Where – or you die !?"

Sami said nothing, felt the warm blood dripping down his cheek, then looked beyond Yusuf.

At that very second Zaffy had come from the restaurant, knife in hand. She silently leapt at the Nubian from behind, her knife slitting his throat. Deep cut. He collapsed to the floor, as the boys rushed in.

Yusuf turned and thrashed wildly back at Zaffy. Blood was billowing from his jugular as he struggled to stand.

Sami floored him as Zaffy stabbed him in his chest.

He grunted and lay face down on the floor.

The monster's body twitched a moment then was still.

The others looked at each other in silence.

It had been him or them.

Zaffy gave the body three furious kicks, for her mother, father, and brother.

Then quietly started to clear up the mess.

*

Suki Carter was exiting from the House of Commons lift and walked straight into Godfrey Young. She'd been avoiding him for days. Now the world knew she was having his baby it was the talking point in every Westminster bar.

"Godfrey!" gasped Suki wishing she was somewhere else.

"Suki!" thinking just the same. "You OK?" It was a tactless question but he couldn't think of anything to say to her. He suspected her marriage was now on the rocks, because of the pregnancy, just as his own partner was moving out from his place that very weekend.

"If you call putting the Sussex home we've lived in for years on the market, OK, then I'm OK!" she snapped.

"Because of the baby?"

"Because of your fucking Land Tax – we can't live there any more!"

"The poor will gain from this, love..." mumbled the P.M.

Suki ignored his answer. "You been trying to knock me off Godfrey?"

"You what?" he answered, apparently puzzled.

"Someone on high's been trying to kill me."

The P.M. felt his throat drying and licked his lips. He could feel her eyes searing into his. He tried to act as naturally as possible. Adjusted his bright red tie a moment and smiled glibly.

"I fear you're having hallucinations my dear. Perhaps the pregnancy..?"

"I'm not a fucking push-over Godfrey," and briskly shoved past him.

He watched her walk away, still attracted to her rear, fearing how this loose cannon would next impact upon his life.

*

Terry Dunn had promised his twelve-year-old son Jake he'd take him fishing at dawn.

He usually did this on his own, and come home with a few mackerel for breakfast, fresh from the sea. Nothing better, with a fresh brown roll from the bakery, washed down with a steaming cuppa to bring the warmth back into your veins after a freezing night out on Brighton Pier.

It took forever to wake the little sod in the dark, but Terry and Jake were eventually heading in his electrician's van along the Marine Parade towards the pier.

It was high tide in about an hour so their timing was perfect.

Terry had taught young Jake the basics of catching mackerel.

You tied chicken feathers to a hook and threw them over the side. These looked like sand eels, the mackerels' dream dish, so usually you'd start pulling in the blighters after a few minutes. If they were around that was.

Terry took Jake to his special spot halfway down the pier.

He had a hot flask of tea and a couple of peanut sandwiches. Should keep them going till brekkie and fresh fish.

Terry rubbed his hands together, opened his fishing bag, got out the line with the string of feathers and hooks and handed it to his son.

"Off you go boy," he said, shivering in the early dawn light. "Good luck."

Jake tossed the line over and both waited. And waited. Terry had a feel on the line. Nothing yet. He started to tell his son that sometimes, sometimes, he'd return home with nothing. He also confessed that sometimes, not very often, he'd nip round the fishing stalls, buy some there, and tell his wife he'd caught them.

But there was a problem.

Jake was pulling on the line and it was not budging.

Terry had a go.

Bloody snagged.

He took a swig from the flask, told his son to stay put, and trudged back to the beach entrance end at the Marine Parade.

Down onto the pebbles and started walking out under the pier, in the sea.

Lucky he'd brought his waders.

Didn't happen very often, a snag, but with the tide coming in fast, he walked out quickly as he could.

The water was nearly up to his waist when he saw him.

A guy was tied to one of the pier's barnacled columns.

Gagged and slumped forward.

The blood drained from his pallid bruised face.

Eyes so sunken and shut he looked dead.

The tide was inches away from his mouth and getting higher.

Terry quickly took out his fishing knife and cut him free.

There was life left in Duffy as the good Samaritan dragged him back to the beach through the incoming tide.

Terry bounced on his chest forcing Duffy to throw up an ocean of sea water.

Another minute or two and our lad would have been feeding the mackerel.

CHAPTER TWENTY

Marky leant over the bath and gently sponged Duffy in the steaming soapy water.

He'd been found by some fisherman under Brighton Pier within minutes of drowning.

Now he was safe. But he'd had a shock. Those guys who took him were lethal.

And was only Marky and the cop siren that stopped them turning the singing detective into a power-drilled pin cushion.

His body was bruised all over, he was still suffering from his near death experience. The first time that had happened was some arsehole drug pushers working out of the East End where he nearly had his throat slit, and was saved by a neighbour's dog biting their goolies. This last was more serious. He'd get even with that vicious pair, sooner or later.

"I think you should stay here for a few weeks Duffy..." said Marky, mopping his brow, patting his hair in place.

"Don't like one place too long Marky, but thanks. Seriously." He took her hand. This girl was a bloody gem.

"What were they after, these guys?"

"Dunno. But it's all linked to the P.M.'s office. It was them that nearly cut me up over that blackmail photo."

"P'raps we should keep an eye on Godfrey Young. Could lead us to them..."

Duffy stood, naked in the bath.

"One place I'd love you lead me now babe..." And collapsed dripping into her arms.

*

Godfrey sat in his office with his enforcer twins, Simon and Justin.

"That's the end of Duffy..." smiled Simon.

"Unless he gets washed up on the Isle of Wight..." smirked Justin.

"More likely shark bait from what you've said," nodded the P.M.

"Don't think he knew anything..." said Simon.

"About anything," laughed Justin.

"We were just about to do some DIY on him..."

"When the fuzz arrived."

"Well done boys – think we've tied everything up now, nice and tidy."

The twins beamed back.

"So. To show my gratitude, I'll take you for a slap-up tomorrow night..."

"Where boss?"

"The Gay Hussar – where else?"

The twins sniggered.

"I'd make it lunch but got to open another fucking hospital wing in the afternoon..." sighed Godfrey. "Bloody NHS."

*

Harry sat in his office with Moggie and Sonny. It was Operation Red Czar minus one.

Suddenly life had got bloody serious. He'd called them in for their tech briefing. Each had a different role. Each was a vital cog in making the job run smoothly. Sonny was running field ops, Moggie back-up.

Harry painted the scenario.

Tomorrow afternoon the target would arrive at the hospital to open the new wing. Sonny, dressed as a doctor, would be the welcome party, as he pushed a patient - Frank - in a wheelchair towards the limo. Frank would be carrying his breathing cylinder, filled with explosives. The hospital staff and patients, would be waiting safely inside for the target's entrance.

"The target'll be in an armoured Jaguar XJ Sentinel driven by one of our boys... escorted by three unmarked Range Rovers carrying eight Royal Protection plods, plus there'll be two Special Escort outriders. As they approach the hospital there'll be a small demo that'll delay the security vehicles a vital minute or two, allowing the target to proceed on their own..."

"The Jag has explosive resistant steel plates under the body, and bullet-proof windows, so target's well protected while inside..."

"We hit him as he steps out of the car..?" confirmed Sonny.

"Exactly... Sonny - Frank still doesn't know you're CIA ?"

"No way boss – thinks I'm gonna die with him..."

"Leave it like that."

Sonny nodded.

"Materials ready ?"

"Got the semtex for the breathing cylinder... Be some firework display."

"So we take out Frank and the target in one hit," added Harry.

"Still feel bad about the old guy," sighed Sonny. "Setting him up like this."

"Sonny. He's my fucking father-in-law. But. He's riddled with cancer. He's in real pain. This is a godsend. Believe me." Right then Harry did not even believe himself. He still felt fucking guilty. Quietly angry. But it was going to happen. It had to. For the country's sake.

"Moggie. You're sniper back-up. We got that room in the Premier Inn opposite. If we need you."

Moggie nodded. "Making it clear sir. If the bomb fails for any reason, and he tries make a run for it, I take out the target?"

"Absolutely. One shot. You're my fail safe," agreed Harry. "And get out of there pretty damned quick."

They all sat in silence a moment as Harry poured each a scotch and quietly raised their glasses.

"Tomorrow. Operation Red Czar..." toasted Harry. "I do love pyrotechnics..."

"One last question boss," asked Sonny.

Harry raised an eyebrow.

"Why don't we just shoot the fucker?"

"Because Sonny, I want the world to think this is the work of a major player – it's gotta look bloody spectacular..!"

*

Tara slid off Charlie's naked body and cuddled up to him with a new-found affection.

They'd been eating in Soho then went to a pub, then a bar, then a club, then bed. Both remembered very little after those three sambuccas on ice in the trattoria. After all her secret escapades she'd forgotten what a really nice guy her reporter mate was. He wasn't adventurous or flamboyant like Duffy, but he was safe, regular, good hubbie material as her Ma would say.

"Got that publishing job, thanks to you Charlie," she said fondly.

"So you told me last night," he murmured. "Well done."

"How long we known each other?"

"Too long."

"You know my bra size, my fave perfume, my worst faux pas," she said. "You ever done anything crazy Charlie, anything mad?"

"Only that night at The Ritz."

"Remind me."

"We were staying the night. I got up pissed, about four, to go to the loo. Turned left, as you do at home, opened the door, went out, and click. There I was standing in the hotel corridor, locked out of my room, stark bloody naked..!"

"... and you climbed up, draped yourself in a curtain, went to reception, and was propositioned by the gay receptionist..."

Charlie nodded.

"Silly boy..."

Tara ran her finger down his nose, to his mouth; down his chin, to his belly button.

"I think, I think it's time."

"Not again Tara – got work..."

"I think it's time you asked."

"What?" asked Charlie.

"To fucking marry me!" shouted Tara.

Charlie looked at Tara. He'd been wanting this for years. Why had she suddenly changed.

"I'd love that Tara, really love that."

Tara sat upright. "Let's do it then. Registry office. Today. Don't tell anyone. Announce it when we're ready!"

"Fuck," sighed Charlie. "Everything comes at once."

"Don't say you're too busy!?"

"Bad timing babe. Something huge breaking …" he said.

"Bollocks! Bigger than our wedding?"

Charlie paused, wondering whether to reveal what he'd been working on for weeks.

"Confidential Tara."

"Spit it out."

He paused again and turned to face her.

"I think the Prime Minister's in danger."

"That tosser – bloody hope he is!" snapped Tara. This was the shit she suspected had been trying to silence Suki Carter.

"I think he's got a terrorist working for him."

"Just saw a flying pig…" She saw from his face he was not joking, and slumped back on the pillow. "Holy fuck."

"Dave Chubb, aka Jazza Al Britani. Frozen food packer from Lowestoft… then became Muslim… joined ISIS, and went head-chopping in the Middle East."

"And?" asked Tara.

"About two weeks ago Godfrey Young employed him as his personal bodyguard."

"He would have been vetted..!"

"Godfrey's sacked all the usual guys – using his own crew now…"

Took a moment for Tara to digest. "Charlie – this is dynamite."

"So big I'm not sure where to go…" he nodded.

"Duffy." she said firmly. "He's a bloody detective… And he's got a gun."

"Sure. But I need to warn the Prime Minister. This little shit could top him any minute…"

*

Frank and Sonny nestled into a back bar at the Hilton. Neither was saying much.

Both knew tomorrow was the big day. Both had secrets they couldn't divulge.

Frank knew he must call Sir Paul and find out what was in that brown envelope; Sonny was hiding that he was CIA and helping run the assassination plot, instead of some random street busker Frank had picked up in L.A.

Sonny rummaged inside his overcoat and pulled out a small paper bag.

"What you got?" asked Frank.

Sonny took out two spliffs. "Thought this might make us relax, before the big day."

"Jeez Sonny – haven't smoked weed in years..." said Frank in awe.

Sonny lit one, handed it to Frank, then lit another for himself.

"Don't let the staff see – they'll throw us out..."

Sonny took a long drag and sat back, enjoying the joint. "This is more like it..."

Frank inhaled. "Great idea Sonny."

"When you last do this?"

"Amsterdam. We were in one of those hash cafes. Girl standing on a tiny bar, doing crazy things with a pile of plastic bananas... Think I passed out. Next morn woke in my hotel bed, covered in ... plastic bananas."

"I once worked in a department store, selling shirts and stuff. Used to get high in the storeroom then come out and not let the customers leave till they bought something – they loved it." giggled Sonny. "Least I think they did."

They both went quiet a moment.

"You know what's happening don't you Sonny," asked Frank softly.

Sonny nodded.

"It's tomorrow."

Sonny nodded again.

"I'm getting briefed first thing, then it happens after lunch. Outside a hospital." Frank paused. "You and me. "

"Knew I had a reason."

"You don't even know what you're walking into... I dragged you to London as my companion... and now, tomorrow, you might get hurt."

"Frank. You're a great guy. I know you're dying. I know you've got me into something scary, but, things don't always go to plan... whatever that is."

"For you I hope not Sonny. You're too young..." wavered Frank.

The cannabis was getting deep into their blood streams as each began to really relax, even to float just a little.

"Death's a funny thing. You never know when it's coming. Except if you knew you were going to die on that day like tomorrow - guess mentally you see that little door at the end of the corridor that'll open and you'll go through... Pop. Everything goes blank. And you're curtains..." mused Frank. Already his thoughts were getting hazy, felt he was rambling.

"Nothing's what it seems Frank," slurred Sonny. "All this fake news shit. I could say a load of stuff to you right now and you wouldn't know if it was true or not,"

"Me too," agreed Frank, taking a long drag on his spliff.

"I could tell you Frank I been with for the CIA for years. That you never picked me up that day on Hollywood Boulevard; I picked you up! That I've known all along what you've been doing... what you've been planning..."

Frank leant over in a fit of giggling.

"And I could tell you Sonny that I had a cancer scan last week... and I don't know the result – I could have a few more days or a few more years but don't let anyone know...it's my secret..!"

"I even did special forces in Iraq and Syria – I'm not a street busker..." smiled Sonny too widely.

"Seems we both been working for the CIA and we didn't know it – if that was true..." and Frank started belly laughing.

"That was during my belly dancing days in Beirut..."

"When I was climbing Everest for charity in a clown suit..!" hooted Frank.

Sonny's eyes were drawn to the bar where an exotic girl in grey blue hair and a cerise kaftan was sipping a tequila through a long straw. He recognised those cheekbones at once, though everything else had changed. The German girl.

Frank struggled to his feet, swaying.

"You OK?" asked Sonny, suddenly sobering up.

"Early night – big day tomorrow..." and Frank tottered slowly to the lift.

Sonny pondered then went and sat beside the girl.

"Ah..." she said . "The man who sells airplanes..." she purred, gutturally.

"Is that what I do?" whispered Sonny, trying to focus. "Where you from?"

"Germany."

"Thought so. I'm Sonny."

"Mia." She liked this guy. He seemed a bit pissed. She felt in control. Her hand went into her bag for the diazepam.

"Drink?"

She nodded and Sonny ordered two tequilas.

"Live here now ?" asked Sonny. He'd already noticed her hand in her bag and guessed what she was doing. He could play the same game.

"Just visiting," she replied. The moment Sonny was not looking she'd drop three pills in his drink.

Sonny's mind had cleared. He'd been drugged once before. In Hawaii. Been tracking a Russian who put some sleeping dope in his drink and the guy got clean away. Never again.

"Been on the London Eye yet?" asked Sonny.

Mia popped the pills in his glass.

Sonny pretended he hadn't noticed.

"Not yet – they say the views..." Mia said.

"I came to London for love and romance..."

"Really?" said Mia.

As Sonny accidentally on purpose knocked his glass to the floor.

"Shit!"

"Let me get another.." said Mia quickly.

"No... busy day tomorrow... thanks."

He stood and wondered.

"Want to come watch some telly..?"

Mia flinched. Thought long. Then.

"Just for a bit ..."

And both walked hesitantly across to the lift, looking wary of each other.

*

Charlie had struggled with his secret about the P.M.'s bodyguard and decided to confide in Duffy. The singing detective suggested they both pitch up in Whitehall near the entrance to Number 10 Downing Street. Duffy would have his bike so when Chubb came out, they could both follow him.

Duffy was gutted that this little bastard was working for Godfrey Young; quietly amused that he was a secret jihadi who any moment could slit the P.M.'s throat. He'd also put a call into Zaffy's soldier boys who had their own revenge agenda, as he'd kidnapped her in Libya to sell at a slave auction. Seems Chubb alias Al-fucking-Britani had a load of guys queuing up to take him out. On a lethal date.

What Charlie didn't tell Duffy was that he was determined to warn the P.M. about the danger he was in. Hence him turning up at the House of Commons and desperately trying to get a meet with Godfrey. But his schedule was too crowded.

He'd happily do a brief interview for the paper the following week. In despair Charlie wrote a hurried note – "Highly Confidential" on the envelope – "For the P.M.'s Eyes Only" – revealing that his personal bodyguard was connected with ISIS and should be treated with extreme care.

Just minutes before he was due to meet Duffy, Charlie, using a special press card, dashed through security into Number 10 and tried to get to see Godfrey's assistant, Wiz. But she too was in a bloody meeting. Charlie loitered outside the P.M.'s outer office then quietly turned the handle and walked in.

He was a strange little man, balding, scarred, bulky, scowling, and carrying what looked like a Maxim 9, a sci-fi pistol with a built-in silencer. Charlie had done a feature on them when they were first on the market from Utah.

"Out!" said Chubb firmly, waving the gun in Charlie's face.

The reporter turned.

"Wait," cried Chubb.

Charlie froze.

"That for the Prime Minister?" asked the bodyguard, nodding to the urgent envelope in Charlie's hands.

Charlie was lost for words.

Chubb leant his head sideways to read what was on the envelope.

"'For the P.M.'s Eyes Only'. Give it here then. I'll make sure he gets it."

He pulled the envelope from a stunned Charlie, who was then shoved from the office and the door slammed in his face.

Charlie stood in the corridor, muttering: "Fuck, fuck, superfuck!"

Moments later he was in Whitehall, telling Duffy what had happened.

The detective was pissed off Charlie had gone and revealed his hand so soon.

"Let's hope that little shite doesn't read it..."

A smoking Triumph motorbike pulled alongside them, revving with a monstrous roar. Chindi and Sami. Each with a long bag on their back. No secret what was inside.

Forty-five minutes later a limo cruised out of the Number 10 car park. Chubb was driving, and he had two passengers. Simon and Justin Holloway. The terrible twins. Duffy gritted his teeth. This looked like a perfect storm. All three vile bastards in one caboodle.

The limo took them north. Marble Arch. Kensal Green. Wembley.

Nearing the Stadium the car picked up speed and started going down back streets at full speed, braking at junctions turning right, then suddenly left.

"They've seen us!" shouted Duffy to Charlie riding pillion behind him.

The soldier boys gave him the thumbs up.

The hunt was well and truly on.

The Harley and Triumph were keeping two cars behind the limo.

They all stopped at a red light.

Chubb peered in his rear mirror. Locked round for cops. Then put his his foot and sent the limo shooting through the red.

The bikes did the same.

Now the game of cat and mouse was over.

One of the twins leant out of their window and took several shots at Duffy.

The limo was doing nearly seventy through quiet tree-lined suburban avenues, avoided black cats and urban foxes, shooting every red light, and heading for Wembley Stadium. It turned into a darkish back street running alongside the sports arena. A dead end. The lights on the limo went out as it parked beside the stadium fence.

Seconds later the pursuing motorbikes rounded the corner, screeched to a halt beside the limo, and the four avengers pulled open the doors.

The car was empty.

There were dents on the roof. Like they'd stood on it.

"They've climbed over the fence – into the stadium!" shouted Duffy, doing the same.

The four leapt onto the limo roof and over the barbed wire security fence, into the grounds of Wembley Stadium. There were CCTV cams along the perimeter so wouldn't be long before the cops arrived.

Ahead of them they saw movement in the shadows, leading to the stands.

They hared forward, Duffy carrying his Heckler and Koch P30 in his mitt, Chindi and Sami shouldering their Uzi's. Charlie had a brolly just in case.

Shots rang out, one grazing Charlie on his ear.

"Near miss Charlie!" hissed Duffy. "Come on!"

And he ran to where the bullets were coming from.

The stands.

They spilt into two pairs. Soldier boys to the left, Duffy and Charlie to right.

Suddenly a large floodlight high above the stands turned night into day.

They were not alone.

It targeted Chubb and the twins who were scurrying along

Row M in the seats.

Chindi shot a burst from his Uzi and one of the twins was down.

The light followed Chubb further with the remaining twin.

Duffy took aim at the jihadi. Missed.

Then a bang and tinkle from above as the stadium floodlight was hit, glass falling onto the seats below, and went dark.

More movement in the shadows. Looked like Chubb had split from Jason or Simon or whoever.

A second light from above came on and found one twin straight across in the stands from Duffy, with Chubb back on ground level, on the edge of the pitch.

"He's all mine..." shouted Duffy, aimed slow and careful at the remaining twin. It was a long shot. About two hundred yards. No wind. Duffy held his breath... squeezed... and saw the surfer boy haircut crash to the ground.

One to go.

The soldier boys were closing in on Chubb. The guy who'd given them so much pain in Libya. Chindi was coming at him from the left, Sami from the right.

There was only one way for Chubb to run.

Across the pitch.

He ran for his life with two Uzi's aimed at his head, and Duffy pointing his pistol very slow.

A single shot rang out from high above.

Dave Chubb collapsed centre pitch in a twitching heap.

And the single floodlight went out.

Everything again in darkness.

Duffy, Charlie, and the boys rushed to the jihadi.

They met each other in the gloom.

A pool of blood lay on the ground but no body.

Dave Chubb was nowhere to be seen.

Simply vanished.

But who the fuck was on the lights and pulled the bloody trigger..?

*

When Godfrey Young came out of his financial meeting, how to make the rich fuckers bleed through his upcoming Land Tax, he spotted the envelope on his office desk. "For the P.M.'s Eyes Only." He was slightly irritated he'd let Chubby have the night off – right now he could kill a drink or two with a mate – as his new minder had become quite a close friend, as they do.

He ripped open the envelope and read the handwritten note.

It was from Charlie Lomax, that cocky reporter from the "Evening News", who'd interviewed Sean a few months back.

What he read was absurd, but for a second made him want to puke. He quickly opened a drawer, looking for something.

"Wiz!" he yelled at his assistant.

She came running.

"Run out of scotch – any spare in your cupboard?"

Wiz nodded and scuttled off to find his favourite Monkey Shoulder.

Godfrey re-read the note.

It was warning him he could be in danger – that his new bodyguard Dave Chubb was a Muslim convert – Jazza Al Britani – who'd recently fought with ISIS in the Middle East.

Godfrey swallowed hard then shook his head.

"He can't be… This is fake bloody news from the Tory press!"

He quickly dialled Chubb's phone number. It rang and rang and rang.

"Shit." Godfrey stared once more at the note, digesting its contents and wondering, wondering if there could be any truth in this fuckwit story.

Wiz entered with the scotch.

"Thanks Wiz," said Godfrey. "Have one yourself…" And poured two scotches. "You see Chubby this afternoon?"

Wiz nodded. "In your office, waiting for you."

"And my meeting overran," sighed Godfrey. "What we got on tomorrow love?"

Wiz, ever efficient, opened a large diary.

"Morning free – just regular office work… then afternoon, you're opening that new Godfrey Young ward at Eltham Hospital. Three p.m. Being greeted by an elderly patient with terminal cancer. Good publicity sir."

"Oh yes…" he sighed. "Think I might pass on that Wiz. See if Jenny can do it instead. Got a bad feeling about tomorrow, dunno why…"

CHAPTER TWENTY-ONE

The day of reckoning had arrived.

Operation Red Czar.

The crimson sun was rising on a clear crisp London morn, where commuters were already choking the roads and clogging the tubes. It seemed like any other dawn, on any other day, except it wasn't.

Today was going to be historic; a date school kids would learn by heart; a day you'd remember exactly where you were, who you were with, and what you were doing at three in the afternoon.

Frank Gruber shuffled in his purple pyjamas to the window of his Hilton bedroom and looked out over Hyde Park.

Down there under a tree was an old Chinaman doing his daily exercises, waving his arms slowly to the left, slowly to the right, stooping to do five shaky press-ups, then, collapsing in a heap from exhaustion; pairs of identical joggers, superglued to their water bottles, criss-crossed the paths like so many robotic dancers; but, most striking, were the twenty soldiers in gold-braided uniforms and feathered busbies, from the King's Troop, Royal Horse Artillery, taking their gleaming black stallions with their steaming nostrils for an early morning canter.

Frank soaked in the atmosphere. He felt numb. This was the day he was going up in smoke.

He had the briefing meeting with Harry at ten.

Still time to get a cab to Heathrow and disappear. But he knew those faceless CIA fuckers would seek and destroy.

Frank picked up his phone and ordered a full English

breakfast, then wondered how Sonny would cope with today's deadly scenario.

*

In the Hilton bedroom next door, Sonny had just woken. Mia still lay in his arms.

Her eyes were closed but she was not asleep. The night for her had been the most exciting of her life, experiencing a passion she never knew existed. She was no longer a virgin. And she was glad. Glad that she'd met this crazy guy. Glad she was in his arms and become a woman.

Sonny gently stirred and slipped out of bed.

She put her arm out to coax him back.

But he was already half dressed.

"Why'd you try and drug me?"

"You knew?"

"Pretty obvious..."

"It's just me. I'm sorry. I wanted to sleep with men but nothing else. I wanted to feel... wanted..."

"You that lonely?"

"When you in a city on your own... sometimes you just want to get close, without all that other shit..."

"But last night... last night was beautiful..."

"Yes. It was. You are a gentleman Sonny... thank you..."

"I'd like to stay but got a real busy day..."

Mia sat up and wondered if this was a one off. She didn't want it to be.

Sonny had gone into the bathroom and was shaving.

She didn't want to get hurt.

Now he was in the shower.

She quickly threw on her clothes, took a photo of the unmade bed, of Sonny behind the steamy shower glass, and was out the door.

*

Just a few miles from the Hilton Hotel, at the other end of Hyde Park, Zaffy sat with Chindi and Sami, having breakfast at a Notting Hill street café. All three were poring over a map of North Africa. They'd made a group decision. A life-changer. To go home. Back to South Sudan. The boys had spent half the night telling Zaffy about trapping Chubb in the stadium, and how he'd disappeared. But now they felt the place they should be was back with their own brothers and sisters. Where perhaps, just perhaps, they all might try make a difference to the country.

"This time not go through Libya," said Zaffy. "No more slave auctions."

The boys agreed.

"Try Niger, Nigeria, then across..." added Chindi.

"And not get caught..!" laughed Sami.

They all knew they were putting their lives in danger again, returning to a war zone. But it was their blood, their people.

They clunked their coffee mugs together.

"Juba!"

*

Suki was sitting with her doctor in the natal ward, discussing her baby. She was two months pregnant and told she'd have to wait another month before the ultra sound revealed a boy or girl. She was in two minds whether to give up politics – the thought of bumping into Godfrey every day while bringing up a child that had his nose or ears, or worse still, brain, filled her with horror. But then, once a politician...

"Would you like to know the sex of your child?" asked the doctor.

"Rather it was a surprise," said Suki.

"So you'll have two possible names?"

"No," smiled Suki. "I've one that'll suit a boy or girl..."

"And?"

"I've chosen... Duffy."

*

Marky sat at her computer with Duffy peering at Chubb's face on her screen. He'd told her about the previous night's adventures, taking out the deadly twin assassins who'd nearly killed him in Brighton, and how they'd seen someone shoot Chubb with a single shot from high amongst the stadium floodlights. Then all had gone dark and his body had vanished.

"Which is why he could be still out there," said Duffy. "Godfrey Young could be in danger from this little shit."

"But who shot him?" asked Marky.

Duffy shrugged.

"Why not focus on the Prime Minister?" asked Marky.

"Meaning?"

"Let me try hack into his diary – see what he's doing today – then we could stop whatever Chubb's up to... if he's still alive..."

"Worth a try, if you can get in there..."

*

Frank had just sat down in Harry's office for the briefing. The room felt brittle, tense, as each knew they were discussing the end of Frank's life.

"Tell it like it is Harry. I'm ready," smiled Frank faintly.

"Still in pain?"

Frank nodded.

"You written a will?" asked Harry, half whimsical, half serious.

"Fuck off."

Harry went to a wall chart and unfurled the plan of Eltham Hospital.

"O.K. Let me take you through it..."

The chart showed the layout of the hospital grounds and car park.

"Here's the main entrance to the hospital where the staff and patients'll be safely waiting, well inside the outer doors.

"At exactly 3pm the target'll arrive at the hospital gates and stop in the outer car park.

"You've been chosen as the lucky person to meet and greet as they get out of their limo.

"Sonny, dressed as a doctor, will push you in a wheelchair to the target. You'll be carrying a fake breathing cylinder packed with semtex. Once you get close we'll remote activate."

Frank took in all the information then asked Harry: "How long after reaching the target will you activate?"

"To make it less suspicious, to let you say a few welcoming words, we thought ten seconds," said Harry.

"Can Sonny escape the blast?"

"He knows what's going on."

"What?" asked Frank, wondering why Harry had seen Sonny without him.

"I explained everything. He knows the dangers…"

"Why wasn't I there?"

"You were at the dentist or something…"

"Oh," muttered Frank, slightly saddened that Sonny knew his fate, that he'd been compromised. He wished he'd been able to tell him himself, not hear this shit from Harry.

"He might just escape," offered Harry. "There'll be cover… we're putting up a load of smoke bombs… I want it to look really big Frank. Be one helluva crater."

"Smoke bombs… when do they go off?"

"Five seconds before the semtex," said Harry.

"Five seconds before. So he might survive…"

Frank went quiet.

"So?"

"So what?"

"So who's the fucking target?" snarled Frank.

Harry said nothing for a moment, wondering how Frank would respond.

"Godfrey Young. The Prime Minister."

Frank covered his face in his hands.

"The fucking Prime Minister! Shit. You know, I half suspected… all that 'state capture' stuff…But… I thought it'd be an Iranian…"

"You want out Frank?"

"Too fucking late Harry, and you know it. Be quicker than a long lingering death from cancer. But…"

"But?"

"Why? Why him..?"

"He's in bed with Iran. We're worried about nuclear secrets…"

Frank thought deep, nodded, then walked to Harry and gave him a long hug.

"Better make sure I got clean knickers. My Mum always said if you're ever in an accident, don't get caught wearing dirty knickers..." joked Frank, his eyes moistening.

He looked at his watch.

Just a few hours to go before he met his destiny.

"The Prime Minister... holy shit..."

*

Godfrey Young, the British Prime Minister, sat at his desk signing papers. He paused and phoned Chubb his bodyguard again. Still nothing, no answer phone.

Wiz entered with another pile of documents for signature.

"Heard anything from Chubby this morning?" asked Godfrey, still puzzled.

"Not a peep," answered Wiz. "But security have lined up another guy for the day, Jeremy something..."

Godfrey nodded absentmindedly. "All bloody strange. Had a note last night from that reporter kid, Charlie Lomax... saying Chubby had been with ISIS in Iraq... someone's taking the piss surely..."

"That's ridiculous sir – he's such a proper gent – him and his military tie, shiny shoes..." laughed Wiz. "Oh. Nearly forgot. That hospital opening. Jenny can't do it – home with a migraine."

"Damn. What about Paula?"

"Some miners' gala in Rochdale..." replied Wiz.

"Paddy?"

"Gallstone operation."

"Double damn! Remind me Wiz– what and where?"

"3pm. Opening the Godfrey Young Wing at Eltham Hospital."

"Ho hum. I'll do it. Must be fate."

Wiz went to the door. "I'll warn the driver."

"And see if you can get that reporter on the phone – try get to the bottom of this Chubb nonsense.."

*

Charlie Lomax was sitting on the biggest story of his life. That the P.M.'s bodyguard had been an ISIS jihadi… that he'd been shot by a mystery sniper last night in Wembley Stadium… that his body had vanished, so could still be alive… and now Tara had other bloody ideas..!

In a moment of extreme weakness and possible professional suicide, the young reporter had bent to Tara's desires.

Then agreed to what she wanted.

Chelsea Registry Office.

That afternoon at 3pm.

They were getting married.

They wanted to keep it a secret from everyone, though Tara thought Duffy would make the perfect witness. He was bringing along his pink-haired dolly, Marky, but wouldn't hang around as they were hot on the track of the wounded Dave Chubb. They'd hacked the P.M.'s diary and found he was opening a new hospital wing around the same time. So once the vows were over, they'd shoot to Eltham and see if Chubb was on the scene.

It was now lunchtime as Tara dragged Charlie to Peter Jones to sample the best wedding outfits on offer, then to the Chelsea Potter to get pissed rotten before the ceremony.

The tawny-haired beauty had at last found herself. No more need of shrinks and all that ghastly confessing; no more playing the amateur high class hooker with all those kinky Arabs; no more yellow tee-shirts and threatening vulnerable innocents in the name of The Equalisers. Suddenly the thought of her and Hooray Charlie – as she used to call him – settling into a quaint mews cottage and possibly raise a family, began to catch her lurid imagination. It all seemed very out of character, but, deep down, perhaps she'd always been a Sloane ranger at heart. Or perhaps she was just growing up at last.

*

Godfrey had had a simple ham sandwich lunch in his office washed down with a beer, and felt quite tetchy about opening another bloody hospital wing in his name. The country was groaning with them. When he first became P.M he was a cult; every student in the land wore shirts bearing his moniker, they chanted his name at Glastonbury, football matches, copied his choice in cardigans, even bought the same pet dachshund that he had. But now he was beginning to tire of it all. Sometimes he wanted to crawl away and hide. If it hadn't been for the bloody Iranians the country would have gone down the toilet; he wasn't proud going cap in hand but least they had the same international ideas as his party, socking it to the Zionists and bloody Washington.

In the front passenger seat sat today's stand-in bodyguard, Jeremy something, looking combat fit, efficient, not saying a word. Nice haircut.

And a new driver wearing an Equaliser teeshirt - Rosko, his usual, had taken a sudden sickie...

But he still wondered about Chubby. Perhaps the laddie had been in an accident and was lying unconscious in a ward somewhere; perhaps the bloody far Right had beaten him to a pulp and dumped him in the Thames, perhaps not.

He thought about his baby with Suki. Big mistake. But it was his. It would grow to look and speak like him. Her weak husband was going along with it. More fool him. Who knows, one day Godfrey might adopt the kid as his own.

On a whim he called Wiz at the office.

"Wiz – send Suki Carter some flowers – dozen red roses – make the message - 'Not forgotten you both, love Godfrey'".

They were halfway to this bloody hospital in Eltham.

Tonight he was booked to take Simon and Jason to dinner at the Gay Hussar.

To thank them for getting rid of that ridiculous toe rag Duffy. Which reminded him.

Quickly called the twins. No answer. But left a message on their answer phone.

Always good company those two.

As they neared the hospital gates it reminded him of his old Ma in her care home. Must visit her soon. Kept putting her off. But she was going senile and sooner or later wouldn't remember him. Took out little red book and made note to remind him. Least she survived Covid...

The new driver, Freddie, turned briefly to Godfrey.

"Just coming up now sir," he said. "The hospital."

Outside the gates there was a rowdy demonstration, protesting about nurses' pay, which allowed their limo to pass, then blocked the three Range Rovers and outriders from the protection squad following behind.

*

Frank saw the limo approaching and entering the car park. He and Sonny had been sat waiting for fifteen minutes.

Behind them across the hospital main entrance was a huge banner, saying:

"We love you Godfrey".

Inside he could see the waiting crowds of doctors, nurses, and patients, primed to burst into song as the Prime Minister walked through their doors.

Frank was on his cell. One very last call. Ever.

"I need to know Paul. I never opened that envelope... About my scan results."

He paused long, straining to hear the response. "Thank you my friend. Thank you..."

And killed the call.

His face turned ashen.

His past flashed before him.

He smelled those Pacific Ocean rollers, crashing and booming, salt and sand on his tongue, lungs burning, as he gasped upwards for air.

His mother's loving face, up so close, whispered silently. Her perfume...

From the hospital reception they started singing "For He's a Jolly Good Fellow..."

Sonny leant over him in the wheelchair, clutching that canister crammed with semtex.

"This is it Frank," he muttered through gritted teeth.

Frank squeezed Sonny's hand and stared blankly. "What a clusterfuck!"

"Go well," said Sonny simply, waving at the approaching limo.

＊

Godfrey looked impatiently at his watch. Coming up for three o'clock.

As his car drove into the vast hospital car park, there standing all alone was a black doctor in a white coat, pushing an old man in a wheelchair. He had a breathing canister across his knees. Looked pretty gaunt; probably one of their terminal cancer patients.

The Prime Minister took a deep breath and sighed deeply. What he did for this bloody country.

The limo parked and the wheelchair couple, all smiles, slowly walked towards the V.I.P. guest.

Godfrey got out of the car, and walked to the old man in the wheelchair.

Frank smiled up at him. "Welcome to Eltham, Prime Minister..."

In his head Frank was reminding himself that once the smoke bombs went off, there were five seconds before they blew the semtex.

Five fucking seconds.

Godfrey shook Frank's hand.

"Nice to meet you – you a patient here?" asked Godfrey, wondering how long this shit would take.

The old guy just glared through him.

Suddenly there was thick white smoke everywhere. No visibility.

Godfrey shouted: "What's going on?"

As Frank and Sonny together pushed the Prime Minister back inside the limo, threw the canister after him, and jammed the wheelchair against the door.

The driver and bodyguard had vanished.

Just thick billowing blinding smoke everywhere.

Godfrey shouted from inside the car.

The singing from reception slowly died away...

And five seconds later, as promised, the bomb was remotely detonated.

Harry got the pyrotechnics he wanted.

A "spectacular" never seen before in London.

A bigger fireworks display than New Year's Eve.

The boom could be heard all over the capital, even in the Chelsea Registry Office. The flames seen from the Houses of Parliament.

The white smoke took nearly twenty minutes to clear, by which time the fire brigades and police had arrived.

It looked like a flattened battle zone.

A burning carpet of unidentifiable debris spread over a 100-metre radius.

The limo had disappeared. There were no corpses, no wheelchair. Just tiny pieces of red hot glowing metal shards and smouldering stinking rubber scattered across the car park. Most of the hospital windows had been blown out.

The police quickly ringed off the killing zone.

This was not just a crime scene. It was a terror scene. The death, probable assassination, of Britain's Prime Minister, Godfrey Young.

But no bodies, just carnage.

Until.

Until, one of the firemen saw something high up on the hospital roof.

Possibly thrown there from the force of the explosion.

A man's severed head.

*

Duffy stood beyond the police tapes viewing the burning black dust covering the hospital car park, knowing that somewhere there were the remains of Britain's Prime Minister, who he might have saved if it hadn't been for Tara's last minute bloody wedding. A wedding that never happened as they were halfway through the vows when they heard the bomb blast and hightailed it to Eltham. For once he'd let his emotions give in to his gut instincts. He should have followed Marky's advice and gone straight to the hospital.

Beside him stood his favourite hacker, along with the stunned and bewildered Tara and Charlie.

It was way too early to know what had happened and why.

Too early to know who else had died with Godfrey Young.

Too early to know which bastards were behind this latest London atrocity.

Though everyone had their suspicions.

Just then he spotted an old Met copper mate, Brian Fox, who was digging around in the debris. He hailed him over and tried to get more info on the head found on the roof.

Foxy wouldn't say a word at first.

Until Duffy asked if he still kept two mistresses – one in Balham, another in Hoxton – and how was Rene, his lovely wife?

Foxy relented. In a sotto voce need-to-know basis.

Head on the roof belonged to a geezer who worked for the P.M.

His old bodyguard, Dave Chubb.

CHAPTER TWENTY-TWO

Harry put down the phone as Sonny and Moggie entered his office.

"Tel Aviv – seems you've made Mossad very happy, boys."

"Blast big enough for you boss?" smiled Sonny, his face still bandaged and bruised from the blast's flying debris.

"I said a spectacular – that was massive!"

"Your wish," nodded Sonny.

"All went to plan," said Moggie.

Harry poured scotch for them all.

"Our boys got out OK – driver and bodyguard?"

Sonny nodded.

"And Frank?"

"No sign…" whispered Sonny.

They raised their glasses.

"To a fine old soldier. Frank Gruber. God rest his soul…" saluted Harry. Least now he was in peace, no more pain.

He was quietly very pleased.

This had all been part of a complex plan and appeared to have worked.

The moment the CIA realized that Godfrey Young and his Marxist crew were becoming victims of "state capture" by Iran, they knew they had to intervene.

Through Harry in London they started surveillance of both Godfrey and Chancellor Sean O'Leary, having endless covert meetings with the international broker Saladine, and the Iranian "consultant", Hussein Sulimann. It was only when each appeared to be accepting secret financial payments from Teheran, that the operation got more serious. Especially when the government stopped talking to Israel, agreed to sell Iran military weapons, and turned a blind eye when they murdered their way into that uranium company in Bracknell. The nuclear threat a reality...

Then Sean O'Leary was hacked to death in his hospital bed, probably by Iran, as he knew too much, leaving Godfrey as their sole asset.

Dave Chubb's arrival on the scene made it much easier for Harry, especially when he started as Godfrey's bodyguard. In normal times MI5 would have shut him down but in this case, he was a very useful idiot...

That night in Wembley it had been Moggie up by the floodlights who'd shot him dead, removed the body, and placed it in the boot of the P.M.'s limo, before visiting Eltham hospital.

And all along the killer blow would come from dear Frank, on borrowed time, who went in as a walking suicide bomber. God rest.

Harry looked at his watch and got rid of his boys.

Charlie knocked on the door ten minutes later.

Next the media spin.

*

Duffy sat with Marky drinking weak tea in a café not far from the hospital.

Both of them were tongue-tied. How the fuck was Chubb involved in the bombing? It all began to point to ISIS, that they instructed their sleeper to take Godfrey Young out on their instructions. But why? As P.M. he was bending over backwards for Iran who were fair weather friends of ISIS, so it didn't add up.

Unless. This was what they were meant to bloody think. That instead this was all a CIA plot to stop Iran covertly running the U.K. government. That they perhaps had planted a dead Chubb in the P.M.'s limo, knowing it, or part of it, would be found after the assassination.

It was all beginning to sound like some wacky conspiracy theory, but guess he had to keep everything open until they got more facts. He'd talk to Harry about his theory on what was happening; least he had contacts in the security world and might have heard some rumours.

He worried about Suki Carter too. Her whole world would change now.

There was a black hole vacuum just opened up in government and if she played her cards right, she could just help fill it.

He'd had a call from Zaffy to say her and the boys were soon heading home, back to their own war zone, and arranged to have a last supper with them. Seemed in the end you couldn't escape your roots. But she'd be missed.

Then there was Tara's wedding to Charlie. All seemed very last minute, and bloody chaotic now they'd have to go through it all again. He hadn't forgotten her sitting on that bloody anthill. Precious.

Marky interrupted his thoughts.

The sun was going down. Time to wash away their gloom in a pool of Merlot...

Duffy had noted Marky's mum was far away in Bora Bora.

It was going to be a long night.

*

Charlie obviously knew that Harry had serious army experience, probably special forces, and was now running his own security firm. He seemed to have close contact with the intelligence services, whoever they were these days.

"Was this ISIS?" asked Charlie, accepting a scotch from Harry.

"Hard to tell yet Charlie," confided Harry. "We're getting reports they found Dave Chubb's head at the scene..."

"He worked for them – I tried to warn Godfrey Young..."

"Indeed he did my boy. Which makes it look like a black and white ISIS operation..." added Harry.

"You're not convinced..?" asked Charlie.

Harry looks at him rather theatrically, under his bushy eyebrows.

"My intelligence suggests – and don't quote me directly – my intelligence suggests, the main player behind your terror attack... was Iran", said Harry quietly.

"Iran?"

Harry took another swig before he spoke.

"We all know Godfrey's been arse-licking them to get their money... but, dig deeper and you'll find bribery, arms deals, nuclear smuggling, and... murder."

Charlie holds his breath. "Jeez."

"Very simply. He was about to be named and shamed by Mossad, our Israeli friends."

"Bloody hell."

"So," continued Harry. "Iran took him out. They didn't want to be dragged down with him, the world finding they were breaking their nuclear sanctions, involved in the 'state capture' of the United Kingdom... "

"Fuck me," sighed Charlie.

"Indeed. But, there's more."

Charlie nodded.

"My wife's Dad – Frank – you met – had been chosen as a terminal cancer sufferer to meet and greet the P.M. as he arrived..."

"Oh no..." sighed Charlie.

"He's gone."

"Does Tara know?" asked Charlie with a hoarse voice.

"Not yet."

"How did they do this?"

"Probably a bomb under the limo... remote detonated..."

"Bastards..!" seethed Charlie.

"Probably pretty hefty – that car's got steel plates underneath..."

"Wow..."

"So there's your scoop."

Charlie leapt to his feet. He had several hours before tonight's print was put to bed.

"Can I call you, if I need more info?" he asked.

Harry opened the door for him.

"Of course," he replied. "But just quote me as... 'an intelligence source'"...

Charlie nodded and scuttled out into the street. His head was buzzing – nearly married to Tara, and a bomb killed Frank and the P.M.

Now he had to write the story of his life.

*

Suki stared long at the dozen red roses sent to her by Godfrey. He must have ordered them from his limo, on the way to open the hospital wing. On the way to his death. It was a strange hollow feeling. She loved him, hated him, and bore his child inside her. Now he was no more. She remembered that night in Cannes. That was romantic. Then wondered if he'd ordered her death through the Equalisers. That was far from romantic.

Already the news reports were predicting an early election, that there was no obvious replacement for Godfrey within his party. There were too many firebrands, too many inexperienced hot-headed activists. Suddenly the vibrant Marxist state looked vulnerable. That the Equalisers may disappear as rapidly as they'd arrived.

Certainly with the finances in such a desperate mess, it was conceivable that the Tories might win the next election. But even they had few charismatic personalities to lead the fight, following reshuffle after reshuffle, the talent had always been sidelined so the bland middle managers could rule the roost.

Suki stood, took a long deep smell of the roses, then threw them in her bin.

Times they were a-changing.

Plus ca change, plus c'est la meme chose.

*

On reading "The Evening Standard" Hussein Sulimann nearly choked on his fizz.

They were blaming the hospital bombing on Iran. Possibly in league with ISIS. They were revealing all their secret dealings with Godfrey Young, his payments, the covert military arms deal, even breaking nuclear sanctions by importing enriched uranium.

They were saying Teheran assassinated the Prime Minister with the help of his bodyguard, who'd worked for both ISIS and Iran. That they did this because they didn't want their secret deal with Godfrey being exposed. But it was too late. Now the world knew.

Hussein grabbed his phone and dialed furiously.

"Hassan? I want revenge!"

"Who did this bomb – it wasn't us!" cried Hassan.

"Mossad or the CIA."

"The CIA," murmured Hassan firmly.

"I agree," said Hussein. "We'll hit the Yankees where it hurts." He paused, then: "I want to activate Surena!"

"Everything's in place sir." replied Hassan calmly. "We can go within the hour."

"Your men are ready?"

"Ten operatives. In a south London park."

"Let's wait a few days – surprise them – I must attend the Prime Minister's funeral. To show we didn't do it."

"Won't they arrest you?"

Hussein laughed. "Diplomatic immunity. I can do anything in this fucking dump!"

"Exactly when then sir?" asked Hassan.

"End of the week. Friday morning – 10 a.m. – when they're in their offices. I want to see the smile on the face of the Great fucking Satan..!"

CHAPTER TWENTY-THREE

Chindi and Sami had finished their shift at the restaurant and were biking along Bayswater Road on a damp drizzly night when it happened.

A dark-haired young guy suddenly leapt over the railings bordering Hyde Park and ran across the wet glistening road in front of their Triumph motorbike.

Chindi braked, too late, and skidded into him.

"Help me, I been shot..." he cried and passed out in Sami's arms.

A hundred yards further down the road they clocked two other men climb over the Hyde Park fence, look up and down the street, then start running towards them, fast.

"He's bleeding..." said Chindi.

"Trouble!" whispered Sami.

The boys saw the approaching men were waving guns, made an instant decision, and roared off down the road with the wounded boy sandwiched between them on the pillion.

*

Zaffy was heading to bed at her nurses' dorm when the soldier boys crashed in with the wounded stranger.

She took one look at the bullet wound in his arm and ran off for antiseptic and bandages. It was not serious. The bullet had gone straight through, missing the main artery, though still a lot of blood.

They sat the boy in a chair and plied him with hot tea.

He was in his early twenties, jeans and tee-shirt, called Bakka.

"Who did this ?" asked Zaffy, washing his wound, then tying a bandage.

He shook his head, saying nothing.

"We're trying to help you Bakka…" said Chindi.

"They will kill me."

"Who?" asked Sami.

Bakka looked at the three, and shook his head again.

Zaffy took out her phone and called Duffy.

"We got this boy – he's been shot – but he won't tell us what's going on – you should see him – please…" she said, knowing that of all the people she knew, he would find the truth.

*

Duffy pulled up a chair and faced Bakka. The kid looked Arab, though could have been from any of those North African countries, even Israel.

"You got friends who want to hurt you. Why ?" he asked.

Bakka looked at Duffy. He was confused. These people were his enemies. But in here he felt safe. Out there they'd cut his head off..

Duffy persevered. "We'll find you somewhere to stay – where they can't find you."

There was little choice.

Bakka looked him in the eye. "I'm from Iran. We are here secret. On a mission…"

"Fuck…" mumbled Duffy to himself.

"I am technical… computers…" said Bakka.

"Go on," said Duffy.

"But. I don't want to kill…"

Duffy nodded, fearing where this was going.

"I tell them I want to go home. They chased me with guns, tried to shoot me…"

"Where are they, your people?" asked Duffy.

"Lorry. We live in big lorry. Somewhere Richmond…" said Bakka.

"And what's in this lorry?" asked Duffy.

Bakka said nothing, looking terrified.

"Answer him Bakka!" cried Sami.

"We just saved your fuckin' life man!" added Chindi.

Bakka cleared his throat. "Drones."

Duffy sat up as if he'd been whiplashed. He stood and turned back to the boy, looking deadly serious: "What's the target?" he snapped.

Bakka shook his head.

"When?"

Bakka shook his head once more and began to sob.

"All I know, is called Surena…"

Just then the boy's eyes widened as he looked out the window into the car park.

Two men had got out of a car and were heading for the entrance.

"It's them!" shrieked Bakka.

The soldier boys recognized them as the shooters from earlier.

"You got a phone on you?" sighed Duffy impatiently.

Bakka took out his cell.

Duffy snatched it and briskly threw it in a bin, pulling the boy to an inner door.

"Come on – let's get out the back…!"

All four scarpered, leaving Zaffy to welcome the intruders.

"Sorry, private property – no strangers!" she shouted, slamming the door in their faces.

The thugs sped round the rear of the building, only to see two motorbikes racing off into the night.

*

Harry was woken by Duffy's phone call. He was not sure about this cheesy so-called singing detective who'd brought the Sudanese nutter into his home, who he'd last seen escorting Saladine at the opera, but he had some earth-shattering info.

The name "Surena" rang bells, big bells. It was what Hussein Sulimann and his Hassan buddy had been plotting in the Turkish baths. Involving ten items. Now identified. As drones.

An attack by ten drones somewhere in London could kill

thousands.

Depended on what they were carrying. Grenades, bombs, even poison gas.

And the target. Could be the Houses of Parliament, Downing Street, Buck House, Oxford High Street. Or, with ten separate aerial weapons, all of the above and more.

The most urgent task was to find that lorry. Pronto.

He called Moggie and brought him up to speed.

There was a large lorry parked in the Richmond area, possibly the park, with ten Iranian operatives and their UAV's. No idea on the target, or when the mission would take place. Imperative to find and destroy that fucking lorry. Soonest.

Or before.

"I'm on it sir," snapped Moggie, as he headed off into the south London dawn.

Just when Harry had thought the fat lady had sung, she hadn't...

*

The funeral of Britain's Marxist Prime Minister, Godfrey Young, was steeped in ideology.

It took place at Highgate cemetery, resting place of the legendary Karl, and was attended by the great and good and bad of left-wing politics. Most of his New Dawn party turned out in their red ties and scarves; several top Tories, including Suki Carter; endless luvvies from the entertainment and movie business; almost every BBC television presenter; William and Kate attended for the Crown; along with Hussein Sulimann, Harry, and Duffy. There were countless weeping young faces in black armbands and Equaliser tee-shirts helping marshal the event, with the Rochdale miners' brass band following the funeral procession.

As no body had been recovered from the bomb blast the wooden coffin was empty, but sat atop was Godfrey's familiar Che Guevara beret with its red star.

The speeches were short and tearful. Everyone had kind words for their Dear Leader but no one seemed to really know Godfrey the person. In many ways he was merely the avuncular uncle figure they needed to get in the wavering voters at each election, while in reality the party was run by hardliners in the shadows.

The speeches were nearly over when there was a loud communal gasping of breath.

The party hate figure and Equaliser target, Suki Carter, had taken the mike, much to the shock of all present, especially her own party leader.

"Godfrey Young – as I know well – and know that you know – was a loving caring human being. He genuinely tried to make the world a better place. He genuinely tried to make people more equal, more happy. I'll be seeing his eyes, his ears, his mouth, till I die, as I'm having his baby. So it's not goodbye Godfrey, more 'a bientot'…"

The crowd stood stunned a moment, then slowly applauded Suki.

This was either the most clever ploy of her career, or simply a heart-moving farewell to an old lover.

Whatever, the speech was seen nationwide and would make millions across the land view Suki in a new light, millions who'd be voting at the next election.

*

Having buried the coffin, a flurry of red doves was released into the air, the crowd ritually sang The Red Flag, then dispersed quietly to the car park. Already, before they unlocked their vehicles, many of the New Dawn party were plotting who should take his place.

Duffy was walking shoulder to shoulder with Harry, both watching Hussein Sulimann chatting ahead of them with the international broker, Saladine. She was beyond doubt the most glamorous creature at the ceremony, swathed in a glistening black silk dress and turban. Duffy craved to catch her up but had more pressing matters.

"I've got snipers on the roofs of our most vulnerable targets in central London," confided Harry. "If something blows before we find 'em, least we can shoot 'em out of the sky…"

"You think he's involved?" whispered Duffy, nodding at Hussein.

"I know it. But can't touch him – diplomatic immunity. So we've put a tracker on his car," smiled Harry. "Hoping he'll lead us to his killers..!"

Harry's phone rang. He answered, listened, then turned to Duffy.

"Moggie. Found the lorry near Richmond Park," said Harry.

Duffy's eyes lit up.

"Empty – looks like a bloody decoy!"

"Shit," said Duffy, taking out his own cell. "I'll get Marky on the case – if anyone can find these rats, it's her..."

*

Around lunchtime that day another memorial service took place. This time at that classic American diner off the Strand, Joe Allen's. Over prosecco bellini and oak smoked baby back ribs, a small intimate gathering celebrated the life and death of a very special person. Frank Gruber.

Tara was about to give a small speech when Duffy and her father Harry, entered, from attending the P.M.'s funeral. Round the table were Viv, Frank's daughter, Charlie, and a still slightly bruised and bandaged Sonny.

"Mumsy and I thought this was the best place to say goodbye to Granpops – Frank. It's American, it's entertainment, it's the food and drink he loved in L.A. We knew he was dying from cancer; we knew he had only a few days left; just bloody bad luck he was chosen to meet the Prime Minister at that damn hospital... I hope he felt no pain, I hope it was quick."

She held up a small plastic bottle. Opened it and dropped something into her hand.

"After that bomb, there was no trace of Frank. Nothing to bury in his memory. Except. This."

And Tara held up a molar tooth in her hand.

"They found this tooth in the car park. Frank's tooth. All that was left of him."

Harry smiled and wondered. Could that old rogue. But no. He was dying.

"He said," continued Tara. "He wanted his ashes thrown

into the Pacific from Santa Monica pier. So. Charlie and I'll soon be going to L.A. to throw, not his ashes, but this tooth, into the Pacific for dear dear Frank..."

She sat midst applause from the rest of the table and ordered more bubbly.

"You're very quiet Daddy," said Tara.

"It's a cliche, but I'm missing him already..."

"His last words were 'what a clusterfuck'..." smiled Sonny.

"Says it all man," murmured Duffy... "says it all..."

"To darling daddy..." said Viv, biting back the tears.

And all raised their glasses to salute the feisty old trooper...

*

Over the next few days Harry and Moggie spent every hour scouring south London – the leafy suburbs, lorry parks, railway stations - for the missing truck with its deadly cargo of armed drones and operators. They suspected they were moving around the country until they were ready for the attack on London. The GPS tracker on Hussein's car led them nowhere – he was spending most of his time eating at The Savoy - while Hassan, his flunkey, had gone to ground.

Marky meanwhile was trying to find something on the dark web that might lead her to the lorry's whereabouts. There was plenty of internet chatter pinging from Teheran to London, but most was regular business.

At Duffy's request she was also babysitting the recovering Bakka who was confined to her apartment, well out of sight, in case his carers were still roaming the streets looking for him. It seemed he was the resident computer geek with the operatives, the very last person they wanted to lose before an attack. Still living in fear, all he'd reveal was these were state-of-the-art monster drones, about six feet across, with six propellers, ensuring they'd keep flying if one prop died in action.

One thing was certain, when the order was given, it'd be well nigh impossible to stop ten robotic drones dropping their deadly cargo over London town.

*

That Friday morning the sun rose at 7.34 precisely. The sky was clear blue and there was an ominous chill in the air.

By 9 a.m. the U.S. Embassy was buzzing.

There were queues of British holidaymakers and homegrown Americans for visa and passport renewals; dozens of secretaries and researchers working at computer terminals in their high-ceiling open-plan offices; junior diplomats and attaches writing and reading confidential documents behind oak doors; the ambassador himself preparing a welcome speech for the new President of Zimbabwe; and uniformed marines, ever alert to defend the complex, sipping cokes with burgers in their hidden quarters deep in its bowels.

This shiny new billion dollar fortress opened in 2018, resembled a glass cube-shaped castle keep with a moat, on the southern bank of the Thames, not far from the old Battersea Power Station.

A place built for shut down safe security.

If there were ever violent riots outside, the doors would swing locked tight and no-one could enter.

It was impregnable.

A medieval stronghold designed for the twenty-first century.

But what they never imagined was a surprise attack from the sky.

*

At 9.30 a.m. the 60-foot HGV sat quietly parked under a tree in Marble Hill Park, sixty-six acres in Twickenham, just across the Thames from the Richmond Golf Club.

It had arrived an hour earlier, and been moving around the southern towns of England from Reading to Portsmouth, so as not to attract attention. Inside the lorry ten Iranian drone operators sat at their computers, facing wall screens, waiting for the command to send their lethal weapons flying up the Thames towards London.

Hassan paced back and forth behind the drone pilots, calmly checking his watch.

Outside on the grass sat the ten six-foot UAV's, hidden under ground sheets, ready to fly within minutes.

Five of them carried bombs that would explode on impact with their target.

Five of them carried deadly sarin gas that could kill thousands when released in the London air.

Their course was simple.

To fly all the way up the Thames, then veer to the right as they approached Nine Elms to attack their target.

Hassan made a call. "Fifteen minutes," he said simply.

*

Marky was peering intently at her computer screen. Watching red blips on a map of London. There was a curious cluster, a sudden spike of cyber activity coming from one static location.

"Got something Duffy! Load of stuff happening – from a park in Twickenham. From like nowhere. Could be the lorry!" she cried.

Duffy called Harry immediately. He'd gone mobile and was cruising the streets near the Houses of Parliament, an obvious target, waiting for news.

"Marky's found something. Marble Hill Park. Twickenham. A spike of data from this one location!"

"Duffy – as planned – you and the boys get to Albert Bridge – if they're coming up the Thames you can pick them off! I'll try join you..." cried Harry.

"Hurry – no time!"

Harry texted Moggie the lorry address, whipped his car around, and drove full pelt towards Twickenham.

His gut told him this was it.

But suddenly the enormity sank in.

Ten killer drones above London.

Just him and a few amateurs to bring them down.

No way.

Get real.

Fast.

Under New Dawn the military had been emasculated, the

SAS disbanded, and most of the rapid response teams put in moth balls. Now the country was without a Prime Minister the city was wide open to foreign attack.

Normally any aerial threat would be picked up by the RAP boys – Recognised Air Picture – from RAF Air Command in High Wycombe, but ten hostile drones flying low level over London could do their dirty work without being spotted.

Harry decided to call in the big guns.

Tried to get through to R.A.F. Coningsby in Lincolnshire, 150 miles away, the nearest Quick Reaction Alert station to London. Their Typhoon fighter jets would break the sound barrier and be down in five minutes blasting away with their air-to-air missiles and Mauser cannons.

But no go.

The suits there wanted proof and double proof before committing.

They wanted to know the targets, which he couldn't give.

And the Typhoons were just coming in for refueling after a training flight over Scotland.

It looked like Harry and his lads were going to do it on their own.

*

It was 9.55 a.m. Hassan pulled the last tarpaulin off the drones and ran inside the lorry.

His men were ready at their computers. He ordered the drone engines to be started, to be warmed up before take off at ten.

Each was armed and ready to go into action.

The operators were locking into their computers the final instructions for their flight plan and attack. The actual distance up the Thames from Twickenham to the target in Nine Elms was roughly twelve miles, so flying at 30 m.p.h., they'd make impact in just over twenty minutes.

Hassan looked at his watch, held his arm high in the air.

Ten o'clock.

And signaled a "go".

The operators jabbed at their computers, activating the

drones' takeoff.

Outside, the ten six-foot drones with their six whirring propellers, looking like giant flying spiders, rose slowly as one from the ground, moving in tight military formation, one line of five in front, another twenty yards behind, turned towards the Thames, rose to a height of one hundred metres, and began their journey of death.

Hassan called Hussein.

"Lift off. Surena has begun."

*

Duffy on his Harley, followed by the soldier boys on their Triumph, was racing across London to Albert Bridge. If anything was coming towards the city, this would be the obvious route for a drone attack. Straight up the middle of the Thames river. Few people would see them, or if they did, they'd think it was some kind of advertising stunt.

He called Marky as he rode.

"Anything?"

"You won't believe this, but just spotted them from the Kew Bridge webcam – ten seconds ago - five in front, five behind – bloody Battle of Britain all over again!"

"Heading where?" cried Duffy.

"Towards the city, towards you!"

"Holy shit!" whispered Duffy, nearly skidding off his bike, as he neared Albert Bridge with Chindi and Sami close behind.

*

Moggie drove carefully into Marble Hill Park. The lorry was parked ahead, hidden under some trees, a load of tarpaulins on the ground.

He parked, took out his M60 machine gun and approached the HGV.

The back door was padlocked. He shot the bolt and looked inside. No-one there. Just the computers.

He called Harry.

"Too late sir. They've all gone."

The operators had put their drones on automatic so they were all flying on a one-stop suicide mission.

"Shit... " sighed Harry. "Now it's up to Duffy."

*

Duffy got the message from Harry, and called Marky. She had a wild idea. Although the drones were on automatic there was a very slim chance she could hack into their flight plan and abort them. If she had time.

"They just passed Putney Bridge... should be with you in minutes," she told Duffy.

Then got back on her computer to try hack into them, fighting the clock.

*

The ten drones were racing up the Thames, looking like something out of "Apocalypse Now."

Dog-walkers along the river bank were stopping and staring, joggers looking up in amazement, drivers nearly crashing as they took in this majestic but slightly sinister sight. Must be shooting a movie.

Harry, who'd been thinking all along of central London locations, realized that in a few minutes the drones'd be near a massive target.

So bloody obvious.

Smacked him between the eyes.

Hard.

Iran getting even with the Great Satan.

Kicking the Yankees where it really hurt.

Their impenetrable super galactic panic room.

The U.S. Embassy.

Could take out hundreds in one hit.

He quickly called their security boys and told them to activate their Marine protection squad, warning they'd just minutes before a possible aerial attack.

Again he hit a brick wall. First they thought it was a hoax call, then even after vetting his security code they wanted to know how certain he was that they were the target...

Harry was beyond frustrated, hundreds could die in the coming minutes, and right now he was stuck in traffic a mile from the Embassy.

*

Duffy and the boys were on Albert Bridge as the drones came into view.

Ten of the bastards.

With only his pistol and the boys with their Uzi's, he felt powerless.

No way could they stop them.

As they all took aim at the approaching lethal flotilla, one of them suddenly dropped silently from the sky, and splashed into the river.

Duffy and the boys were baffled.

Marky came through on Duffy's headpiece. "Yeeha - I got one!" She'd hacked into its flight plan, shut it down, and was now working on another.

The nine were now a hundred yards from Albert Bridge, travelling around thirty miles an hour.

Chindi and Sami fired wildly across the front five and two went down. One of them limping on just three propellers like a wounded albatross, spinning and spinning out of control, before exploding in a massive blinding fireball on the river bank.

Duffy took aim. Missed. Tried once more. Breathing slow. Real slow. Bingo.

Marky came through again. She was into another one. Killed it dead. Which Duffy saw plummet into the water.

And then there were five.

The boys were in their element. Back in the warzone. Yelling at the drones.

"Come and get us..!" Another two shot to smithereens in mid-air like a kaleidoscopic firework display...

In the distance they could hear sirens.

Three left.

The drones had passed over Albert Bridge.

Last chance to take them out before they reached the Embassy.

And the certain death of many hundreds inside.

Suddenly a police car screeched to a halt, sirens blaring, blue lights flashing, cops leapt out, flung Duffy and boys to the ground, grabbed their weapons, and slapped them in handcuffs.

At that same moment Marky seized control of another drone.

She had a strategy. A crazy plan. Knowing there were three about to hit the Embassy, she quickly weaponised her captive asset and turned it on one of the others, sending them both crashing into each other like robot wars in the sky...

A blinding flash, a deafening boom, a dense black cloud, then silence.

Leaving one sole surviving drone, just seconds from impact.

*

Outside the Embassy Harry stood waiting.

He saw it coming off the Thames.

Deadly, determined, relentlessly homing in on its target.

Those gigantic buzzing propellers carrying a cargo of death.

Getting closer.

Harry lifted his AK47, breathed in carefully and...

Whoosh!

Suddenly from over his shoulder, a flash and whirr as a young Marine fired his RPG at the incoming.

Too fast, too low.

Missed.

Only metres from the Embassy's walls, Harry eased his Kalashnikov trigger.

Nothing.

Jammed.

Turned and grabbed a pistol from another Marine behind him.

Sig Sauer M18.

And pumped all twenty-one rounds into the air.

The lone drone exploded with an ear-splitting blast and

blinding flash, a cough and spit from the U.S. Embassy.

One of its six propellers scythed past Harry's head, nearly parting his hair, thudding into the ground, like a jagged metal boomerang.

The Marines, who'd all come late to the party, cheered...

As two gigantic Typhoon fighter jets thundered out of the sun, skimming low over the Thames, flew a wide circle, saw the battle was won, did a salutary spin, then roared back up into the clouds.

Harry's heart skipped a beat.

"Surena" had been a near miss, a bloody near miss.

CHAPTER TWENTY-FOUR

Harry sat in his office with Duffy, Marky, Chindi, Sami, and Bakka, the reluctant Iranian whistleblower.

"Bakka – if it hadn't been for you, hundreds of people would've died in that Embassy," said Harry, firmly shaking the boy's hand.

"Thank you, is good to be alive…" smiled Bakka.

"As for you lot – Duffy, boys – the cops nearly screwed it, but you did well… and you Marky, our super hacker… smashing job."

"Close thing Harry, close thing," murmured Duffy.

"But we got there." Harry paused a moment. "Listen, with all these government changes, looks like they're bringing back MI5 with me in charge. If that's the case I'll see you all get rewarded…"

"Money?" asked Chindi eagerly.

"We'll see… perhaps a medal," corrected Harry. "Now. Loose ends. Need to clear up a few untidy things like our Hussein Sulimann who's behind this whole bloody mess."

He called Moggie into the office.

"Moggie's going to take our Bakka to the airport – we've a ticket for you to stay with your sister in Turkey…"

Bakka took his holdall and followed Moggie to the door.

"Thank you thank you," he bowed to all and exited.

*

Moggie led the Iranian to an underground car park, unlocked his boot, and motioned Bakka to throw in his bag.

His instructions were to shoot the boy from behind and dump the body.

He hesitated.

This little critter had delivered the goods, help solve the drones riddle, and foil the attack. Sure he was working with the enemy but he was only a kid. But then so were those jihadis who laid mines in Iraq and Syria and killed our boys. And this little sod was their computer mastermind who turned coward under pressure.

He shot Bakka through his heart and lay the body in the boot.

"Sorry mate. Loose ends," and drove off to dispose of the corpse.

*

Harry had tracked Hussein from the Savoy to the Turkish baths, and was sitting outside in his car, waiting for him to come out. Instead he was surprised to see Hassan walk past his car and enter.

Now he had the two key players together in one place, responsible for the drone attack on the embassy. Harry decided to give them ten minutes then join them.

But, within five, Hassan had emerged and driven off in a hurry.

Harry wondered what had gone in there and quickly went in, undressed, grabbed a towel, and walked into the steam room.

Hussein was evidently enjoying himself, totally relaxed in a corner, eyes closed, soaking in the heat.

Harry went and sat next to him.

Then saw the bullet hole.

Straight through his temple and the sphenoid bone.

Seemed the Ayatollahs were also keen to tidy up loose ends...

*

Some would have called it the wedding of the decade. Others would have seen it as a bloody good piss-up.

Tara and Charlie had at last completed their vows at the Chelsea Registry Office and the party was at the Chelsea Barn where Duffy had got done over in the bog by the jihadi Dave Chubb. Seemed light years ago.

Right now the singing detective was on a bar-stool crooning Whitney's "I Will Always Love You"... smiling across at the bride, who was slow dancing with her new hubbie Charlie.

Beside them Harry was robotically moving with Viv in his arms. He was another world away, probably planning on how to turn the country back into a Tory nation now that Godfrey was gone, especially as he was back amongst the power brokers.

The D.J. took over from Duffy who led Marky to the dance floor and barely moved as they tightly held each other cheek to cheek.

Tara then grabbed the mike and asked for a moment's silence for Frank, reminding all that she and Charlie would be carrying his tooth with them on honeymoon to California, where they'd throw it off Santa Monica Pier into the Pacific, as her Grandpops had requested.

It was an "aah" mellow moment in the room.

Marky whispered in Duffy's ear.

"Everything that goes around, comes around..."

"Meaning?" he asked.

"Karma. Perhaps it's our time ..?"

Duffy realized she meant marriage, but right now decided to get them both another tequila...

*

Godfrey Young's death had turned British politics on its head. The New Dawn Party fought like skunks in a sack trying to choose a suitable leader and eventually decided on a young female Muslim activist from Luton, who'd been a social worker.

Nigel Warrington, the Tory leader, decided to retire due to illness, leaving Suki Carter very much the front runner in any election. Indeed, if the polls were anything to go by, it was almost a certain bet that she was to be the next British Prime Minister.

Irony of ironies that she was carrying the last one's baby. But then this was already proving an election winner and seemed Suki was scooping up a new following from both parties; vote for Suki and you get a New Dawn kid thrown into the bargain.

She'd also observed with interest that, following New

Zealand's Labour Prime Minister, she in the U.K. would be the only other Western leader to have a child while in power.

It was with this near certainty of winning the election that today she'd welcomed international broker, Saladine, to her office, who brought along the Saudi Foreign Minister, Prince Saad Abdullah. Harry Wickham, the new head of MI5, was also present, in an advisory capacity.

"Prince Saad is willing to make immense investments in Great Britain," explained Saladine, looking like an eastern princess herself in her gold-braid outfit and chandelier gold earrings. "He understands, that under New Dawn, the nation has become financially indebted; he understands, that should you become the next Prime Minister, your party will double your trade with Saudi Arabia, your arms shipments, and nuclear research..."

Harry leant across and whispered to Suki.

"We're not sure about the nuclear research..." she said.

The prince nodded. "Not at first – I understand. But in return for our money we'd also like to donate the building of fifty new mosques across your great country..."

Suki looked at Harry.

"Ten," smiled Harry.

Suki nodded in agreement.

"And of course in these deals there are always personal rewards..." added Saladine, grinning from glittering ear to ear.

Harry grinned back. "Not our sort of thing..."

"And I'm not Prime Minister yet," cooed Suki.

Harry chuckled. "Oh I think I can guarantee you will be, ma'am..."

*

Imagine buying a home on a ship that cruises the world's hotspots forever. Where the residents decide the global itinerary each year, where "another day in paradise" is a wish come true.

Such was the fantasy dream of The World, launched in 2002, which, combining private yacht with a luxury vacation home, was the largest residential ship ever, constantly circumnavigating the planet, with its very rich, very pampered passengers.

This week this floating heaven on earth had sailed from Sydney, Australia, down to Auckland, New Zealand, offering one of the most attractive harbours in the southern hemisphere.

Some of the more adventurous residents had helicoptered across to Waiheke Island, to sample the native delights and vineyard eateries.

Lounging on the deck of the Verandah Café at the Stonyridge Vineyard, you could see dolphins cavorting with each other in the crystal clear Pacific waters below.

"Best oysters I've ever tasted," laughed Sonny, washing them down with a Cabernet Franc, made from the local grapes. He leant across and threw one down the throat of his companion.

Mia gulped, then laughed. "You nearly choked me darling!" she said, mockingly slapping him across the face. The German had gone back to her natural blonde look and reneged on changing her appearance every other day. There was no need to, as she'd found true love and friendship with Sonny.

He too was totally relaxed, having taken the promised CIA bonus of a million dollars, left him by the deceased Frank.

Cruising the world had brought him peace, and he and Mia were planning to wed when they visited their next destination, the Antarctic, hopefully on an ice flow with penguins as their witnesses.

But they were not alone.

Sonny had chosen to share a two-bedroom residence with an old buddy from the past. He was single but always seemed to find female company wherever they docked.

Today she was a beautiful Samoan girl, around thirty, Kiri, with a stunning melodic singing voice, who'd been serenading them on the beach with her guitar and Polynesian love songs.

"Give us another tune doll," urged the old guy, downing his Merlot.

And she started to sing a gentle lilting lullaby, that had others around them burst into applause.

Frank Gruber leapt up like a sprightly young lad and kissed her on the lips.

It was the first time he'd felt really happy in years.

And no-one could touch him.

*

Duffy and Marky were farewelling Zaffy and the soldier boys at Heathrow, flying back to their South Sudan warzone. Harry had paid for their tickets, given Chindi and Sami a cash reward for defending the realm, and was relieved Zaffy had found the real killers of her family.

The singing detective held Zaffy close and long. She was special. Impulsive, inspiring, and bloody gorgeous. Perhaps another time. Another life. Kissed her gently on the lips, clipped the boys affectionately around the ears, and walked away.

Duffy would miss the gang, but right now he had other plans.

He and Marky were off for a month to pig out on the Greek island of Ios, totally zone out of life and let everything flow over them.

"Got a good feel about this Duff," she said, squeezing his hand.

They'd just checked in and were going through security when a rowdy bunch of footballers barged past them. All wearing numbered sports shirts, one bouncing a ball, their leader shoving them through, jumping the queue.

Duffy nearly kicked off but decided those days were over, for now.

The team captain glanced back as they cleared security.

Duffy had never seen him before.

Otherwise he'd have recognized Hassan, and his ten drone pilots.

Moments later Duffy was thrown a life-changing dilemma from nowhere.

He and Marky had just bought two flat whites and were at the exchange bureau getting their Euros for Greece when a sultry voice hailed him from behind.

"Duffy darling…"

He froze. He knew without turning.

Saladine, in a full length mink coat, and those lashes to die for.

"I'm off to Cuba for a week. Spare ticket. Wanna come babe?" she purred, ignoring Marky.

For once the singing detective was speechless.

He looked at Marky on one side, with her short tomboy pinky hair, nose stud, tinted glasses, and torn tee-shirt.

He looked at Saladine on the other, with her seductive perfume, smouldering eyes, moist lips, and that bloody fur coat.

One wanted to marry him.

One wanted to buy him.

And made his choice.

ABOUT THE AUTHOR

Tony McLaren was born in Scotland and raised in New Zealand, where he did a BA degree, was a newspaper journalist, then worked his way to London as a merchant seaman, acting on the West End stage and on screen. After many years creating and producing drama and entertainment for ITV he went solo, selling his formats around the world from Holland to Germany, Italy to Argentina, Turkey to the USA. He now writes and dog walks in the New Forest.

Printed in Great Britain
by Amazon